A cloud of black smoke hovered over the prairie, and where the occasional lonely tree had stood, there remained only a smoking black sketch of a tree trunk. Seth braked the wagon.

Coming through a veil of smoke, the rider was just the silhouette of a man on horseback. Ashes, some still flickering with fire, fluttered past the rider. "Seth Coe!" the man called out hoarsely. "What you got there, an ax? How's that going to help you? I'll tell you what you do. You throw your money belt down over here, and I'll let you go without a scratch!"

The chances of Hannibal Fisher letting him go seemed slim to none. Fisher wasn't going to let Seth go to raise an alarm.

"Hannibal Fisher!" another horseman called, riding out of the smoke. "Drop your weapon!"

Seth felt his heart leap when he saw the badge on the rider's vest.

This is a lucky draw, Seth thought.

Fisher turned his horse about to his left, shouting, "I'm dropping the gun, Sheriff!"

"He's still got the gun!" Seth shouted, but as he was saying it, Fisher was firing. . . .

RALPH COMPTON

PRAIRIE FIRE, KANSAS

A Ralph Compton Western by
JOHN SHIRLEY

BERKLEY
New York

BERKLEY
An imprint of Penguin Random House LLC
penguinrandomhouse.com

ISBN: 9780593102329

First Edition: November 2020

Printed in the United States of America
1   3   5   7   9   10   8   6   4   2

Cover art by Chris McGrath
Book design by George Towne

THE IMMORTAL COWBOY

This is respectfully dedicated to the "American Cowboy." His was the saga sparked by the turmoil that followed the Civil War, and the passing of more than a century has by no means diminished the flame.

True, the old days and the old ways are but treasured memories, and the old trails have grown dim with the ravages of time, but the spirit of the cowboy lives on.

In my travels—to Texas, Oklahoma, Kansas, Nebraska, Colorado, Wyoming, New Mexico, and Arizona—I always find something that reminds me of the Old West. While I am walking these plains and mountains for the first time, there is this feeling that a part of me is eternal, that I have known these old trails before. I believe it is the undying spirit of the frontier calling me, through the mind's eye, to step back into time. What is the appeal of the Old West of the American frontier?

It has been epitomized by some as the dark and bloody period in American history. Its heroes—Crockett, Bowie, Hickok, Earp—have been reviled and criticized. Yet the Old West lives on, larger than life.

It has become a symbol of freedom, when there was always another mountain to climb and another river to cross; when a dispute between two men was settled not with expensive lawyers, but with fists, knives, or guns. Barbaric? Maybe. But some things never change. When the cowboy rode into the pages of American history, he left behind a legacy that lives within the hearts of us all.

—*Ralph Compton*

CHAPTER ONE

Abilene, Kansas, 1871

IT WAS A hot, dusty day, but Seth Coe was in a good mood. The long trail drive was over, and he had been paid. Seth, Franklin, and Jake were standing by the corral gate, at the big holding on the north side of Abilene, Kansas, in the bright summer sunshine.

"How's it come I got only a hundred dollars for all my work on this drive, Seth, and you got a hundred eighty?" Jake asked, counting his money.

"I'll tell you why," said Seth, smiling as he turned away from the cattle pen that sunny afternoon. "Besides being a drover, I was remuda wrangler, seeing as how Henry Graham died two weeks into the drive, and that means I got me an extra forty dollars—and I saved your bacon by pulling you out of that flash flood, so Cullin give me another forty as a bonus."

"A bonus for saving me?" Jake demanded, scowling. "Why, saving a man's life should be done out of pure decency."

Franklin snorted. "Jake, Seth almost died himself pulling your chestnuts from that gully washer!"

The cattle jostled and mooed and snorted on the other side of the raw-timber fence, stirring up a cloud of dust as the three cowboys walked away toward downtown, pleased to be leaving the beasts they'd driven north for more than two months.

Franklin Trotter, Seth's longtime pal, was a year older than Seth. He was six feet three and wide shouldered and heavy bellied. He had long brown hair, thick swooping mustaches, and a broad, affable face, his small blue eyes always glinting with mischief. Like the others he was still wearing his chaps, his red calico shirt, a bandanna tied around his neck, rough tan trousers, and a gun on his hip. "Here's what should concern you, Jake," said Franklin. "Seth was paid a forty-dollar bonus for risking his neck saving yours. That means Cullin figures your life's only worth forty dollars!"

"Also means my life, too, is only worth forty dollars," said Seth. "Jumping in that flood was a fool thing to do." He grinned. "I think I should've gotten eighty."

"Why, if you profited by me," said Jake, a middling man with a weak chin half hidden by a slapdash beard, "I should have half that money, shouldn't I?"

"You should thank your stars anyone bothered to go in after you, Jake Hersted," said Franklin. "Now, who's for going to the Prancing Lady with me for a drink?"

"Suits me," said Jake.

"I'll have a beer and something to eat if it's truly edible," said Seth. "Then I'm for a bath."

They picked up their pace as they headed toward the saloon, their boots clomping the wooden sidewalk, and fingering his money poke, Franklin said, "I think I'll play me some Spanish monte."

"Odds are bad with Spanish monte, my pa told me," said Seth. "A little better in draw poker if you're careful."

"Then why don't you play poker?" Franklin asked. "Been at the railhead with you three times. You never played a hand."

"Because I don't see why I should risk my money, whatever the odds," replied Seth. He was at least a head shorter than his friend Franklin and stocky; he had scrappily cut black hair—he cut it himself to save money—and big brown eyes he'd inherited from his half-Mexican mother; his stub nose he'd gotten from his Irish father. There was said to be some Lipan Apache in there, too. "I've gone to a power of trouble to save up money. Now this is my fifth trail drive, and on my oath, my *last*! I've saved three hundred and forty dollars on the last four drives, and I aim to save a hundred and sixty from this one. That's five hundred dollars!"

"You are the savingest cowpoke I ever met," said Jake. "Never buying new clothes, always patching up the old ones."

"That's why they call him Patches," said Franklin.

Seth frowned at that. He despised the nickname. "They're going to call you Busted Nose if you don't quit saying that, Franklin."

Franklin grinned. "Why, you're so short, you couldn't reach my nose!"

Jake laughed at that. They came to the Prancing Lady and paused at the door, seeing Marshal Hickok, resplendent in a cream-colored suit, French cuffs, and a broad-brimmed yellow hat, standing on the wooden sidewalk across the dusty street, glaring at them. He had shoulder-length honey blond hair and drooping blond mustaches. Hickok glared at everyone he didn't know. It was a clear enough message. *Whatever it is you're a-thinkin' on pullin' in my town, don't.*

"I don't care for the idea of staying in this dust bowl of a town long, Franklin," murmured Seth. "I saw Hickok there shoot a man in Hays City for getting on his nerves—seems like he'll shoot you if you look at him cross-eyed."

"He had a good reason for that gunning in Hays," said Franklin. "Why, he never shot a man who didn't need shooting."

"Still and all—he makes me nervous, and I've done nothing wrong. Well, come on, I'll have a glass of beer with you fellas and watch you lose your money. Then I'm for a bath at the Drover's Inn, might even spring for a haircut."

The trio of cowboys went into the Prancing Lady Saloon—which was already half full, though it was not yet three in the afternoon—and made straight for the bar. Seth ordered a beer, and the other two ordered whiskey. A gangly saloon girl, who looked more like a saloon matron to Seth's eye, leaned back against the bar, eyeing the three cowboys. She had a horsey face much coated with white makeup and daubed with rouge, and sausage-curled peroxide-bleached hair. Her smile seemed genuine, though, if a little sad. "What can we get for you gents today?" she asked.

"What's your name, miss?" Seth asked.

"Caroline."

"Caroline, my name's Seth. Say, does this saloon have luncheon?"

"You could call it that, Seth," she said.

"Between you, me, and the gatepost—is it worth eating?"

"Well—anyhow, it won't kill you."

"That's good enough for me. Do you suppose I could hope for a sandwich with any meat but beef and some cheese?"

"I'll see to it, Seth. How about you boys?"

"I'll have two such sandwiches," declared Franklin, whose appetite was legendary, "and another whiskey."

"Another whiskey for me, too," said Jake, eyeing the faro table.

Seth and Franklin ate passable sandwiches, and Seth turned to contemplate the saloon. There were five tables, four of them ringed by cowboys Seth knew well, including Rudy Rodriguez, Gus Rossner, and 'Baccy Smith from the Cullin Ranch drive, who were playing poker with a tall, gaunt man in a lavender-colored bowler hat. A potbellied stove stood in a back corner, unused now, and in the other was a Mulatto dealer presiding over a semicircular green felt table, chattering at the three drovers who stood gaping at the cards. In between, against a wall, was a tobacco-stained upright piano, highly unlikely to be in tune.

Franklin nudged Seth with his elbow and whispered, "Tell you what, Seth—there's two seats at that poker table yonder. I'll wager tomorrow's breakfast, all you can eat, that the card wisdom your pa taught you won't be worth a hill of beans at that table, and you'll fold your tent before I do."

"You'll wager what?"

"Whichever one of us quits first buys breakfast tomorrow."

Seth frowned. He didn't like to risk his money; he was saving in the cause of a long-term plan, which was something else his pa had taught him. But he didn't like to spurn Franklin's wagers—they were an old tradition between the two—and he said, "I'm not promising to go broke on that table, but if I'm careful, I can sure outlast a tyro like you. You're on!"

Ten minutes later Seth was seated across from the gambler in the lavender hat and laying his first bet on the table. . . .

RUSK RUSKETT HAD been a bounty hunter for five years, and he'd never learned to like it. He mulled this sad fact over as he rode his roan stallion on the wide dirt trail to Abilene under a brooding afternoon sun. Every single time he went out after a man, he swore it was his last. But by jingo, he made enough in bounties, four or five times a year, that the rest of the year he could sit on his porch, drinking hard cider, smoking a pipe, and listening to his Sioux wife sing Injun songs as she worked. Bounty hunting seemed worth it, in the long stretches between hunts. He could go fishing when he wanted to; he could hunt game; he could make merry with his Nawaji. Otherwise he'd be slaving away on some other feller's ranch all for a verminous bunk and a puny poke of dollars.

But this whole business of a man all alone hunting outlaws was dangerous and grueling. Rusk had been wounded twice on the job, once by knife and once by gun. The long, hot days in the saddle, the dealings with lawmen who didn't approve of him, the endless interviews with those who might have seen the outlaw he was chasing, and the tedium of it all—it just didn't seem worth it sometimes.

Now he was tracking a man who wasn't even "wanted dead or alive." That meant to get his bounty he had to drag this Hannibal Fisher owlhoot back to Judge Isaac Parker *alive*. Most tiresome, that was. Much easier to just shoot them and sling them over his pack mule. But it was in most places a legal hazard to shoot his quarry even in self-defense—because often enough it was out in the Big Lonesome somewhere, without witnesses. How was he to prove it was self-defense?

Hannibal Fisher was likely a dangerous man. The gambler in the lavender hat was wanted for stabbing a businessman to death in Kansas City over some bunco scheme gone foul. He had shot a faro dealer in Tuscaloosa, too, but that was ruled a legal killing. As Fisher had not yet been proven to be the murderer in the stabbing case, it was not a question of dead or alive. He must be tried. Rusk was therefore not permitted to shoot the man from cover and get it over with.

Rusk scratched in his thick black beard and shook his shaggy head. A most chancy hunt, this was.

Rusk's stallion trotted him around a curve, and he saw the rooftops of Abilene some distance ahead. He patted the shirt pocket holding the lavender, the plant itself. Searching for Fisher, Rusk had discovered that

few knew what the color lavender was, so he brought
the flower.

"He always wears a bowler hat this color," he would
say, brandishing the blossom. "Last seen here in
Abilene. Got a face like an undertaker. You seen him?"

T HE ITINERANT GAMBLER sitting across the poker
   table had a long, gaunt, clean-shaven face that
made Seth think of an undertaker. The expression on
the man's face could have belonged to an undertaker,
too, somber but rather blank.

But there was something in the gambler's gray eyes
that made Seth think of the points of well-sharpened
knives. The man was angry because Seth had won five
hundred eighty dollars from him. The gambler had
held what he supposed were winning hands—three
queens one time, two pair, jacks and kings, another.
But Seth had been lucky and shown a full house against
the queens and triple deuces against the two pair. Seth
guessed the gambler must've been having a string of
good luck before this game, as he'd had a goodly poke
to bet from; but maybe bad luck before coming to
Abilene, for the man's pin-striped dark blue suit, which
must've been fine once, judging from the fabric and the
tailoring, was frayed about the cuffs; one shoulder
seam was coming loose, and his lavender bowler was
badly scuffed. Now this gambler was even poorer than
he'd been before, Seth reckoned.

It was Franklin's turn to deal, and he shuffled the
deck and dealt the cards. The gambler discarded two,
Franklin discarded one, Seth tossed two cards into the
deadwood, Jake folded, and so did the half-drunk red-

bearded farmhand. Seth had started with a king and queen of spades and a four of spades. His two new cards were a deuce and jack of spades. He had a king-high flush.

Franklin bet ten dollars; the gambler made it twenty; Franklin called the raise, and slow-playing his flush, Seth just called. The gambler, his face stony, raised the pot fifty dollars. Franklin swore under his breath and folded. He'd probably been hoping to fill a straight, Seth figured. Seth raised, risking eighty dollars—since he had won more than that already.

The gambler stared at him for a long moment, then said, "Make it one hundred forty." And he threw the rest of the cash he had on the table into the pot.

Seth knew he risked losing the hand if he called. The gambler could beat him with an ace-high flush, a full house, or four of a kind. But he figured if he lost this hand, he'd still be ahead. Unlike most cowboys, he had no trouble quitting while he was ahead.

"I expect I'd better call you," he said, and showed his king-high flush.

A blaze of red showed on the gambler's face, and his lips compressed to a bloodless line as he folded his cards.

Franklin whistled softly as Seth scooped in the pot.

"Well, I am done losing money to you, Seth," said Franklin, shaking his head ruefully. "I'm going to quit while I've still got a nickel or two left to buy that breakfast."

"Catch you round the mountain," said Seth, stacking his winnings as Franklin stood up.

The gambler turned in his chair, bent down, and took off his boot. He reached into it and pulled out ten folded twenty-dollar bills.

"My turn to deal," he growled, tossing the money on the table.

"You got another two hundred in the other boot?" Franklin asked innocently. He sat down again. "Think I'll keep an eye on this game."

Shuffling the deck, the gambler glared at him. "You mean something by that?"

"Just what I said."

The gambler dealt the cards. He examined his cards and discarded three, casually fanning them at the edge of the discard pile—which seemed dodgy to Seth.

Not liking the looks of his own cards, Seth discarded three as well, keeping only a ten of diamonds and a jack of clubs. Jake discarded two. The farmhand rubbed his chin, muttered inaudibly, then tossed three. They received their replacement cards, and Seth found he had an ace-high straight. He decided he needed a bet but not so big it'd induce the others to fold. He tossed twenty into the pot.

"That all you going to bet, Seth," Jake asked, "after getting your pay, that big bonus, and clutching the rest of the money you saved like a—"

"Jake," Franklin interrupted coldly, "shut up."

Seth nodded to himself. In a country where the outlaws far, far outnumbered the lawmen, loose talk about a man's cash wasn't thought suitable.

"I raise you eighty," said the gambler, tossing four twenties into the pot.

"Whee-ew," said the farmhand, folding his cards. "Too rich for m'blood."

Jake sighed and folded as well. "I'm gonna get me a drink. Maybe folks are friendlier at the bar. Last time I play cards with you, Seth Coe. You're too damn lucky."

He got up, put what remained of his money back in his pocket, and went to the bar.

"That girl at the bar will be as friendly as you can afford 'er to be, Jake," said Franklin as Seth counted out the money and tossed it on the pot—and then added a hundred more.

The gambler smirked and smacked the side of his right hand, the one holding his cards, on the table hard enough to make it jump a little.

But Seth had kept one eye on the deadwood cards and saw it when the gambler—having drawn their attention to his right hand—flicked a card from the discards with the tip of a finger so it shot under his left hand.

"Mister, it's against the rules in any house to monkey with the deadwood," Seth said coldly.

The gambler went stiff in his chair, and he fixed Seth's eyes with his own. "What the hell did you just say to me?"

"I'm saying you set up those three cards you discarded in case one was good for you later, and now you've got one palmed under your left hand."

"If you are accusing me of cheating, I'll see you in the street!"

The room got very quiet. Everyone stared.

"I'm not a gunhand," Seth said, shaking his head. He simply wasn't going to get in a gunfight. He was no great hand with a pistol, and he did not believe in gunning anyone except in the direst circumstances of self-defense. "I'm not going to meet you anywhere, mister. But I'm not going to let you use that card in your left hand either."

"You accuse me of cheating—then you forfeit all!" the gambler said.

"I missed that one in the poker rule book," Franklin said dryly. "You were caught, mister."

The gambler put the cards in his right hand carefully on the table, facedown, and then stood up, reaching under his coat for his hideaway gun—and froze when he saw Franklin's Colt whip up to point at his liver. Seth heard three distinctive clicking sounds and looked over to see Rudy Rodriguez, Gus Rossner, and 'Baccy Smith at another table with their guns pointed at the gambler, cocked. Their faces were grim. All three men had ridden the range with Seth many a time.

Out of the corner of his eye, Seth glimpsed Caroline hurrying out the door of the bar.

"I don't believe," said Franklin softly, his gaze hard and steady on the gambler, "that you're reckless enough to pull that pistol, mister. Not with four of us ready to cut you to pieces. Now, you open your cards faceup on the table. The cards in your right hand. And you let go of that card under your left."

Trembling with frustrated fury, jaws working, the gambler did as he was bade. His poker hand showed ace high—a busted flush with four hearts. The losing hand.

The farmhand stretched out a hand and turned over the card the gambler had extracted from the deadwood. A ten of hearts. "Why, that would have given him a flush! And he knowed it! He's crooked as a Virginia fence!"

Seth turned up his own hand, showing the ace-high straight.

"Tinhorn," said Franklin, "you lost the hand."

"I was just fixing to boot that son of a sick dog out of town," said someone at the door.

Seth turned to see Marshal Hickok, leaning casually on the frame of the open door, looking amused. He had one hand on the butt of his Colt Navy. "What's the cowboy's hand?"

"He's got an ace-high straight, Marshal," said Franklin.

Hickok nodded. "I should run you into the pokey, Fisher," he said, glaring at the gambler, "but it's full to bust right now. Get your carpetbag, get on your horse, and get your rump out of Abilene."

"Marshal, they were all in it together—they set me up to be robbed!" Fisher said, the pitch of his voice rising close to a whine.

"A lady I trust says different. You were monkeying with the deadwood, and you've got a losing hand. And you tried to force a gunfight. Leave all that money on the table. And your gun, too. Put it down there, real careful."

"Marshal, it's dangerous out on the prairie without a firearm!"

"You there, the big man with the gun—holster it, take his gun, and bring it here."

Franklin did as he was told. Marshal Hickok looked at the pocket gun. "Thirty-eight-caliber Hulbert and Merwin pocket revolver. Not a bad little weapon. I carried one myself in the war when I was scoutin'." With a few practiced movements of his long, thin fingers, Wild Bill emptied the little gun of its bullets and put them in his pocket. "You three men, put away your guns, too. By God I've gotten slipshod. I should've collected your irons when you came to town, the whole shootin' match."

They holstered their guns, and Hickok crooked a finger at the gambler. "Come here, Fisher."

Fisher, cowed by the famous gunfighter, took a deep breath and gave Seth a chilling look. "You have not seen the last of me," he said in a low voice. But he walked over to the door meekly enough. "Yes, Marshal?"

"Any other weapons? You lie to me, I'll break your hands so you can't hold a card anymore."

"No, sir. Well, there's a knife in my boot."

"You just keep it in your boot." Marshal Hickok tucked the .38 under Fisher's coat, then took him by the ear and dragged him out the door.

The Prancing Lady Saloon erupted in laughter.

H ANNIBAL FISHER FELT a profound bitterness. The humiliation of having been caught cheating, of having had four guns drawn on him, of having been dragged from the saloon and driven summarily from town in a gale of laughter, stung him deeply. He was already raw inside from having lost his last dollar.

Now, as he rode his swaybacked horse south to a shady spot with a spring he knew of, he knew he could not rest till he had made the brown-eyed cowboy pay for every inch and every speck of that humiliation. . . .

He had heard one of the cowboys call the man Seth Coe. And when they'd first joined the table, he heard Coe and Franklin agree to head south on the morrow, directly after they had breakfast.

Fisher had a Henry rifle on his horse, and he would wait at the spring south of town, within sight of the road. He reckoned on shooting both cowboys off their horses. Firing from the cover of the trees, he'd stand a good chance to come out unscathed. Then he'd rob their bodies, get his money back and a good deal more.

Maybe take one of their horses as his own, sell the other, and . . .

Fisher's thoughts were derailed by the sound of pounding hooves behind him. He turned to see a stranger ride up on a roan: a black-bearded, shaggy-haired man with a floppy, sweat-stained hat—and a pistol in his hand.

"Hannibal Fisher!" the man called. He grinned at Fisher as he reined in about fifteen feet away. "I'm taking you into custody. I've a warrant for your arrest to answer charges of murder in Kansas City!"

Fisher cursed himself for not reloading the hideaway gun. But this man had the drop on him, anyhow, and he had the look—including the long buckskin coat—that spoke of an experienced bounty hunter.

"Now, who'd you be?" Fisher demanded.

"My name's Ruskett. I've got the warrant and poster on you right here in my coat pocket."

"Who's that you called me? Fisher, you said?"

The bounty hunter laughed, showing crooked yellow teeth. "Marshal Hickok confirmed every last thing about you! Most assuredly I have my man. Hickock thinks I'm going to bring you back to Abilene, but I don't know as he'd give me the bounty—he don't care much for bounty hunters. But I do a power of business up in Newton, and that's where we're going. Now, you take out that hideout gun and toss it down."

His head spinning with the endless dark flow of his rotten luck, Fisher tossed the gun on the ground. "What bounty have they attached to this false charge?"

"Four hundred dollars."

"Why, I can get you more than that!"

"You couldn't raise that much money if you sold

every gold tooth in your head and that sickly nag, too. Now, shut up and take up that rifle by the barrel and toss it over to me."

Fisher was looking down the muzzle of Ruskett's gun. He didn't see much choice. Very well. This was another man he'd have to have his revenge on. He tossed over the rifle, reflecting that it was a long way south to Newton from here. He would kill this man Ruskett, soon or late.

As he let the bounty hunter shackle him, Hannibal Fisher swore in his heart to kill anyone who would stand in the way of his getting revenge on the man who'd taken his last dollar at the poker table—the man who'd occasioned his humiliation as he was driven from town. . . .

Seth Coe.

CHAPTER TWO

"Y OU AND YOUR damn sheep farm!" Franklin laughed
as he and Seth rode south in the misty morning.

"It's not a sheep farm. It ain't even a sheep *ranch*,
Franklin," Seth said patiently. He didn't mind being
teased by Franklin. Bantering with him made the time
pass on a long ride. "I merely propose to get me a small
herd of sheep, along with everything else, because it's
good land for it there. Don't paint me as a sheepherder.
You'll get half the cowboys in Texas after me. I'll have
some cattle, but mostly I'm going to raise remuda
horses."

"Hold on. You forgot the cotton fields!"

"Good land for cotton, too. My pa raised cotton, and
I know just how to do it."

"Why quit there? Why not build a railroad!"

Seth grinned. "One thing at a time." He patted his

horse's neck; she gave a soft whinny in return. Then he added, "What I want to do isn't so much, Franklin. It's just that I got to save money to make it happen. Once you know you want something, why, you got to set a goal, my pa said, and if you have to, work your way there an inch or a nickel at a time. I got money stashed in the bank at Chaseman—nearly two thousand dollars. My pa willed me and my sister and brother a thousand dollars each. I still got that, and I've saved a thousand more."

"You worked hard enough at it," Franklin admitted. "Two and three jobs at a time back home. Wore me out just watching all that work."

"With that and what I won off that gambler, I might could buy the land and the start-up stock I need. Now, I figure I'll need help running the place. Going to need two kinds of partner. The ugly kind and the pretty kind. The ugly kind—that'd be you. The pretty kind, that'd be my wife."

"You ain't got a wife. You ain't even got a sweetheart."

"Going to find one. She's out there. I know she is. I'll know her when I see her."

Franklin chuckled, shaking his head. "Well, it's a long way to Chaseman, Texas, Seth. Maybe you'll meet her on the way."

"Not likely."

"How'm I going to be your partner, anyhow? I've got a couple hundred dollars at home, but it's not enough to buy in on anything."

"Why, you'll be my foreman, and I'll cut you in on the profits. You'll earn your way into it!" It had never occurred to him that Franklin wouldn't want to be his partner. He always had been, one way or another. "Thanks for backing my play with that tinhorn, Franklin."

"Don't like his type—you, I got used to." He shook his head. "But, Lord—you're planning to turn me into a durn 'alfalfa desperado.'"

Seth gave him a narrow look. "There's no shame in farming—and it ain't just a farm. I guess you don't much want to be a foreman. Too much work!"

"There's no working a ranch that's just dreams, Seth."

"Supposing I get it out of my dreams and plant it into the dirt down there, south of Chaseman?"

"Well, I expect I'd have to hang around and do my part, to keep you from embarrassing yourself."

Seth smiled. "I'll hold you to that. You remember anyplace on this road we could camp, come sunset?"

"We can't stay in some town somewheres? Oh—I shoulda knowed it. Can't do that because then you'd have to spend a dollar or two." He sighed. "It's going to be a long, long ride back."

THE COURTHOUSE IN Newton was a big two-story frame structure, with the courtroom at the front and jail cells at the back, offices up top. The jailer, name of Sam Mundy, a white-bearded old man in overalls, locked Hannibal Fisher into his cell as Sheriff Dawson and Rusk Ruskett looked on with approval.

"Enjoy your gloating while you can," said Fisher. He was doing some quiet gloating himself: the hideaway knife in his boot had gone undiscovered. It was small and slim and well disguised, for the boot was designed to conceal it.

"Fisher," said Dawson, "you'll be here a week or more till I can get you escorted to Kansas City, so you'd better keep a civil tongue in your head if you want to be fed."

Old Sam chuckled. "That's right. You talk smart to me, Fisher, I might forget to feed you—and forget to empty your thunder mug." With that, swinging the key ring on one finger, he shuffled off to read the newspaper at the far end of the row of cells.

There were three cells in a row, divided only by bars. The far one was empty, but the one abutting Fisher's was occupied by a man he recognized: an outlaw getting close to middle-age, name of Curtis Diamond, now taking his ease on his bunk, hands clasped behind his head. He wore a long frock coat, even lying on his bunk, striped trousers, and down-at-heel black boots. Fisher recalled him wearing a diamond stickpin, to go with his name, and he noted now that the stickpin was there—but the diamond was gone from it. Had to sell it, most like. Or lost it gambling.

"Take a couple of days to get your bounty, Ruskett," said Dawson. He was a tall, clean-shaven man with a weather-lined face and cold blue eyes. He wore his Stetson tipped back. "Where will I find you?"

"I'll find me a room over to Hyde Park, Sheriff. Probably I'll be round about the Red Front Saloon of an evening."

"To hell with that, Ruskett, I'm not going to look for you. You just come and check with me in two days. If I'm not in town, check with the court clerk."

The two men strolled down the passage to the door, Ruskett talking of nothing much, as Fisher sat on his bunk. "That you, Diamond?" he said none too loudly.

Diamond opened his eyes and looked over. "Yep. I seen you come in, Hannibal. What they accusing you of? Card cheat?"

Fisher scowled at that but said only, "Somebody got killed in Kansas City, and they didn't have a suspect. So they picked me 'cause I knew the man."

Diamond sat up, stretching. "I've known that to happen. Now, me—they're fixing to hang me, all thanks to a bunch of damn liars. Somebody got shot in a robbery, but I was . . . Well, I was somewheres else."

"When's your send-off?" Fisher asked, noting that Dawson and Ruskett had left the jail area, and the old man was out of earshot.

"Not quite a fortnight."

Fisher moved to the end of his bunk closest to Diamond and spoke in a low voice. "How good are you at keeping your mouth shut?"

Diamond looked over at him with sudden interest. "I'm quiet as the grave, is how."

"I've got a knife in my boot. Comes the right time, if you can get your hand around that old man's mouth, I can cut his throat. Then I'll get us both out. I'm going after some money, and I'm going to need some help to get it. You throw in with me, why, you've got nothing to lose and everything to gain."

For Fisher had evolved a new plan on the way here. And it would take men like Curtis Diamond to help him pull it off. . . .

* * *

W HAT THE HELL kind of a name is Prairie Fire for a town?" Franklin asked musingly as they rode past the town's welcome sign.

"Name based on its history, I'm guessing," Seth replied. "Big ol' fire sometime."

"A black-omened name seems to me. If I was contemplating settling in Kansas, I'd move on past any burg named after a prairie fire. 'Sakes, it must be prone to them! I've seen only one, and that's one too many."

It was sundown as they rode in, and fittingly enough its red glow was setting the town of Prairie Fire ablaze as their horses clopped up to the barnlike building with the words *FEED, GRAIN, and LIVERY* painted above the big open doors.

"We stopped in this town once, two years ago," Seth reminded Franklin as they unsaddled their horses. "It was on the way up, when Cookie Nick sent us in for coffee and bacon. Nice enough place. But we weren't here long. Don't want to be here long this time either."

"Seth, I had above two months sleeping in my bedroll, coming to Abilene, and I am right sick of it," said Franklin, pouring grain into the trough for his horse. "They got a hotel in this town, I expect."

"Don't want to spend the money. You could do it and pick me up at the camp," Seth said. "There's a creek to the south, Black Creek, with some cottonwoods round about it. I can camp there, close enough to the road you can find me." He patted Mazie. The muscular brown-and-black mare snorted and nuzzled at his hand. "Back pretty soon, girl."

"Seth," said Franklin in a tone that wasn't far from exasperation, "there's every kind of road agent out there on the prairie. You haven't got a big hire of cowboys to scare 'em off."

"I ain't some little lost calf, Franklin."

"Ain't you, though?"

The two cowboys headed out to the dusty street. It was still warm, the day's heat rising from the aggregate road, but a fresh breeze was blowing in off the prairie. As they strolled down the main drag, Seth observed the town had the common layout for frontier settlements, with a main street right through its middle. The street was rattling now with a procession of high-sided freight wagons carrying the first summer wheat harvest, and the sounds of a laughing girl in a frock and pinafore rolling an iron hoop. Shops lined the road at the center of town, mostly small false-front stores. Beyond the stores, two cafés, and a tailor shop, there was a pool hall called Henry's, a grange hall, a modest two-story building that looked like a city hall, and a church steeple sticking up down at the end of the street. Apart from that, there were houses set on side streets and not much else of note.

"Anyhow, here's the general store," said Seth. "I don't think it was open last time we was here. Had to buy from a farmer selling out the back of his wagon."

A small brass bell on the door jangled when they entered the Prairie Fire General Store, F. Dubois, proprietor. A vinegary-faced man in a long white apron was counting out change to a lady in a yellow bonnet. She watched the process with an eagle eye. The man was F. Dubois, Seth assumed. He looked vaguely familiar. And Seth reflected that he'd known a family named Dubois back home in Texas when he'd been a boy. The shopkeeper's oiled black hair was parted in the middle, his small black mustache overwhelmed by heavy cheeks. The lady departed, primly avoiding eye contact with the dusty cowboys. Dubois twitched his long nose and looked markedly unenthusiastic about the two cowboys approaching the counter.

"Yes?" he asked, in an accent Seth had heard before. French Canadian . . .

"Evening," said Franklin. "Need us a pound of cornmeal, two pounds of bacon, quarter pound of sugar, two pounds of coffee—"

Dubois was scribbling the items on a pad. "Ground coffee or unground?"

"Don't usually ride with a coffee grinder," said Franklin. "Make it ground. Now, sir . . ."

Franklin went on with the order, but Seth couldn't seem to hear him anymore. The young woman coming in from the back room had arrested every last speck of Seth's attention. She was a small woman, her tawny hair half up and curled. Compact, perfectly proportioned, she was almost like a child's porcelain doll, with her elegant little Cupid's bow lips the color of bing cherries and her large blue-green eyes.

It can't be her. She was so like the little girl he'd known in childhood, but grown into a womanly figure. After a moment, he was sure of it. This was Josette Dubois.

"May I assist you, sir?" she asked Seth as she reached behind herself to tighten her frilly pink-and-white apron.

Seth was staring at her delicate white fingers. There was no wedding ring.

Should he tell her who he was? Would she remember him? Somehow, he felt it might embarrass her.

Seth cleared his throat. "Ma'am, my friend is . . . is ordering our goods but, ah—I was considering on"—he was suddenly self-conscious of his patchy red calico shirt—"on a new shirt."

"We do have one left," she said. "The milliner also does some haberdashery and such like and would have more." She, too, had an accent, though not as pronounced as her father's. She said "such" like "sooch." Seth found it to be most charming. "But we do have a nice new blue cotton shirt."

"I'll take it," Seth blurted.

She looked startled. An adorable sight. "Well—I have only one, and I'm not sure it would fit you. Might be a whisker too big."

"Oh, I could adjust that. We cowpokes, why, we learn to mend and such."

"I see!" She smiled. "That is most admirable. Most men do not seem to trifle with sewing."

"'Course, I'm not *just* a cowpoke—I'm starting a considerable business of my own"—he licked his lips—"down in Chaseman, Texas."

"Chaseman! I lived near that town when I was a"— she blinked and peered at him, head tilted, lips pursed—"a child."

"Josette—"

"Josette!" Dubois roared.

She jumped a little at that, and her shoulders tensed. Seth had to suppress the urge to take her hand and comfort her.

Josette turned to her father. "There is no need to shout, Papa."

"I was calling to you twice, girl! You ignore me, no? Go—" He pushed the list on the pad to her. "Fill this!"

"Yes, *oui, certainement*, Papa," she murmured, consulting the pad. She glanced furtively at Seth and made a small gesture to Seth—it was just a hand motion that said, *Wait a moment*. But it made his heart leap.

Seth found he was breathing hard as he watched her bustling about the shop, gathering up the order.

"Seth?"

He thought about asking if he could carry those things for her.

"Seth!"

He turned, blinking. "Well—*what*?"

Franklin seemed amused by something. "You look a mite petrified there, Seth. Like you seen something that's froze you on the spot."

"It's Josette, Franklin," Seth whispered.

"It's who?"

"You knowed her. She went to our school."

"Why, I seem to remember the name. You're saying she's from our corner of Texas?"

"I spent most of a summer running with her— chasing round with our dogs, trying to get kites to work, making a raft on the Pendleton River—we near to drowned. Had a fine time. Then her Pap . . ." He nodded toward Dubois, who was seeing to a heavily bearded man with the look of a prosperous farmer. "Well, he had to leave town. Dragged her off with him. Ran up here, I expect."

"How old were you two?"

"Eleven."

"Seth, I'm mighty impressed with your memory," said Franklin. He joined Seth in watching Josette tie up their purchases in brown paper. "She must've had quite an effect on—"

Seth made a slashing motion with his hand to shut Franklin up as Josette came over to him with two packages.

"Thank you, ma'am . . ." Franklin said. "What's this package here?"

"Why, your friend bought a shirt."

"Will wonders never cease," Franklin said.

She once more looked at Seth with her head crooked to one side. "It cannot be . . ."

"It's Seth Coe, is what it can be," said Franklin.

"Oh! *Seth!* That was it!"

Seth winced. She hadn't remembered his name.

"I went to the same school as you did myself, ma'am," Franklin said.

"Josette!" her father barked, slapping another list down on the counter.

"Excuse me. . . ."

"Close your mouth, Seth," Franklin said, "before you catch a fly. Let's go."

Seth drifted numbly after Franklin to stand on the sidewalk outside. "There you were, Franklin, pretending you remembered her from school—!"

"Why, I *almost* remember her. There was a tiny little female with legs like sticks running after you." He chuckled. "I noticed she couldn't remember *your* name, Seth! But you sure remembered hers!"

Seth looked over his shoulder, ducking his head a little to look through the window in the door for a glimpse of Josette. "She signed me to wait and talk to her later."

"Sure, she did. A pretty girl like that? She probably wanted you to introduce her to me."

"Now you're the dreamer round here."

Franklin handed Seth his wrapped-up shirt. "Seemed to me that pa of hers didn't like our looks."

"For some reason, fathers are right prejudiced against cowboys," Seth said. He looked down the street. "Eastern Road Inn, it says there. Let's get us a room."

"What happened to sleeping in the damn bushes again?"

"My back was hurting me some this morning."

"Oh, is that what it is?"

"Franklin, shut your piehole, and let's go get us that room and some dinner."

OLD MUNDY WAS bringing Fisher and Diamond their supper, whistling a tune between the space in his front teeth. He was careful to keep a step back from the bars as he set the tin plates and cups on the floor and slid them through the horizontal slot. "Fried chicken tonight, Diamond," he said. "You're getting the fine eats to set you up good for hanging."

"Twelve days to the hanging," Diamond said. "That's a lot of good meals."

"That lying bounty hunter get his blood money from the sheriff?" Fisher asked, picking up his plate. He gave a nod to Diamond as he did so: the sign that this would be their chance.

Diamond gave a small nod without looking at him. Fisher had the knife tucked into the back of his belt, and the timing seemed good, but you never knew. Mundy might not fall for it. . . .

"Ruskett got paid an hour ago," said the old jailer. "Headin' out this very evening. In a hurry to get out of town. Owes some money over to the gambling hall."

"Now who's the crook?" asked Diamond. He remained standing, not far from the bars, as he ate. Fisher sat on the edge of his bed. They had this all worked out.

He and Fisher ate their chicken with their hands and used wooden spoons for the fried potatoes. Diamond washed his food down with well water.

"Condemned man should get whiskey," Diamond observed, looking disapprovingly at the tin cup.

"When we're fixing to hang a man, we don't waste good whiskey on him," said Mundy, chuckling.

"Bad whiskey be all right," Diamond said, wiping his mouth with the back of his hand.

Fisher finished his meal, drank a little water, put the cup on the plate, and stepped up close to the bars. Diamond put his plate, spoon, and cup through the slot.

"Here you go, you old coot," he said. "Tell 'em I want pie next time."

"Pie now, is it?" Mundy shook his head, coming closer for the dirty plates.

Fisher waited till Mundy was about as close as he usually got, then shoved his plate clumsily at the slot, purposely knocking it into a crossbar. "Damn it!"

The plate and cup clattered down, the mostly full tin cup sloshing its water as it rolled under the slot. Acting on reflex, Mundy bent to pick it up—having to bend closer than usual.

Fisher's hand went to his knife as Diamond lunged, his hands darting between the bars, one hand clapping over the old jailer's mouth, the other forcing him closer—as Fisher's knife swept up and sliced through Mundy's throat and windpipe.

Gurgling on blood, squirming, Mundy tried to pull free—but it was no good. Fisher had him by the beard now, and the two men held him fast till enough blood gushed out so that the old jailer sank, shaking, to his knees. His eyes fluttered . . . and he died.

They let him fall, and it was the work of a moment to pull the keys from the jailer's belt and two moments more to unlock the door. Sadly, Mundy had no gun to seize, but Fisher found six dollars in his pockets, which was some consolation.

The two men, stepping around the spreading pool of blood, went to the door to the hall outside the little cellblock. This being a courthouse, Fisher hoped the sheriff wouldn't have an office on this floor. And this time of night he'd be off getting his dinner.

Fisher's luck was with him at last—when they opened the door, they saw no one in the hall. "We'll walk out cool and calm," said Fisher. "We'll steal us some horses and see if we can find that Ruskett. He told me where he lives—we'll find him on the road going east."

"What we want with him? He's just trouble."

"He's got guns, for one thing, and he's got four hundred dollars on him. . . ."

"Alls of a sudden, meeting up with him does sound appealin'. . . ."

CHAPTER THREE

"SETH, WHAT'D OLD man Dubois have to leave town over? I never heard much about it."

"My pa told me. He knew Josette and I were pals." They were finishing their dinner at the Prairie Fire Café, Seth relishing the tartness of the green-apple pie. "Dubois was supposed to supply the Apache reservation with flour and potatoes and such. He kept back half of it and charged for the whole amount. Sold the extra on the side."

"That's plenty crooked! Taking food from the mouths of them families!"

"That's about the size of it. He got found out, left town one night before he could be charged. And here we come to find he's started a store all the way up to Kansas." Seth poured a little more coffee into his cup. "I never liked him—'cause he didn't like me. Didn't want me around his daughter. But when I heard that story about the reservation, why, I sorrowed that Josette was stuck with such a man. She has no mother—he worked her to death, seemed like—and no one else but Dubois."

"They were talking French, weren't they? Where they start out, New Orleans?"

"Nope. French Canada. Quebec. She taught me a few words in French. I remember 'em, too. *Como-tally-voo.*"

"What's that mean?"

"Means 'how y'all doin' or some such. Well, that was a good meal. I expect the store's closed now. . . ."

"You going to buy another shirt?"

"Just hoping to walk her home, not that it's any of your never mind."

"I expect he chased her off home to make his supper. *Have it ready when I get there*, he'd say."

Seth nodded. That sounded exactly like F. Dubois.

He paid his share of the tab and went to see if the store was still open. Nope, it was closed. Seth stood there on the street, telling himself that this could be an omen. Likely Josette was closed to him altogether. He ought to just ride on out in the morning with Franklin. . . .

J OSETTE WAS STILL stirring the gravy when her father came in. He stumbled into the back of a chair, and it fell with a clatter. She knew at once he'd been drinking. He often told her, when they closed the store, that he would stay there a while to do his business sums, but she knew he would soon be off to the saloon out to the edge of town. Sometimes she made supper for him, and he didn't get home till late, and then he com-

plained the food was cold and inedible. Last time he'd
thrown the pot at her head.

He needed to be wrangled like a horse into the loco-
weed at a time like this. She commenced spooning
dumplings onto his plate, to go with the wine-cooked
rooster, so she could get the food to him quickly and
keep him calm. The plate was china, blue cornflowers
decorating it. Her mother had picked it up, and sometimes, looking at the china, Josette felt an aching lone-
liness deep down inside. Josette missed her mother
badly. Mama had died of the pneumonia, maybe
brought on by overwork in the cold, for her father had
had Mama out in the barn every night, no matter how
cold it was, churning butter to sell along with the goods
he'd lifted from the reservation.

Josette looked out the warped glass at the waning
moon rising over the prairie. It made her think about
what a big world it was and how there was surely something more for her out there, somewhere.

She'd thought about leaving her father. She was of
age, after all, and he could take care of himself if he
had to. She had little devotion to him. More than once
he had hit her—as when she'd tried to walk out with
Jeff Koenig. He had struck her mama when he was in
his cups, too.

What would she use for traveling? He had sold her
horse, and he did not give her a salary for working at
the store—it was simply expected of her. "I give you
house, food, clothing. I raise you. That's enough!" her
father told her. How was she to move away with no ap-
preciable money? She had managed to save some money
by doing some sewing for neighbors and selling extra

butter and eggs, but—it was so very little. Perhaps she
could save a little food up and take the weekly stagecoach with what little money she had to Kansas City.
There she might find work. But—she might not. She
could end up wandering like a ghost on the street.
Would the Church help her? Josette, like her parents,
was Catholic. Her father had almost never gone to
Mass, and there was no Catholic chapel in Prairie Fire.
She missed going to Mass, hearing a Catholic choir, being able to pray before the Holy Virgin. In Kansas City,
surely there would be a Catholic church. Perhaps—

"Josette!" Dubois barked. *"Où est mon souper!"*

"Voilà," Josette said meekly, placing the plate and
the silverware on the table before him.

"Sit down," he told her in Quebecois French.

"I will eat later, Papa," she replied in the same language.

"I said, *sit down!*"

She sighed—and sat. "Is this good, or would you
prefer me to sit with my hands in my lap?"

"Do not talk peppery to me, girl!" He was chewing
with his mouth open as usual and talking at the same
time. "I will have you listen now. I've found some property I wish to make my own. It is on this side of the
Cimarron River where cattle herds are forded across.
I want that land so that the trail boss will have to pay a
toll to take his herds across. I will begin a new store
there, too." He swallowed a great lump of food and
then crowed, "Maybe I even start a little town! Imagine that, eh? Dubois City!"

Josette nodded patiently. She was used to her father's
harebrained schemes. One of them had almost landed

him in jail in Texas, so they'd had to ride out in the night and start over here. That memory put her in mind of Seth Coe. Curious, his coming into the store today. He seemed to glow when he looked at her. She remembered their time together as children. Funny, how—

"Josette!"

"Yes, Papa?"

"You are making the wool gather! Listen to me! Now, this land I want, I cannot afford. It is owned now by the Kelmers."

"Yes?" She knew the Kelmers a little, mostly from the store. The Kelmer patriarch, James, was the most powerful rancher in the county. He had used his money and influence to make Lem Chilroy, his accountant, the mayor. James was part owner in the bank, too. He was a superficially affable man, always with a big smile for her, but he was well-known to be ruthless underneath.

She knew his son, Heywood, a little more, a man who talked a good deal without saying much, interrupting other people to do it, always playing a part of some kind. He'd hinted at taking her to the summer dance. She had not yet said no. He was wealthy, he was good-looking, and one could get used to a man's annoying ways. Perhaps she could learn to like him if he courted her. Other men had tried to court her—but her father had driven them away. The son of James Kelmer was too powerful to drive away.

"I spoke to James," her father went on around another mouthful of chicken, "to try to come to a deal. He did not want to change the price. Then I spoke to Heywood—always so friendly. I thought maybe he would speak to his father for me. He said maybe so. But he said, 'I am in need of a wife, and your daughter is the prettiest unmarried girl in town.'"

Her mouth dropped open. "Papa! Are you thinking of . . . of trading me for land?"

"In the old country, in many places, such things are done, and why not? You moon about, wishing for a man, and here he is—a fine-looking man with money! Me, I will find a squaw to do your work."

She shook her head in wonder. Traded to the Kelmers? It was true she wanted to be married. Partly to get away from her father; partly because she was lonely for tenderness. And she loved children. But it was not unthinkable for her to live without a man. Why not? If her father was any measure of what men were like . . .

Admittedly, despite her indifference, at best, to Heywood Kelmer, there would be money. She might have a housekeeper and perhaps be able to raise the sheep and goats and horses she'd always wanted. A woman should be practical, shouldn't she?

"But," her father went on, "there is no completed deal as yet. He wishes to . . . to walk out with you."

Josette frowned. How far did "walking out" go with Heywood? She had heard a rumor of another girl and a baby given away. Did he wish to ride the mare before he purchased her? Well, she knew herself to be a strong woman. She would keep him on the other side of the corral fence.

"Very well, Papa. I can let him court me, and we will see. What is the harm?"

What, indeed? But she had some nagging inner prompting, some instinct, that told her Heywood himself might be the harm. . . .

* * *

WELL, THAT WAS a good breakfast," said Franklin. "Had to have them hot cakes. Never could make 'em myself."

"I'm about filled up to bust," Seth said, gazing out the flyspecked window of the café.

The two cowboys were used to rising with dawn most times, and they'd been waiting at the door of the café when it opened a little after seven. It was a trifle after eight now as they finished their meal. They sat by the window at Seth's insistence so he could keep an eye on the sunny street.

"Be good to ride out of town right smart, Seth, before it gets hot out. Hell, it gets too hot, we can find a little shade and take us a siesta this afternoon."

"Oh—no hurry," said Seth, setting down his coffee cup. "We might want to buy some fresh eggs to take along."

"Last time we done that, you busted them in your saddlebag."

"I'll pack 'em right on top this time, and take good care."

"I suppose some eggs would go good tomorrow morning. Where you reckon to get them? Oh—I have me a notion. The F. Dubois General Store. They might have some eggs in from Farmer Brown or Farmer Green. That it?"

Seth dabbed at his lips with the plaid napkin. "And why not?"

"Why, I bet we'd get a better price just stopping at a farm on the way," said Franklin, grinning and watching Seth's face.

"I just thought . . . She's my old friend. Dang it, Franklin. Why shouldn't I see her once more?"

"Fine and dandy. Then we ride out?"

"I reckon so."

But Seth wasn't so sure.

They went to see to their horses, brushing them down themselves to save on the fee and because the horses liked it better; they saw that they were grained and watered.

Back on the street, noticing the blacksmith already at work, they strolled over and Franklin asked the big, yellow-bearded man if he could fix the failing belly buckle—jury-rigged now with rawhide—on his saddle. The big man agreed, and they brought the saddle back, Seth the whole time keeping an eye on the general store.

At last, as they were watching the blacksmith repair the buckle, Seth saw Josette and Dubois walking up to unlock the store.

Seth shifted his feet impatiently, waiting a couple minutes so he didn't seem like he was rushing at Josette. He looked at the blacksmith. Then he looked at the store. Finally, he said, "Franklin, I'm going to see about them eggs."

Not waiting for a reply, Seth crossed the street, entering the store moments after the wooden sign reading *Open* was hung in the window.

Josette looked up as he came in, met his eyes, and smiled. That smile was so bright and lively, he almost stumbled over a crate of apples.

"Well, my goodness, don't fall and injure yourself, Seth," she said, leaning on the counter. He didn't see her father; he supposed he must be in the back room. That was good luck, anyhow.

Seth strode over to her and said, "Would you . . . Could we . . . go for a walk? After you get off work?"

"I have to go prepare my father's meals then. And do many other chores after."

"He doesn't give you any time to take your leisure?"

"Precious little." She glanced over her shoulder and lowered her voice. "The store is closed on Sunday, and being as I often pick berries out along Black Creek this time of year . . . in the morning, round ten, a little to the north . . . I—"

"Josette!" Dubois roared, coming in. "What do you say to this cowboy?"

"I . . ." She licked her lips. "He was asking if we had any fresh berries. I told him I hoped to have some in on Monday."

Dubois scowled, his lower lip half covering his upper. "You—cowboy! What you want? More supplies?"

"I . . . You got any fresh eggs, Mr. Dubois?"

"We do not!"

"Mrs. Emery's farm—they'd have some," Josette said. She gave her head a little shake as if to warn Seth to say nothing more.

"You think I am a fool, cowboy?" Dubois demanded. "You think I don't see what it is you do here? You are looking at my daughter like a bull at the cow!"

"Papa!" Josette hissed, turning to him, her eyes flashing. "To say such a thing!"

"*Soit silencieux!*" Dubois snarled. "Into the back room, Josette!"

"No! I am not a child!"

"You go, or I throw you there!"

Seth felt his hands ball into fists. It was going to take some power of will not to throw a sockdolager into this man's loud mouth.

The door jangled. "Seth?"

He felt Franklin's hand on his shoulder, a firm but not unkindly grip. "Franklin—this man—"

"Please . . ." Josette shook her head at him. "Go."

He saw the glimmer of unshed tears in her eyes. Then she turned away and almost ran through the curtains to the back room.

His emotions churning, first this way, then that, Seth turned away.

"Stay away from her!" Dubois called after Seth. "I have the shotgun! She is loaded!"

Outside, Seth couldn't keep from slamming the door shut.

"I have the shotgun! She is loaded!" Franklin said, mimicking Dubois. "Well. This here's a good town to leave behind, Seth. And right now . . ."

"Leave?" Seth looked at him as if he were the one speaking a foreign language. "I'm going collecting berries on Sunday. By hook or by crook."

"Sunday! That's more'n two days off!"

Seth shrugged. "What's your durn hurry?"

THEY'RE GONNA COME lookin' for these here stolen nags, Hannibal," said Diamond.

"You complaining?" Fisher snorted. "They were going to hang you! I got you out. You stick with me, and I'll get you riches, too."

It was dark on the prairie. There was the making of

a summer storm off to the north, where lightning flickered blue-white in a bank of dark clouds. But nearer at hand, the sky was full of stars and a rising moon.

"Hold up. My rump's fair worn away by this damn greenhorn saddle."

They reined in under a big sycamore tree. Some startled animal, maybe a possum, clattered its way up the trunk into the shadows of the foliage. They'd been riding over rough ground, trying to stay off the main road, and it was hard on a man's behind, along with these new saddles. They'd taken the horses from a big barn at the outskirts of Newton—a new barn for a new ranch with new horses and even new saddles. The barn had smelled of green planks. Fisher had taken charge of a loaded Henry rifle holstered in saddle gear hanging on the barn wall.

"Tried to make it look like the horses busted loose and run off," Fisher said. "Maybe they bought into it. We've ridden so twisty out on the prairie, up creeks and across rock, they'll have a deuce of a time tracking us."

"What makes you think we're nigh to that bounty hunter?"

"He was gnawing on a corncob pipe when he was taking me to Newton. Mentioned he goes through two or three a month. Well, I saw just such a pipe with the smell of his tobacco at the last campfire. It's him—and that was last night, just plumb on the route I said he'd be on. Now, if we stay on this route and watch for a campfire . . ."

"I need me a rest." Diamond climbed off the horse, rubbed his rump with one hand, with the other taking up his canteen. "Nothing but water to drink . . ."

"We'll get some whiskey soon enough. Ruskett carries a jug in his pack."

"You sure this Ruskett's worth chasing?"

Fisher thought about that for a moment. Then he said, "I'm as sure as can be. I'll tell you something. The world just decided, sometime this year, to be contrary to me, whatever I did. Run out of one town after another. That ruckus in Kansas City fairly gave me the blue devils, Curt. Then I made up my mind, next time I was going to ride right over anyone who was in the way of getting myself ahead. I had a warmish run of luck at cards, and I went to double my winnings. And first that Coe wins most of my ready, then calls me out so's I get on the wrong side of Wild Bill! Then a bounty hunter rides me down. That's enough of that now! When I make up my mind to something, I follow it all the way to hell and back. Ruskett tossed me in the jug, so he's going to pay for it. That Coe's going to pay. They're going to bite dirt!" He jabbed a forefinger at Diamond. "And don't you run afoul of me, or you'll get the same!"

Fisher could see Diamond's eyes go cold at that. He didn't like being threatened—especially when he was unarmed.

"You stick by me, Curt," Fisher said in a milder tone, "and I'll fill your pockets with cash, both gold and folding."

Diamond grunted and peered down their back trail. "First thing is to get ourselves clear of the law."

"Then let's ride on!"

"Not quite rested yet. Nor is my mount."

They rested the horses for half an hour, Fisher chafing at the delay, and started out once more. "Let's go down to the road, and just keep quiet, listen for anyone tracking us," Fisher said. "He won't be far off the road."

"'Bout time we get out of the toolies," Diamond said.

Two hours more, and they were crossing a log bridge over a creek when they saw a light twinkling off to the south. It had the red flicker of a campfire. "Could be him," Fisher whispered. "Let's walk the horses into those willows yonder, and we'll move in slow to see whose fire it is. . . ."

"I'm not feeling so charitable I care whose fire it is," Diamond growled.

The horses tied up in the willows, they crept through scrub brush a few steps off the creek, approaching the firelight, Fisher carrying the Henry.

They were within six yards of the campfire, when Fisher got a good look. It was Ruskett all right, sitting on a folded blanket by the fire, taking a pull on a jug he'd propped on one shoulder. Fisher signaled to Diamond, and both of the stalkers stopped where they were. Seeing the shotgun cradled across Ruskett's lap, Fisher tried to figure how to come at Ruskett without catching a bellyful from the ten gauge. Was he close enough for a sure shot with the Henry? Maybe so.

Fisher raised the Henry and took aim—and Diamond whispered, just a little too loud, "Careful not to hit that dang jug!"

Ruskett swore to himself, dropped the jug, and swung the shotgun their way—Fisher had to take his shot.

It went right home, hitting Ruskett in the heart, and the bounty hunter jerked back with the impact, falling on his back, twitching, calling out what might have been an Injun name . . . and then he went limp.

"Got him, by God!" Diamond crowed.

"Damn your noise, anyway!" Fisher muttered, pushing through the brush to the campfire. "I wanted him to know who it was! I wanted him to know why he was going to die!" He kicked idly at the body. "I'd've got the jump on him. . . ."

Diamond had already scooped up the jug. "He's a considerate gent, ain't he?" He took a slug of the corn liquor. "Whew! Yes, sir, he built us a campfire, left us all his gear, and even bought us a drink. What about the money, Hannibal?"

Fisher knelt beside the body, dug around till he found a leather bag, tugged it free, and, hands trembling, forced it open. "Considerable sum in here. Looks like about two hundred dollars." In fact it looked to be above four hundred.

"He was supposed to have four hundred!"

"Maybe sent the rest on."

"Let me look at that purse!"

Fisher swung the rifle toward Diamond. "You going to call me a liar?"

Diamond stood there, glowering at him, his face taking on flickering red tones in the firelight. But he was unarmed. After a moment, he said, "I reckon not."

Fisher tugged out some bills from the leather bag, tossed five folded twenties at Diamond's boots. "There's your share."

"How about his horse? His saddle?"

"You been complaining about your saddle. You can have his. We'll sell his horse and share the money. And you can have that shotgun. I'll take his six-shooter."

Diamond bent over, reaching for the shotgun.

"Nope, not yet!" Fisher snapped. He prodded Diamond with the muzzle of the rifle. "Back up."

Diamond stepped back, his scowl deepening.

"One more step," Fisher said.

Diamond hesitated—then took another step back. Fisher put the small leather bag of cash in his pants pocket, then picked up the shotgun. He tucked his rifle under one arm, quickly emptied the two shells out of the street cannon. Then he tossed the weapon to Diamond. "When I decide I can trust you, you can have those shells. But I'm not sure right about now—I saved you from hanging and gave you a hundred dollars, and you're calling me a liar! And, Curt—I need you to know who's boss."

Diamond let out a long breath. "Let's put it behind us. I didn't mean nothing. Let's see if he's got anything to eat. . . ."

"Right after you drag that body off into the brush."

"Yep. He's poor company the way he is."

"Just sling him behind that pile of rocks back there."

"Where we going after this, Hannibal?" Diamond asked as he came over to take the corpse by the collar. "I mean—for the plan and all."

"Back west a ways. Then we ride hard to the south. The road to Texas. I'm going to find that cowboy that took my money. We'll take it back, and I'll take a good deal more out of his hide. . . ."

CHAPTER FOUR

"Y OU MOONING OVER that girl isn't going to win her, Seth," said Franklin. "She didn't seem the type to disobey her father. And you don't really know her—what you remember is a little girl. She's a grown woman now and has 'most forgot about you."

They were in the Gypsy Saloon, in the early afternoon, sitting at the bar. The saloon was a little east of Prairie Fire, as if deliberately set apart from the respectable part of town. It was set a bit back from the road, too, as if to make it yet more inobtrusive. Four men—three ranch hands and their boss, it looked like to Seth—were crowded at the far end of the bar, grousing about something in an undertone.

"I was always sweet on that little girl," Seth mused, "but I was too young to say so. I knew it wasn't the time."

"Now you're old enough to know it's clearly not a

winning proposition, Seth. The man threatened you with a shotgun! Even if she eloped with you, he'd have the sheriff chase you down. She may be of age, but out here, it's expected that a man's children do his bidding right along."

Seth shrugged. "I just knew when I saw her, Franklin. What a wild roll of the dice it was, me finding her here at a time when I've got no further plans to ever come back to Kansas. I had one chance to come across that girl! I'll tell you what it is—it's fated by providence!"

Franklin made a little scornful puffing sound. "Providence! Your pa tell you about that?"

"My ma."

"Oh, it would be, too, wouldn't it? How long do you reckon to chase this here will-o'-the-wisp?"

"We're meeting to . . . to have a kind of picnic. Well, anyhow, I'm gonna help her pick some wild berries, come Sunday. Then I'll have her alone enough we can talk it over. If there's nothing doing, I'll give up then and there."

"That's tolerably fair. But what're we supposed to do round here while you're waiting for your glorious berry-picking expedition, Seth?" Franklin asked as he dumped a shot of whiskey into his mug of beer. "Because all the activity I can figure to round up is getting drunk and playing gamblin' games I end up sorry I played."

"There's a pool hall in town," said Seth. "And we could do some hunting."

"I done spent enough time on the prairie. Some billiards now, that might go. You know this town hasn't even got a whorehouse. Doesn't seem quite civilized."

Seth drank a little of his beer and looked out the warped glass of the saloon's only window. A big sorrel horse, tossing its head, was pulling a buggy in toward town; seen through the cheap glass, it seemed to ripple and dance as it went. "We could find some work to pull in a handful of cash. Day's worth of work or so."

"Ain't that just like you?" Franklin said, shaking his head. "Looking for every last chance to wear yourself out. And me with you."

Seth turned to look at the four men at the other end of the bar. He had heard them talk about branding cattle and having too much of it to do in the time allotted. He turned to the bartender, a sallow man with a plump face, muttonchops, and eyes so small and dark, they were like raisins in dough. "Say, friend, those fellas down there"—he kept his voice low, using the discretion of frontier men avoiding offense—"they work at a ranch hereabouts?"

"Black Creek Acres," said the bartender, scratching somewhere under his greasy apron. "That tall fella, that's Heywood Kelmer. His pa owns the place. Biggest spread for a hundred miles."

Seth nodded and sauntered over to the cowboys, lifting his beer in greeting. "Gents." He touched his hat to the tall man. "Would you be Mr. Heywood Kelmer?"

"I am," said the tall man, looking at Seth with a faint expression of disdain. He was wearing a riding suit with a black-velvet tailcoat, shiny black boots to his knees, and a riding cap tilted back on his thick curly black hair. Seth had only seen riding suits in magazines till now, in illustrations of plantation owners out in the Carolinas and suchlike places. Heywood Selmer looked like a man from a magazine in another way, too—his features were so regular, he was like some paragon of male beauty in a lithograph. Paler than the other men here, with a mustache that closely followed the supercilious curve of his lips, he looked at Seth as if he were about to laugh. But Seth soon learned he looked at most folks like that.

"My name's Seth Coe, sir, and I heard you speak about a power of work to be done and not much time to do it. My pard and I, we just finished the Cullin Ranch drive. We done it twice in two years. I was second ramrod for Mr. Cullin. We've both done as much branding as any man alive, and we work quick."

"Little pitchers have big ears," chuckled a cowboy with long gray hair, a bushy mustache—so bushy it quite hid his mouth—and a curled-back hat on his head.

The other two cowboys grinned at that.

"Kind of short, aren't you?" said a big man with a low-crowned hat and bristling black beard. "We breed the biggest cattle in the state!"

"Never found one too big for me to rope. I rode a couple, too."

"Rode them!" Heywood's perfectly formed sable eyebrows bobbed in surprise. He gave a small affected laugh, like something he had practiced. "We prefer to herd them, ha-ha!"

The other men dutifully laughed.

Seth grinned. "Rode 'em in competition, down to Dallas. They're not made to be ridden, and they let you know it! If a man can stay aboard for half a minute, why, he wins ten dollars."

"Remarkable!" said Heywood, snorting. "They have branding competitions, too?"

"Roping and branding, yes, sir. I won second place. Y'all don't have rodeos in Kansas?"

"Haven't time for such things. Well, we may have a day's work for you. Come over to Black Creek with us, and if Vince here thinks you're all right, you can get started this evening." He turned to the cowboy with the bushy mustache. "Vince, you and the boys take him and his pard out to Black Creek. See how they do. If they're all right, put 'em up in a cabin, and they can work tonight and tomorrow."

He turned his back on Seth, then, bending to talk to a compact hand with a ferret face and a door-knocker mustache.

Seth was surprised to be dismissed in that way. Most men in Texas settled wages and then shook a man's hand at a time like that. But it was short-time work, and he decided he wouldn't let it stick in his craw.

He returned to Franklin and said, "Got us a free place to stay and something to do!"

"I heard! You got us a miserable bunk, a lot of work, and you didn't even ask how much they're paying." Franklin sighed. But his partner had made a deal for the two of them, and Franklin wasn't inclined to buck it. Kicking now wasn't the cowboy way, after riding with a man for so long. "Hell—let's go and get it done."

JOSETTE WAS SURPRISED to see Heywood Kelmer ride up on his palomino quarter horse; he was wearing a tailcoat and a funny little cap that tied under his chin. She'd never seen a man in a riding suit before either. Must be showing off a new acquisition.

She was on the wooden sidewalk in front of the millinery, on her way back from the café, bringing her father a covered dish with thick oxtail soup, for he'd given over his breakfast and now found himself famished. Bread and cheese to accompany the soup could be had at the store.

"Hello, Josette," said Heywood, touching his hat and bowing a little in the saddle.

"Afternoon, Heywood," she said, nodding. She paused, squinting up at him in the bright sunshine. What a picture of a man he was. Tall and straight in the saddle, riding in finery, and that look on his face like a man giving a child a treat. As if she were lucky to encounter him. "I'm just taking my papa his lunch."

She expected him to get down and offer to carry it for her, but he didn't. "You know the summer ball is coming up," Heywood said.

"I seem to have heard it remarked upon."

"How coy you are! You're coming to it with me, aren't you? Your father spoke to you?"

"He mentioned it. Are you so sure no one else has asked me first?"

"Mr. Dubois gave me to understand he wouldn't permit such foolishness."

"My father thinks he can speak for me. Maybe he can. Maybe he can't. Still and all, I might be persuaded to go to the dance with you. If I choose to go at all."

"It's at Black Creek Acres, you know."

"I do know that. It was there last year and the year before. My father allowed me to watch but not to dance."

"This year he's promised you'll dance with me!"

"Has he? You will have the wooden dance floor set out?"

"With flowers and bunting! We'll have a bigger band this year, too. Musicians coming all the way from Kansas City!"

She shrugged noncommittally. "It's two weeks off, so there's still time for you to decide if you prefer to escort Maybelle Skupper."

"Maybelle! You saw me riding with her once, and you jump to conclusions."

"Or Georgiana Potts. I hear from Melody Winters you've been escorting her to Sunday services."

"Pah!" But then he chuckled. "Most interesting to find you have been on a gather of my doings!"

"You belittle me with such remarks, Heywood. The ladies at my sewing circle tell me of your doings without my asking—as they report everyone's doings." Josette smiled. "We'll talk on it later. This pot's getting heavy. Good afternoon, Heywood."

She made the faintest curtsylike bob, as her mama had done when taking leave of folks, and hurried off down the walk to the store, clasping her covered dish and thinking that Papa would have wanted her to be far more agreeable to Heywood. And Heywood himself seemed surprised that she didn't do a little girlish dance of delight at his invitation. But some instinct told her to wait, to just wait and see what happened.

T HE SECOND DAY of work at Black Creek Acres was a long one and more pressed than the first by reason of a different supervisor. Seth didn't mind the first day under Vince's bossing; he rather liked Vince. But Saturday morning, Heywood Kelmer had taken over.

"In the name of efficiency," he'd said.

Chance Grogan, the little man with the door-knocker mustache, had muttered to Seth that Heywood was "like to talk of efficiency, since he come back from that business school out east."

They were working in a cattle pen out by the biggest barn that Seth had ever seen. The barn contained dairy cows on one side and horses on the other.

To the north, between here and the tree-lined Black Creek, a quarter mile off, was an alfalfa field, ripe for harvest. The place interested Seth because the Kelmers seemed to be doing something—successfully, too—that Seth himself wanted to accomplish: a sizable spread with a mix of enterprises. Should one enterprise fail, the others would keep the business alive. It seemed to have worked for the Kelmers; a good distance off, Seth could see the splendid three-story white house, done up in the Colonial style complete with pillars.

A warm breeze lifted dust up around the cattle bunched at the far end of the pen, away from the branding fire, and Seth, at four in the afternoon, had sat astride his mare since their short, Spartan lunch. Grass lariat in hand, he waited for Franklin and Sweeney to separate out a yearling for roping and branding. Sweeney was a gangly fellow with sunken eyes and a curtain of lank brown hair around his half-bald pate—the others called him Peanut, maybe because of the shape of his long head.

"How is it you prefer a grass lariat?" Sweeney had asked Seth.

"Why, it's lighter, and the leather ones can crack on you."

Sweeney shook his head in disapproval. "Stock needs a good firm leather loop."

The black-bearded fellow, naturally enough called Blackie, was working with Vince, the two of them tending the red-hot branding irons at the stone-ringed fire. Chance sat calmly on his horse, waiting his turn to rope a calf. There were eighteen more hands off on other chores around the property, not counting the sharecroppers working on the alfalfa.

Heywood Kelmer mostly watched from the fence, calling out suggestions, which usually slowed things down. Now he strolled up beside Seth's horse, thumbs hooked in his belt. Heywood was wearing a spotless white hat with a high-peaked crown, a white cotton shirt, and blue dungarees tucked into shiny black riding boots.

"You do most of your cowboying on a mare?" Heywood asked, cocking his head to look up at Seth. "I figure a gelding is better."

"Why, some prefer a gelding, but all that matters, to my mind," said Seth, cricking his back to the left and right to ease the stiffness, "is how biddable a man's horse is for the job. Now, mares are a little smarter, I find, and take training right quick. And if they like you, they'll work harder for you."

"If they like you!" Heywood snorted. "Around here they like what the whip tells them to like."

Seth shrugged, dallying one end of his lariat around the saddle horn with his left hand and grasping the rope just under the loop with his right. "My pa used to say there's a place for the quirt, but getting a horse to bond, why that reaches deeper, makes the horse more loyal."

Heywood's brows knit at that. "Your *pa*, huh?" He snorted again and pointed. "Well—there's your calf. Let's see how quick that mare of yours can be."

Franklin and his mount had nudged the young beef away from its protective, moaning mother and out into the middle of the pen. It was more a yearling than a calf, and was looking for someplace to run as Seth nudged Mazie into action. She had seen the yearling and knew just what to do, immediately dashing in a tight circle, pushing the yearling away from the other cattle, making it run. Seth whirled his loop, then whipped it out flat for a heel catch, sending it unerringly to slide under the yearling's rear hooves. Leaning back in the saddle, he said, "Ho!" to Mazie, and she dug her hooves in, the rope tightening from the saddle horn and, the honda closing the loop, jerking the yearling off balance. The horse began backing up, pulling the calf in reach of the branding men.

Blackie held the yearling down with his knee, driving the sizzling brand home on the bawling beef, while Vince made a couple of quick cuts in one of its ears for an additional branding mark.

On the work went for a few hours more, with Seth and Franklin and sometimes Blackie trading off jobs. Sometimes Sweeney branded or cut out the calves, but he didn't seem to have the skill to rope them. Heywood watched, did a little branding, made some more unhelpful suggestions, then went off to some unknown business in the barn.

Almost time for supper—and for Seth and Franklin, being paid off for their work over the last couple days—the men had just finished branding for the day when Sweeney made his bet.

"That horse of yours, Coe," he said, "that's a sound horse. Kinder quick, too. But I bet you she's got no legs for jumping."

"Mazie can jump over the moon, she wants to," declared Seth, untying the mare from the fence.

"That right? Boss has a horse can jump over that fence there. Seen him clearly like a breeze. Bet your horse cain't do it. Not without dropping you along the way."

"Is that so?" Seth said as Heywood returned. "I'd take your bet on that."

"What bet is that?" Heywood asked.

"Wouldn't do it unless it was okay with you, boss," said Sweeney meekly. "Just that he thinks his mare could jump over that fence like your stallion. I'm saying it's not a jumping horse."

Heywood took off his hat as he looked over Seth's horse. He took a blue kerchief from his pocket and dabbed sweat from his forehead. "Could not envision that horse jumping a fence myself. Tell you what. As the day's work is over, and if we use that fence over there, the one missing the top board—balance another board so's if the horse hits it, we don't get a broken-leg horse lying in the way round here—why, I'll put twenty dollars on it."

Sweeney suggested raising it to forty dollars, and Heywood consented. Franklin bet forty on Seth, and Seth took the bet himself.

Vince shook his head. "Not a-gonna bet on this. I reckon this man knows his horses. And I am sure not going to bet against the boss."

"Here's one condition," said Sweeney. "She's got to carry you over without you falling out of the saddle!"

Seth shrugged. "Never going to fall out of this saddle."

No one else took the bet, and Vince went to get another piece of lumber to set at top-board height on the section of fence where it was a mite low. Seth calculated that the distance across the pen was more than enough for Mazie to do it. She was the only horse he had ever felt comfortable jumping—for he didn't like risking a horse ending up with an injury, nor himself either—but he couldn't keep that mare from jumping when she was of a mind to do it. She loved jumping over any obstacle at all, with or without a rider. Seth handed Sweeney the reins, took the board from Vince, and went to place it himself, making sure it was balanced right. He wanted it to be set up so one clip of hoof would knock it down. He didn't want Mazie hurt.

He walked Mazie back to the far end of the corral, talking to her as they went along. "We're gonna jump us a fence, girl. . . ."

Seth climbed up in the saddle and set himself for the jump. "Seth, wait!" Franklin called. "Maybe check the—"

But Mazie was already running, picking up speed to a gallop, leaping—and the saddle gave a sudden lurch, throwing Seth into the air. He was half over the fence when it happened, and he fell on the far side, deliberately turning in the air to catch the impact in a belly flop, the only way, at this angle, to keep from breaking a bone.

The mare sailed over the top board, coming down beside him, taking another ten steps before digging in to stop. Seth was gasping, the air knocked out of him, and then coughing in the dust, when Mazie came over and nudged him with her muzzle.

"I'm"—he coughed—"all right, girl." He got to his feet, and, still wheezing, stared at the saddle—it was askew on the horse.

Franklin vaulted over the fence and put a hand on his shoulder.

"You bust anything?"

"Don't believe so. What the hell happened to my saddle?"

"I was trying to tell you. . . ."

"You lost, Coe!" Sweeney called. "You fell off! Pay up! You other gents, too!"

Franklin and Seth went to Mazie and looked at the saddle. Seth swallowed a cussword. "The damn strap's been loosened!"

"I tried to tell you I saw that Sweeney foolin' with your saddle. He was making it look like he was being sure the strap was tight, but I don't trust him and . . . well, off you went!"

Seth didn't anger easy. But he had a mad on now. He might've put his hand on his gun, only none of them wore a gun for this kind of work.

He turned and shouted, "Mr. Kelmer! Will you—" He had been about to say, *Get over here and look at this!* But he thought better of it, not wanting his pay docked for talking rough to the boss, and called, "Would you mind having a look at this?"

Vince opened the gate, and the men followed Heywood through to inspect the horse.

"I've ridden with this man for years, Mr. Kelmer," Franklin said. "He has never buckled his cinch loose."

"I thought it felt kinda funny when I got on," Seth said, "but I figured I imagined it, since I knew how I cinched it, which was good and tight!"

Heywood bent and looked. "It's loose, all right. Quite loose."

"Are you looking for a way to welsh on a bet?" Sweeney demanded.

Franklin rounded on him, fists taut. "I thought I saw you fooling with that cinch! You made sure to say you win if he falls off—and then you made sure he fell off!"

"That's a lie!" Sweeney snarled, but stepped back out of Franklin's reach.

"Now, I don't know . . ." Heywood muttered, scratching behind one ear. "Coe—you think this man did what your partner says?"

Seth glared at Sweeney. "Not a speck of doubt!"

"Vince, what do you think?"

Vince tugged thoughtfully on his mustache. "I did see Sweeney put a hand on the horse and wondered at it—couldn't see what he was doing. But by God, I've watched this man Coe all day, and *that's* a horseman! He's not the man to make a green mistake! And he'd have fallen off before now if that cinch was loose—it wasn't loose till Sweeney was fiddling with it!"

"Yeah," Heywood said reluctantly, "I reckon so. Well, then . . ."

"Now, look here!" Sweeney began. "I've been working on this ranch for a full six weeks, and this man just got here and—"

"You're *done* working on this ranch," Heywood interrupted. "You're fired! Vince, pay Peanut here off and escort him off the property. Right away."

"What about the bet?" Franklin asked. "That horse cleared the fence, and it wasn't Seth's fault he came off!"

Heywood turned to him and Seth, narrowing his eyes. "That bet is canceled on account of . . . of all this.

It was invalidated." He seemed testy now that Franklin had challenged him about the bet. "You two, stay for supper at the chow shack, and Vince'll pay you after. Then hit the trail. And don't be gossiping about this!" He turned and stalked away.

Seth shook his head and went to pick up his hat, which lay on its crown in the dirt.

HANNIBAL FISHER ELECTED to take Ruskett's horse for his own, since no one yet knew it was stolen. At a small ranch to the south, they got forty dollars for the one he'd taken from that barn outside Newton. The horse was worth more, but the hard-eyed old rancher must've guessed it might be stolen, and what with him having two armed, grown sons at hand, Fisher wasn't inclined to argue.

They'd traveled most of a long, hot day south, fast as they could without doing real harm to their mounts, and just in the last afterglow of sunset, they saw smoke rising from a low, rocky hill about five hundred yards off the road.

"Somebody's got a camp out there," Fisher said as they reined in.

"You supposing it's this Seth Coe you're looking for?" Diamond asked.

"I reckon they could have taken their time, heading south—and this could be their camp. There's but one way to find out."

Just as they'd done with Ruskett, Fisher and Diamond tied the horses in the brush off the road and stealthily worked their way toward the camp, being careful where they set down their boots. Fisher had the rifle, Diamond the shotgun. Fisher had given him the shells but kept Diamond in front of him as they started up the hill.

The hill was stubbled with small, scrubby trees around low, mossy boulders. They followed a deer trail, winding between the boulders, toward the top of the hill just above the camp. That way they could have the drop on the cowboys. But getting into position, lying belly down on a shelf of rock about thirty feet above the camp and peering through a partial screen of juniper bushes, they saw by the campfire glow that Seth Coe and his friend Franklin were not there at all. Instead, there were four men; a tubby, shirtless man with a mane of red hair was squatting by the fire and cooking, the other three passing a mostly empty whiskey bottle and grumbling at one another.

"Too warm for a fire," said a bearish man. "We got the lantern."

"Got to cook the stew with something," said the tubby man, stirring the cast-iron pot with a stick.

"That tub without his shirt," whispered Diamond, "is Smiley Briggs. I rode with him and Buster Gaines—the one shaped like a big ol' bear. We had a run at a stagecoach, didn't get but three hundred dollars out of it. I know the half baldy with the high forehead there only by sight—him with the scraggly brown beard and the suspenders. Name's Sweeney, is all I know. Horse thief, mostly. Don't know the younger one."

With the three men—and yet somehow not with them—was a lean young man with a worried, quizzical look on his face. He sat a little apart from them, his hat hanging from a broken branch on a tree beside him. He was holding a canteen in his lap, tapping it absently with his fingers as he gazed into the fire. He looked to Fisher like a fella who usually went clean-shaven, but he hadn't had a chance at a razor for a few days. He took off his blue bandanna and wiped sweat from his forehead.

Fisher saw he wasn't wearing his gun belt, but it was in reach, and he had a Winchester by his side. The other three had guns handy and rifles. It would not do to startle them.

"What you look so sour for, Bettiger?" Smiley asked. "Gettin' a free meal, ain't you?"

The younger man shrugged. "I'm just weary, is all. And I've earned my meal same as you, Briggs."

Fisher gestured to Diamond to pull back, and they wriggled to deeper cover. "I would confer with those men," Fisher whispered, "if you think we could talk to them without getting in a fight."

"I expect so, if we do it right."

"They might've seen Coe on the trail. And I might be able to use them. . . ." *I need such men,* Fisher thought. "You call out to them, real careful—tell 'em your name."

Diamond nodded and cupped his hand. "Hello the camp! We are friends!"

"Devil take it—some lying posse snake!" Briggs growled, reaching for his rifle.

"It ain't the law, Smiley. It's Curt Diamond! Me and my partner here saw your fire! We want to talk, is all! Can we come into the camp! We got half a jug of corn liquor left!"

There was a brief whispered colloquy at the fire. Then Briggs called out, "Come on in, but hands up."

"Can we trust them for that, Curt?" Fisher asked softly.

"Sure, I've ridden with Gaines and Briggs, and we parted with no sourness. Come on, Hannibal."

They wended their way down the hill and emerged into the firelight, guns held over their heads.

"Howdy, boys," Diamond said, chuckling. "How'm I going to get that jug up to camp with my hands held up like this?"

"Well, leave your gun, and go get it," said Gaines.

"You act like you don't trust me!"

"It'll make the others feel easier," said Gaines.

Diamond nodded and handed him the shotgun.

Fisher handed over his weapons without complaint and said, "Mind if I sit down?"

"I know you," said Bettiger. "Hannibal Fisher. Wanted in Kansas City right about now."

"I won't deny it," said Fisher. "I hear you boys have spent some time in the willows yourselves."

Briggs grinned. "We're there now! Looking for some way to skin us a hog and get enough bacon to head for Mexico."

"I might could help you with that. I'm looking for a man carrying a good deal of money that belongs to me. And his partner's got some, too. Along with that, I figure it's time to make a withdrawal from a bank. . . ." He had a vague plan forming about using these men to rob a bank as cover for settling the matter with Coe.

"Pull up a log and set," said Gaines. "Tell us about this fella holding your money."

"He's a cowboy," Fisher said, sitting on a small fallen tree trunk. "Likely on his way to Texas. Black hair, dark eyes. Maybe a 'breed. Name's Seth Coe. Rides with a tall man called Franklin."

"Seth Coe!" Sweeney burst out. "Why, I saw him and that Franklin not but three hours ago!"

Fisher went rigid, staring fixedly at Sweeney. "Did you now. Whereabouts?"

"A few miles outside of Prairie Fire, 'bout five miles southeast of here. I was working out on Black Creek Acres, about to set up some horse rustling. Gaines and Briggs here, they were coming to meet me, help me with the herd. I had a plan to get every last horse off that spread so's they couldn't come after us."

"A plan that went tails up, what I hear!" Bettiger snorted.

"Only because I got fired! And why? Seth Coe! He spoke against me! Him and his partner, they got me fired. Boys, I'd throw in with Fisher here if it'll help me get back at that Coe! I'd like to see him dead!"

CHAPTER FIVE

S UNDAY MORNING, WEARING his new blue shirt, Seth
was trotting Mazie east along the town side of
Black Creek in search of Josette. He had some aches
and pains from pitching off the horse, and he had slept
fitfully in the hotel in town, but he was feeling surprisingly good this summer morning. There was thin cloud
cover and just enough breeze to offer some coolness,
and a pretty girl was waiting for him among the gooseberries. Or so he hoped.

Twenty minutes more, he spotted her yellow polka-
dotted shade bonnet lying on an old multicolored quilt
beside a covered basket. He rode a little closer and saw
her in the shade close to the creek. Josette was crouch-
ing down to pick gooseberries, which she dropped into
a tin bucket. He saw she had close-fitting leather gloves
on; the vines, in a shrub about five feet high, bristled
with sharp thorns. She was wearing an ankle-length

yellow summer dress, with puffy shoulders, and white button-up shoes.

Seth nudged Mazie a little closer and climbed down as Josette turned to look at him with a curiously crooked little smile on her petite lips. It was that funny little smile he remembered from childhood.

"Morning, Josette!" he called as he led the horse over the creek. He tied Mazie where she could reach the water and the small patch of grass on the bank.

"You remembered!" she said, dropping a few berries into the bucket.

"Never was a doubt I would," Seth said, strolling over to her, just as if he were calm and collected, though inside his heart was thudding. *Calm down, you damn fool,* he told himself. "What you got there, most of a pail?"

"Oh, yes, several quarts."

"Red gooseberries, are they? We used to eat the ones that were kinda yellow and green down by the river in Texas. You remember?"

"Those are sweeter. These are a bit tart."

"Why, I like some tartness. Maybe that's why I always liked you."

"Oho!" She pretended outrage. "So you think I'm sour like a pickle?"

"More like a Kansas gooseberry. Had a green-apple pie yesterday. My favorite. Can I help you?"

"You have gloves?"

"Heck, I don't need gloves if I'm careful."

"Then you must be very careful indeed."

He plucked at some berries, got one free, and accidentally crushed the next one.

"Now you crush them, Seth! You don't remember how to do it at all!"

"Well-l-l . . ." He tried again—and immediately ran afoul of a thorn. "Ouch!"

"Did I not tell you? You need gloves."

"Maybe you're right." Seth went to his saddlebags, found a pair of leather gloves, and pulled them on as he returned to her. He tried to pick another berry— and crushed it as he attempted to pull it off the vine. "Dang it!"

"Yes, it's more difficult with those cowhide gloves. Now, I'm using some old kid gloves. You can pull the vines out of the way for me so I can reach toward the back. . . ."

Glad to have something he could accomplish for her, he held the vines back, and looking at the creek, he asked, "You remember when we swam in the river? You in your . . . your knickers. Me in some old cutoff britches."

She adopted a prim expression. "Yes—I was just a little girl then. Do not expect to see me swimming in my knickers today."

"No, ma'am." He pulled another vine down to her and said, "I was remembering this morning you nearly drowned in the river one time, and I pulled you out—"

"What! It was I who pulled *you* out!"

"That is not how I recollect it! You fell off the raft, and on account of the current—"

"You were swept away, and I took your hand and pulled you to the shallows."

"Why, it was the other way around!" But he was laughing as he said it. "You *are* a bit sour, ain't you?"

Josette brushed something off a particularly large gooseberry. "This one would not survive in the bucket. It's too ripe." She turned to him with that peculiar, teasing squiggle to her mouth and then held the berry up to his lips. "You can have it."

Somehow feeling breathless, Seth opened his mouth, and she placed the berry on his tongue. He had never tasted anything so vividly before.

"Now, that's the finest fruit I ever tasted. . . ."

"You see? I know how to choose them. Voilà, I have enough berries. I think I have enough for two pies and some preserves. Let's sit down."

"Shall I put this bucket in the water, keep it cool?"

"Yes, in the shallows there. Not close to your horse! She'll eat them all!"

He set the bucket in the water and went to sit by her on the old blanket. "You make this quilt?"

"It was the first one I tried to make. Very badly. It's only good for sitting on the ground." She was poking through the basket and drew out a jar full of what he assumed was well water.

"Looks like corn liquor in that jar!"

"What a wicked notion! That is water! You think I'm drinking like my father?"

"I was only joshing. The old fella go back to the pump a little too often?"

"Back to the pump? Oh . . ." She averted her eyes and said almost inaudibly, "Yes."

She looked embarrassed, and he was sorry he'd asked her about it. But he was worried Dubois might be a brutish drunk. Her father had angered quick when he'd thrown Seth out of the store.

Josette changed the subject, nodding at Mazie. "That

is a fine horse. We have only a mule now. Papa sold my horse, Marie, this spring. . . . I miss her so."

"Why'd he sell her?"

"He said we did not need her. He wanted the money. But I needed her. She loved me, that horse."

She looked as if she might cry and turned away, busying herself taking picnic items from the basket. Seth was gratified to see Josette had clearly packed enough for two. She had been expecting him. She'd wanted him to come.

Seth wanted to take her in his arms, to comfort her— not just for the loss of the horse, but for the sadness he sensed she carried with her. But that was something that would happen between two grown-ups of long acquaintance, not the friends they'd been as children. Most likely Josette thought of him as that childhood friend, not as a suitor. He figured he should let it alone.

And yet, watching Josette take out a loaf of homemade bread, a jar of preserves, butter in a ceramic jar, two plates and silverware, two red napkins, and then neatly arrange it all on the quilt, he marveled at the way she brought grace to the simple act of unpacking a basket.

He was shaken, realizing how affected he was by her. He had known a good many women; some were as good on a horse, as good at ranch work and at working a gun, as he was. Josette was a town girl, but he knew she was a strong woman. It was right there in how she carried herself and how she spoke.

Seth knew right then and there. He cast away all doubt. He wanted to marry Josette Dubois.

Franklin would say it was foolishness. *Why, you've known her as an adult but for a few minutes here and there!* But it felt as natural as the springtime thaw of ice into fresh water.

Seth couldn't ask her now. It wasn't proper. A man and a woman needed courtship. Josette would need time to be sure.

He glanced around. "I don't see that mule. . . ."

"No, Papa has him. Probably rode into town to the saloon. I walked here—it is only half a mile."

She sliced two pieces of bread and began buttering them, and a startling thought came to him. Maybe she wouldn't take to him in a marrying way at all! He wasn't a tall, handsome figure of a man. But women had always seemed to like him, anyhow. Bernice Clumm had hinted broadly of matrimony back home.

Still—he wasn't a landed, moneyed man. Not like, say, that Heywood Kelmer. A good-looking, wealthy man like that would have much more to offer.

Seth found himself wondering who might be courting Josette. She had to be the prettiest girl in Prairie Fire . . . so someone must be courting her.

She gave him some bread and poured water into a chipped mug and handed it to him.

"I thank you kindly, Josette. Here, now—should I be calling you by your Christian name? Maybe I should say 'Miss Dubois' or 'ma'am.'" He knew he was fishing for some sign of her regard, and he was a little ashamed to do it.

"Don't be silly. We are old friends! Josette is right and proper."

"Would your father approve of that familiarity?"

"I suppose not." She made an eloquent dismissive shrug that seemed to derive from some distant European ancestor. Then she gave an impish smile, and he sensed he was about to be teased. "But it's true he did not seem to take to you, Seth. Some rough cowboy off the prairie!"

"I'm nothing like that! I'm a rough cowboy from Chaseman, Texas!"

Chewing her bread, she laughed without opening her mouth and nodded. There was a twinkling merriness in her eyes that he remembered from childhood. She swallowed and said, *"Exactement."*

"These are some fine strawberry preserves, Josette. You lay 'em up?"

"Certainly, I did."

"And you made the bread?"

"Of course. But the butter is from the store."

"Dang good bread. Here you are, pretty as the dickens and a good cook—I expect half the men in town are swooning after you."

"Swooning? I have had some offers. None of them were acceptable to Papa."

"You're old enough to choose."

"You do not know Papa. Anyway—none of them were men I wished to fight for. Also—I am Catholic. Maybe not many men want to marry a Catholic girl. We are the only Catholic family I know of hereabouts." She sighed. "I miss going to Mass on a Sunday morning. . . ." She looked around at the fair day, the trees shimmering their leaves in the soft breeze, the chuckling stream, and added, "Perhaps this is Mass enough."

He cleared his throat. "You know—back down in Chaseman, we've got the mission church. My grandma was Catholic, and she married there. Now, if you wanted to go to a Mass, if you came to Chaseman, why—"

"Oh—it is not so easy to move away from here. And you? Do you go to church?"

"Once a year on Christmas, I go to the mission church with the Catholic folks. But I don't know if I'm a religious man."

He almost said, *I'd become one for you, Josette*. But he held his tongue.

They finished their bread and jam, and she handed him an apple. He tossed it up and down in his hand and asked as casually as he could, "You never thought of going back to Chaseman?"

"I don't know. This is a nice town. But I do miss Chaseman. Papa would not go there again." She smiled ruefully. "He left Texas in an awful hurry."

"He did at that. Well, now, me, Josette—I've got some land picked out there, two miles south of Chaseman. Lord willing, it'll be there when I get back. I've got enough money saved to make an offer on it— and start my own spread. Now, I'd start with raising horses for cattle drives—for the remuda, you know— and then . . ."

Seth told her, at some length, of his plans. She surprised him by seeming captivated. At last she said, "Oh, but that sounds wonderful!"

He wondered if she understood why he was telling her all this. He dared not be more explicit, not yet.

She looked over at Mazie and said, "You know, there is one man who has asked permission to court me. And Papa said yes. His name is Heywood Kelmer."

Seth's heart sank. "Is that right?" He drank a little water and said, "You know, I worked beside that very gent all yesterday. Staying over for a few days, why, I wanted some work . . . just till I head south . . . and he had me and Franklin ropin' and brandin'."

"Truly? How was he to work with?"

"He didn't get his hands dirty, which is maybe good—most of the time he didn't get in the way."

Seth felt a little guilty for giving what might have been a prejudiced opinion of Heywood Kelmer to Josette—considering that he was a rival. But then, he reflected, he'd only spoken the truth.

He dabbed at his lips with a napkin. "So your pappy wants you to marry Heywood?"

Josette gave a different sort of shrug now—a resigned one. "Yes, I think so. He has some understanding with the Kelmers. There is land Papa wants to buy from them to start another business, and he cannot pay the full price of it. But if I am to marry Heywood, then they give it to him at a good price."

Seth rocked back a little at that. "Why, trading you for land, that—that's . . ."

She grimaced. "Papa says that the money for the land is like a dowry—in Quebec, a dowry is still the custom—and the land like a wedding present. But . . . I don't know. . . ." She drank a little water from a mug and said, "He hasn't made it, what would you say, *official*—not yet. Heywood has asked me to the summer dance, out at Black Creek Acres, and I am expected to go with him. It's in about two weeks. Maybe there he will ask me to marry him."

Two weeks, Seth thought. *That's some time yet. . . .*

"What do you think you'll say if he asks you?"

Josette blushed. "That is a very personal question."

"I'm sorry." But he badly wanted to hear the answer.

"Oh, I don't know, Seth. It would be wise to marry him, I'm sure. He's got money. And . . . he's a man of . . . of influence hereabouts."

She didn't seem any too certain of Heywood, Seth told himself.

The cloud cover was burning away as the day warmed, and even here in the shade, they began to sweat. Gnats rose up from the brush and darted at them. "Well," she said, looking around, "it will soon be hot, and perhaps I'd better start for home."

"Josette—I'd be honored if you'd let me . . ." He began to offer her a ride on the back of his horse but was not sure that would be proper, the two of them on one horse. "If you'd mount Mazie there, she's a good 'un with the ladies, and I'll walk her back to your place. I'll carry the berry pail."

"You're sweet, Seth! But—I don't know if Papa is home. He might be. He was threatening you with a shotgun!"

"I remember it clearly!"

"Still—yes, that would be nice. But likely it'd be best if I walked the last little ways myself. . . ."

She put on her sunbonnet, packed up the basket and blanket, tucking the blanket under its handle. He went to get Mazie and the bucket of berries. She climbed onto the horse with no hesitation or awkwardness. *Grace in everything,* he thought. He handed her up the basket, took the reins, and they started off on a path between two harvested fields. She could have ridden without his leading the horse, but it felt more gentlemanly this way. It encouraged him that she permitted it.

After a while, she said, "I expect you'll be on your way back to Chaseman soon?"

Seth knew Franklin wouldn't want to cool his heels in Prairie Fire. But that was just too bad for Franklin. He would find his pard again down in Chaseman.

"Oh, I might linger about awhile," he said, "if I can get a little work. Don't think I'd cotton to working for the Kelmers again." He told her what had happened with Mazie and the bet.

"And he would not pay the bet? That doesn't seem honorable. Look!" She pointed at a goodly farm across a field from them. "That's the Hamer place over there. Sol was talking of needing a hand to do some farmwork. If a rough cowboy would consider such a job . . ."

"Why, I'm no stranger to farmwork. I'll ask the man tomorrow."

Seth smiled to himself. That farm was not far from the Dubois place. Maybe that was just by chance. But maybe it wasn't. . . .

L ANE DAWSON RODE into Newton on a warm, moonless night, leading a column of weary townsmen. After dismissing the tired, discouraged posse, Sheriff Dawson gave his horse over to the care of the livery and walked wearily up the stairs of the courthouse to his office. He felt like he was rode hard and put away wet.

Charlie Buford was leaning back behind Dawson's desk, booted feet up on it, reading a newspaper in the glow from a gaslight wall lamp, a crooked cigar smoking in the carved-horn ashtray. The old lawman had white hair that grew long because he didn't trouble to cut it much, a square-cut white beard, and pale blue eyes in a florid face. Charlie had a silver sheriff's star on his chest, and as soon as he saw Dawson come in, he tossed the newspaper aside, took the badge off with a pleased grunt, and tossed it on the blotter. "Glad you're back. Tired of being sheriff."

"Don't look like you're wearing yourself out doin' it, Charlie," said Dawson, bending over the desk to sort through the mail.

"Had to drag three men for street fighting to the calaboose about an hour ago, me and that no-account you call a deputy."

"Which no-account exactly?"

"Pierson. Some deputy!"

"He's not much use—it's true. Why didn't you get Hornby?"

"Hornby fractured his leg trying to work on his barn the very day I came out looking for him."

"Well, the damn fool," Dawson said, straightening up. "I'll get you Harry Shug to help you."

"Wait a damn minute—did you come back without catching that Fisher?"

"Lost their trail. Roved over the county and beyond, looking, asking everyone. Could not find hide nor hair."

"And you're going back out again?"

"The man killed my jailer, Charlie. Him and Diamond, they killed my jailer, stole two horses, and made us all look like fools. They're looking to hang him in Kansas City for another killing, so Kansas City ain't pleased neither."

"That old fool Mundy was to blame, not you! He knew better'n to get close to that cage!"

Dawson tossed a wanted circular aside. "That *old fool* was my friend!"

Buford sighed and swung his legs off the desk. "I spoke too hastily, Lane. I'm sorry. But I'm in a foul mood, trying to keep up with this job. I'm going to be sixty-eight in a month, and that's too old for sheriffing—"

"You're still the best lawman this county ever saw!"

Buford grabbed his cigar and puffed it alight. "The best *retired* lawman, anyhow."

"I'll chuck you right back into retirement soon's I get back, Charlie. People here trust you, and I need you to watch the town while I hunt down Fisher and Diamond. It's the shame of this town that they got away—and killed Mundy in the bargain. They were pretty rough on us in that newspaper you were reading."

"Hows about you get Shug to do it. He can be interim sheriff as well as I can."

"No, he can't. He's too young. I'll get him to watch the jail tonight. You go on and have your drink and get some rest and be here tomorrow after breakfast."

"You do know that I can say no to that, don't you?"

"I know you, Charlie—and I know you'll do the right thing."

"That always was a failing of mine." Buford stood up, cigar clenched in his teeth, and stretched. "I'm going. You look like you need a good night's sleep."

"I'll sleep like a drunk sow soon as Pierson takes over. I'm riding out at eight in the morning. . . ."

"To where? You lost their trail!"

"Been thinking on it. I calculate he'll go south toward Mexico. I'll just see if I can catch up."

"No posse?"

"They'd slow me down too much."

"Don't try too hard to bring those owlhoots back alive," said Buford, heading for the door.

Dawson nodded grimly. "I won't. I surely won't. . . ."

PAPA WAS STILL asleep, having come home last night fully drunk, and Josette knew he'd be late to open the store this morning. It gave her time to have a talk with her mother.

Mama's grave was a pretty one at the moment, bedecked as it was with wild prairie flowers—the daisy-like yellow tickseed alongside flamelike petals of red catchfly and golden butterfly weed. There was still dew on the blossoms catching the morning light. Josette, standing by the grave, smiled though her eyes stung with tears. Mama had admired the wildflowers of the prairie.

The grave was tucked into a corner of the town cemetery, half circled by chokeberry bushes where yellow finches fluttered, twittering cheerily as they fed on the berries. The cheap wooden marker was tilted askew now; it had cracked from many frosts, and Mama's name was scarcely readable. Josette was afraid that if she tried to straighten the marker, it would break off entirely.

Losing their home in Chaseman, fleeing in disgrace, coming here, and starting over that hard winter—all of it had contributed to killing Mama. Much of Papa's money had been seized by the court, and leaving in haste, they'd had to abandon most of their furniture in Chaseman. They'd slept on the floor for close to a month, and Papa had started his general store in little more than a shack. He'd invested some of their

remaining funds in four milk cows, having heard
there was a shortage of butter locally, and compelled
Mama to work at milking and churning in the crooked,
drafty little barn that had come with the property he'd
leased, whatever the weather.

When she wasn't milking cows and churning butter,
Mama had worked from dawn and into the night,
keeping house, cutting wood, washing, making most of
their clothing, cooking, scrubbing pots, helping to load
the wagon for the store, looking after the stock. That's
how it was day after day, in a fiercely cold winter, when
there never seemed enough wood for the stove, and it
made Mama bone weary. Though just a girl, Josette
had helped, but there was always more to do. Mama
came down with pneumonia and died after ten days of
sickness. The next day, Papa sold three of the milk
cows.

The memory of that ice-shrouded winter made Josette shiver, even in the midst of a warm summer morning. She sat by the grave, laying a rose among the
wildflowers, and said, "Mama, I don't know what to do."

It was a curious thing, the way folks talked to the
dead at a cemetery. Curious but commonplace, for
the dead were good listeners. Josette did not suppose
the corpse in its coffin was listening, but she had a
foggy notion that the spirit of a dead loved one, somewhere in the next world, would listen if you spoke at
their grave. She had no genuinely close friends. No one
else to talk to.

"Papa seems to be sinking ever deeper into the
downing of spirits," Josette said, speaking to her mama
in French, "and sometimes he throws a pot at me or a

boot and curses at me! He has picked up his shotgun and waved it about right there in the kitchen! He threatened Seth with it at the store. . . ."

Josette grimaced. She had been mortified when Papa had driven Coe from the store. "You remember Seth Coe from Chaseman. He was just a boy then. He's a man now, Mama, a drover, and he came into the store on his way to Texas! We renewed our acquaintance—we even had a little picnic—and I believe he's hinting that he might make a good husband for me. I am not certain I could ever care for him so much as that, but then again, perhaps I'm too old for girlish romances. And, Mama, Heywood Kelmer, too, seems to be honoring me with courtship—he seems to think it's an honor for me! If he proposes, I should say yes, because it will profit Papa, and because Heywood is rich and a fine figure of a man. But he is only a gentleman on the outside. The last time I was alone with him, for a few minutes at the dance last year, he tried to kiss me—and I told him no, I was not ready for such familiarity. And, Mama—he tried to force me to kiss him! He left bruises on my shoulders!" She shook her head and closed her eyes. "I pushed him away and ran back to the dance. He has never apologized. I have been kissed, it's true, a time or two. Once by a handsome drummer passing through, but I kissed him willingly. Now, Seth—he would never behave as Heywood did. He would know the proper time."

A crow lit on the wooden fence nearby and tilted its head as it regarded her, seeming to wonder whom she was talking to. "Oh, yes, Mama, I know I should be sensible and marry Heywood. Are not all men beasts, with their pawing hands, after all? But something in me rebels against that man, even when he's on his best behavior. Seth, now, I do enjoy his company. He is a hard worker and has plans for a sizable acreage in Texas. . . ." She brushed an ant off her dress and went on. "I don't know if I could fall in love with Seth. But I do know that he is a good man. I can feel it."

She reached out, picked one of the flaming-red flowers, and sniffed at it.

"It may scandalize you, Mama, to know that I have thought of simply leaving Papa, even without marrying. He says himself he can get someone to take care of him—and I might find work in Kansas City or Dodge. But I have little money for such a trip . . ." She sighed. "I should go and make his coffee. Perhaps set out some willow bark for his morning head. I'm sorry to complain so much. You should enjoy the fields of heaven and not have to sully it with worrying about me!"

Josette stood up, brushed herself off, tossed the wildflower onto her mother's grave, and started toward home, daydreaming about simply passing the house and keeping on to the next road, the next town. . . .

She knew, though, that she would only go home and start Papa's breakfast.

Franklin shook his head in disgust. "Two weeks!"

"Well," said Seth, hooking his thumbs in his trouser pockets, "she's got to make up her mind and . . . you can't rush a lady, Franklin."

"You haven't really proposed to her, Seth."

"No, I haven't. But . . . I will!"

They were standing on the wooden sidewalk in

front of the little hotel, shaded from the bright morning sun by the porch roof. Down the street, in front of
the Wells Fargo office, a group of people was gathered
around the stagecoach, which had just trundled and
bumped its way into Prairie Fire. People getting off the
stage were being greeted, and one of the greeters
looked to be a local newspaperman, for he had a pad
and pencil in his hand and was scribbling something
about the new arrivals. The *Prairie Fire News* would
be out tomorrow with a column about visitors to town.

"Well, I will here and now inform you, Seth Coe,
that I will not remain in this town for two weeks more,"
Franklin declared. "I've got a girl myself I hope to see
back in Chaseman. My brother expects me to go hunting with him. I told him soon's the drive was over—"

"Franklin—you can keep the rest of your almighty
plans to yourself!" Seth said. "I'll follow you—only I
can't follow you to Texas, not right now. I'll be back
there soon enough. I'll not hold it against you if you
ride south this minute."

Franklin's face had gone glum, not a look that was
usual to him. He took off his hat and slapped it against
his hip, something he did when he was making up his
mind. Then he nodded to himself and put it back on
his head. "I'm riding out. I need me some time off, and
being as I'm not in love with a pretty store clerk, there's
nothing to do here but work! I have sworn off work for
a month or more!"

"I know you better, Franklin. You'll be repairing
your mama's fences and milking her cows for her
within a week of your return. But by God, I wish I
was going to Texas with you. Only—I just can't." He

clapped Franklin on the shoulder. "And I'm sorry for it."

Franklin nodded his head just once. "I'm going to get my rig," he said resignedly. "I'll look for you in August. It's going to be a lonely ride."

"Oh, you'll probably meet some other no-account cowpokes along the way and fit right in. Just don't get drunk and get yourself stabbed again."

"Hell, Seth, that was two years ago. I've grown up some. He hardly stabbed me at all. . . ." He managed a grin, winked at Seth, and then went back into the hotel to get his change of clothes.

Seth figured Franklin would go from there to the store for a few things, then to the livery and lickety-split for the road to Texas.

Seth let out a long breath, then turned away and strolled down the sidewalk. He had not much sense of where he was going. Mostly he wanted to walk and think. Was he being foolish, waiting around for Josette to suddenly fall in love with him and elope?

But when he tried to imagine riding off without her, the picture just would not form in his mind.

He came to the Town Marshal's office in a small building—smaller than the livery—between a two-story building containing Delbert's Leather Goods, Hardware, and Tackle Store and a structure almost as big with the sign *City Hall*. The marshal's office seemed dwarfed between the two.

A lean fellow, not much taller than Seth, was using a tack hammer to nail up a wanted poster outside the office. He had a lined, florid face and an ash blond mustache; a shield-shaped badge was pinned to his white cotton shirt. The silver ribbon of his badge was etched *L. Coggins, TM*.

Just as well, Seth figured, if he was going to be here a while to meet the Town Marshal. "You'd be Marshal Coggins, I calculate," said Seth.

Hammer in hand, Coggins turned and looked Seth up and down. "And you'd be who?" he asked in a gravelly voice.

"Seth Coe, Marshal."

"Got something you want to confess to?"

Seth smiled. "No, sir. Looking for work hereabouts and visiting an old friend."

"Is that so! Who's your friend?"

"Miss Josette Dubois. We kind of grew up together down in Texas."

"Oh, Miss Dubois! Why, I was tempted to ask her for a dance last year. Afraid I'd bust her toes, though. Pretty girl. Smart, too. You a drover, Mr. Coe?"

"You can call me Seth if you're a mind to, Marshal. Yes, sir, that's what I've mostly done. But this year I hope to own my own spread."

"You sound like you're from, where, the Panhandle?"

Seth had noticed a Texas drawl in the marshal's voice, too. "Little south of there but not so much. Chaseman."

"Oh, why, that's nothing when it comes to south—I hail from Laredo!"

"You don't say! Any farther south and you run out of Texas."

"Every blame winter I tell myself it's too cold here, and I'm moving back to Laredo. But never quite get there. On account of my wife, Lou Ellen, is from right here, and she doesn't cotton to Texas." Coggins transferred the hammer to his left hand and stuck the right out to shake. "Seth Coe, welcome to Prairie Fire. My name's Luther, but you can call me Slim—most everyone does."

They shook hands, the marshal's fingers feeling softer than most handshakes Seth experienced, except for one—the man's trigger finger. There was some callusing there.

Coggins let go of Seth's hand and gave the tack another tap with the hammer, and Seth looked over his shoulder at the poster. What he saw sent a coldness through his belly. He instantly recognized the halftone photo of the wanted man.

~WANTED DEAD OR ALIVE~

$1500. REWARD
Hannibal Fisher
For Murder of a Jail Employee
in Newton, Kansas
Also Wanted for Jailbreak and
Suspected Murder in Kansas City
Last Seen in Southern Kansas
May Be in the Company of
Escaped Murderer Curt Diamond
Contact Sheriff's Office, Newton, Kansas

Last seen in Southern Kansas? Prairie Fire was in Southern Kansas.

And Seth remembered the last thing Fisher said to him before Wild Bill took him away. *You have not seen the last of me.*

CHAPTER SIX

SETH FOUND SOL Hamer in the barn, trying and failing to saddle a draft horse. The stocky, broad-shouldered farmer had the saddle crookedly on the big Clydesdale's back as he struggled to tighten its belly strap. The horse, used to plows and wagons but not saddles, was shifting restlessly and snorting.

"Mr. Hamer?" Seth said, coming in.

Startled, the farmer straightened up and scowled at him—a very big scowl from a very wide mouth. He had a shovel-blade face encircled by a brown beard sprinkled with gray. "What do you suppose you're about, trespassing in a man's barn?" he demanded.

Seth took off his hat. "I'm sorry, sir. I asked your wife, and she said—"

"Well, whatever it is, we don't want it! I've got three lost cows and"—he shook his head and turned in exasperation to the saddle—"and this durned saddle . . . !"

"Mr. Hamer, Josette Dubois said you might need some help round here. Just generally, like."

"Well, I don't! Can't afford it!"

"Be pleased to put that saddle on for you, sir. No charge! Being a cowboy mostly, that's a job I know as well as any."

The scowl became a squiggle of uncertainty. "Hmm—very well, since you're here."

Sol stepped out of the way, and Seth put on his hat and went to introduce himself to the horse. After a few moments of patting the horse and murmuring to it, he straightened the saddle, adjusted it a little farther back, hitched up the belt, and stepped clear. Pondering his handiwork, he shook his head doubtfully. "Well, Mr. Hamer, that will serve for a short ride. Best that can be done. You see, that saddle is not meant for a horse this size. A mite too small."

Sol took hold of the straps of his overalls and looked skeptically at the saddle. "Don't have another saddle, and don't have another horse. Got a mule, but it'll buck any rider except my missus. The blamed thing loves my Daisy." Sol Hamer had a big belly, but he seemed a strong man, the red shirt under the overalls barely constraining his muscular arms. "Had that saddle for twelve years. Haven't used it. Need to get after those cows. The bull knocked down a fence, and the cows are all to heck and gone. Miles off!"

"Now, if you're saddling it so you can bring in some cattle, why, there's no need for that if you'll trust me some. I'll do 'er for you. My mare's right outside, ready to go, and we've got nothin' to do for most of the day. It'll do me and my pony good to get out there and chase some stock down. I'm right natural with a lasso, and that horse is trained for the job—we'll get 'em for you."

Sol stuck out his lower lip and knit his thick brows. "Told you—can't afford it. Haven't got the money from the first harvest yet. Ten days at least."

"Tell you what, Mr. Hamer—trade me supper, and a place to sleep tonight and that'll pay me for today, anyhow. If you like my work and keep me on for a time—and I can do farmwork as easily as ranching—why, you can pay me when you've sold your goods."

Sol looked at him dubiously. "I don't even know your name!"

"Seth Coe, sir." Seth stuck out his hand, and after a second's hesitation, Sol shook it, his own large, callused hand fairly swallowing Seth's.

"Feels like you've done some work."

"Yes, sir, I have."

"You fix a fence?"

"Easier'n combin' my hair!"

This struck Sol as funny, and he chuckled, showing a mouthful of big yellow teeth. "Well, now . . . we've known Miss Dubois since she was a little girl. . . ."

"So have I, Mr. Hamer."

"Have you, now? If she says you're all right, I suppose you are. And she sent you here, so"—he gave a brisk nod—"you can take that saddle off Goliath here for me and get yourself after that stock. There's five of 'em, counting the bull. I'll point you the way. If you can get it done before supper, we'll feed you, and I'll ponder on your doing some more work round here. But see here—I've got no cabin to put you in and no spare room in the house!"

"This time of year, a barn's more comfortable of an

evening than a hotel room. Leastwise for me it is. Now, suppose I was to sleep up in that hayloft?"

"That'd do you?"

"I surely spent many a night sleeping in barns, Mr. Hamer. Comfortable as my mama's arms."

S ETH COE, YOU have straw in your hair!" Josette declared as he approached the store's counter, hat in hand. "I am scandalized! Surely that means you've sweet-talked one of the local girls!"

She looked at him with raised eyebrows and her head cocked to one side—but then she grinned, and he grinned back in relief.

"Slept in Sol Hamer's barn last night, Josette."

"So you did get some work with him! That's dandy. But this . . ." She reached out and plucked a piece of straw from his hair. "You look like a hayseed."

"Brought in some lost cattle for him yesterday and fixed the fence they busted out of. Got supper for it, and he's hired me as a hand for a while."

"You are an enterprising one. Come in to buy something?"

"Need some more nails to fix a cow stall."

"We only have household nails, two and three inches. You probably need Elmer's down the street. They have all that."

Seth lowered his voice and said, "I must confess I'm not really here for nails. . . ." He'd only mentioned nails in case Dubois was listening, but Seth couldn't see him around. "I was wondering if this evening you could—"

The door jangled as someone came in, and Seth turned to see, to his dismay, Heywood Kelmer. Heywood was wearing a string tie, a brand-new gray Stetson, and a denim jacket with leather panels in the shoulders. He had something between a smile and a leer on his face as he strode in his gray soft leather boots to the counter, put his hands on it, and leaned close to Josette, just as if Seth wasn't there.

She took a step back. "How can I assist you, Heywood?"

"Why, you can sell me a jar of that Gimble's Hair Cream, and you can tell me if you've made up your mind about a certain something. . . ."

Crowded by Heywood, Seth stepped to the left, and from there, he could see into the back room, where Dubois was taking a long pull on a pint bottle of spirits. Josette's father was standing by a table, looking blearily down at an account book. He corked the bottle and thrust it to the back of a cabinet.

Josette was wrapping the hair cream. "And what was the other matter?" she asked, acting as if she'd forgotten.

"Why, you know perfectly well, Josette!" Heywood declared, grinning. "What a teasin' coquette you are!"

She frowned. "A coquette!"

"Yup! Josette the coquette! Makes a charming rhyme! Well, have you made up your mind about the summer dance or not?"

"But should you be seen there with a flirtatious 'coquette'?" she asked innocently. "It'll ruin your reputation!"

Heywood scowled. "Now, look here. There's good reasons you should be treating me better than this!"

"If there's nothing else, Mr. Kelmer, I was just talking to this gentleman about certain other matters. . . ."

She turned to Seth—making his heart leap—but Heywood pointed at her and said, "I insist on an answer, Josette!"

Seething inwardly, Seth was about to warn Heywood to back off when Dubois came in, walking almost steadily. "What is this? She is refusing to speak to you? She is rude?" He shoved Josette toward Heywood so she had to grab the counter to keep from falling. "You will serve the gentleman!"

Seth's hands tightened into fists at that.

"I will not be pushed about in this way!" Josette said, her voice cold and sharp. "I shall not serve Mr. Kelmer!"

"Mr. Dubois," said Seth, "the man was talking to her like she was a bar girl!"

"You!" Dubois snorted. "Go away!"

Eyes tearing up, Josette turned toward the back room—but her father grabbed her by a wrist and flung her against the counter beside Heywood. He kept hold of her, squeezing, so that her eyes shut with the pain. "You will serve that man and be glad of it!"

Seth saw red, and—scarcely aware he was doing it—he vaulted over the counter. Roaring, "Get your hands off her, you drunken old fool!" he straight-armed Dubois, knocking him back away from Josette so that he fell on his rump.

"What the devil, Coe!" Heywood snapped, agog. "You'll see the marshal now!"

"Yes, yes, call the marshal! *Vite!*" Dubois said, struggling to stand.

A little stunned at his own actions, Seth turned to Josette, who was just standing there, shaking her head, as Heywood, backing toward the door, shouted, "Who're you to step in, saddle tramp!"

He rushed through the door, its bell jangling like an alarm with his hurry, and shouted for Marshal Coggins.

Josette had braced herself with a hand on a shelf and helped her father to stand. His face was red, and he shook with fury.

"Papa, he didn't mean it—"

"You!" Dubois jabbed a finger at Seth. "I will find my shotgun for you!"

"I'm sorry, Josette," Seth said. "I expect I got too . . ." He didn't know quite what to say. He turned away and walked around the end of the counter, thinking to head toward the door—but he stopped in the midst of the store, wondering if Josette was safe with Dubois. Had he made things worse for her?

"Papa," Josette was saying, "just calm down. You've bruised my arm! Seth saw that, and—"

The door jangled again, and Coggins came in, looking grave. "What's this I hear about an assault, Coe!"

"I . . . I was afraid her father was like to break her bones, the way he was manhandling her, Marshal. . . ."

"So you knocked one of our merchants on his backside?"

"I didn't hit him. I was just trying to push him away, but in the heat of—"

"That's not the way Kelmer tells it," said Coggins as Heywood came in.

"You want to keep your job, Marshal," Heywood snarled, "you'll arrest that man, lock him in a cell, and lose the key!" His face looked savage in that moment.

"Yes!" Dubois called. "He has made assault on me! Arrest him!"

Marshal Coggins shrugged. "Seth—you'd best come with me. You're under arrest."

* * *

Right curious that this cowboy could have as much money as you claim, Hannibal," said Sweeney as the six men rode across the prairie in the gathering dusk. "Seemed willing to work for a day or two just for spending money."

They were headed roughly east of the town, planning to camp somewhere along Black Creek if they could find a spot that provided enough cover. Six men could arouse some interest, and it was best they kept hidden, not so easy out on this flat prairie land.

Their horses cantered through the knee-high yellow grass, past a copse of shrubs, moving steadily but not too quick, for there was some doubt about where they were to hole up. Jackrabbits scurried and prairie chickens flurried as the group of horses clopped by. Hoping for a handy supper, Gaines fired a couple of pistol shots at the grouse—missing both times.

"Sweeney," said Fisher, "that cowboy took a pot off me bigger'n any you've ever seen! Cheated to do it, and his friends backed him up with their guns."

Fisher had indeed exaggerated how much money Seth carried on him. He needed to motivate this ragtag gang. Seth was staying over in Prairie Fire, and Diamond, who had passed through the place, knew it to have a capable marshal. The marshal had several men he deputized at need, too.

"We can take him and that Prairie Fire bank, too, if we're wise!" Fisher said.

Several antelope, roused by the thud of the horses' hooves, rose up from their resting place in the high grass and went bounding away. Gaines peeled off from the group of riders to pursue them, tugging his rifle free of its saddle holster. He galloped after the antelope, and the others reined in, waiting where Gaines could find them.

"Damn, I'm tired of sitting on a horse," said Diamond, arching his back and stretching in the saddle. "Give me a train anytime. Even a stagecoach is better."

"You complain too damn much," said Fisher, wiping his forehead. Without the wind in his face of riding, he was feeling the heat.

"He does, at that," Briggs said, taking up his canteen. "Always did."

"This bank—anyone here look it over?" asked the young man. Luke Bettiger his name was. He'd worried Fisher once by mentioning that his father had been a Texas Ranger, but it seemed there was naught but bitterness betwixt them.

"I gave it a look when I was through there," said Diamond. "Small bank. Does not have its own guard at night, so far's I saw. *Does* have a stout vault."

They heard several more gunshots from Gaines, and Fisher glanced around to see him, some ways off, afoot now.

Fisher slowed his mount to a slow walk, and the other men slowed, too, so as not to get too far ahead of Gaines. "I never robbed a bank myself," Fisher admitted, "though I saw it done once, fairly slick." He looked at Bettiger. "You ever try it, Luke?"

Bettiger shook his head. "Nope. I took some money off a man who owed it to me and wouldn't pay. Shot him in the leg to do it. I shouldn't have done it. But I sure did. And I took my money back, too. They called it robbery, so I'm in the willows with you fellers."

"You done more than shoot that welsher," Briggs observed. "You helped us rob that freight wagon."

Bettiger shook his head in disgust. "Come out of it with forty dollars apiece and an extra pair of boots!"

"Boots aren't cheap," said Briggs. "That crate of boots was worth getting. I sold most of 'em to a trading post in Sedgewick. The trader didn't ask no questions."

Bettiger sighed. "Anyhow, for me it started with shooting that crooked varmint in Sweetwater. May as well hit a bank, I do suppose, and try to get enough to start over in Old Mexico."

Unsure of Bettiger's trustworthiness, Fisher prodded him with "Be a funny thing if you were chased down by your own pappy!"

Bettiger's head snapped around, and he scowled at Fisher. "He's retired."

Diamond chuckled grimly. "Texas Rangers never quite retire, way I hear it."

Bettiger shrugged. He looked toward Gaines, who seemed to be dragging something through the grass to his horse, and let his silence speak.

I shouldn't have done it, Bettiger had said. Fisher had taken special note of that remark. He was thinking that Bettiger might quail at some of what needed to be done. He might decide to change sides. Luke Bettiger might be one man too many for this expedition.

It just might be necessary to arrange for that gloomy young man to die.

THE JAIL CELL was windowless and so hot that Seth removed all his clothes except his underdrawers. He lay on his back atop the rough blanket, staring into the darkness, sometimes wiping sweat from his eyes with the back of his hand. Marshal Coggins had said the judge could give him as much as thirty days. How would anyone bear thirty days and nights in here?

Over and over Seth ran through the events that had brought him to the jail cell, and he couldn't see he'd had a lot of choice, this side of sheer cowardice. He wasn't usually so hot tempered. But it was Josette. . . .

He slept little till close to dawn. Around eight in the morning, the marshal came in and woke him by clacking a key ring on the bars. "Get dressed, Seth. You're going before Judge Twilley."

Grateful to be out of the cell even for a visit to the justice of the peace, Seth hurriedly dressed, splashed his face with water from the bucket in the corner of the cell, and was soon standing in the city hall before a judge seated behind an oaken table. The justice wore a linen sack suit, a mite too big for his spindly frame, and it seemed to Seth this Judge Twilley was at most in his late twenties. A chestnut beard and stately mustache did little to disguise the judge's youth. Seth felt a little put out at being judged by one so young.

A middle-aged clerk with a short graying beard and an alcohol-reddened nose sat at a small table to Seth's right. He was likely the clerk for many jobs in the city hall. There was no one else in the small courtroom— Heywood Kelmer was noticeably absent.

In a voice that seemed as callow as his unlined face, Twilley said, "Why, here's the desperado!" He quirked his mouth to one side, enjoying his own wit. "And yet he's not shackled, Marshal?"

Coggins chuckled. "Somehow, I think I can keep Mr. Seth Coe reined in, Your Honor."

"Mr. Kelmer would seem to be less certain of that," the judge remarked, looking at the papers before him. "He describes the man as having 'viciously assaulted' Mr. Francois Dubois, and he demands that Mr. Coe be given the maximum sentence, to be followed by an escort out of this county and preferably out of the State of Kansas entirely. But Mr. Kelmer did not think he needed to be here today, once he gave me what he conceives to be my orders, and I dislike having my judgments determined by high-handed landowners. In the matter of Mr. Francois Dubois, I remember when he was up before my father a time or two, and I suspect there's more to the story. Well, Mr. Coe?"

Seth cleared his throat. "Well, sir, Your Honor, Heywood Kelmer was treating the lady like a bar girl and worse. Then Mr. Dubois, who wishes Josette to . . . well, to please Heywood, he gave her a shove and like to've knocked her down. The lady said she was not going to take it and made to leave, and he took her by the wrist and fair threw her at Heywood—he was hurting that girl, Judge! And—" He cleared his throat once more. "I could not bear to see her mistreated so. I know Josette—she is the friend of my childhood. I expect it's true I acted more on instinct than on good sense. But if you'd been there . . ."

"I wasn't, Mr. Coe, and must rely on testimony. The lady being unable to testify—" He looked at the marshal with lifted brows. "That it, Slim? She's unable?"

"As to that, Your Honor, I cannot rightly say. Dubois wasn't willing to let me speak to her, and he *says* she refuses to testify. That's his story. I will just add that I could see no evidence of injury on Francois Dubois. It would help if we could speak to Miss Josette."

"I am unwilling to compel the lady's testimony," said the judge a little regretfully.

"I will just add," the marshal went on, "that when I came back to the store to interview her, I spied Dubois ushering her into the back. And I saw bruises on her arms. He told me she didn't want to talk to me. She did not call out anything different."

"She's afraid of her papa," said Seth.

"I'll let you know when I want anything further from you, Mr. Coe," said the judge, squinting down at the paperwork. "I have Heywood Kelmer's statement and the marshal's here . . . and I've heard your side of it." He looked at Seth speculatively. "I understand that you're working at the Hamer farm?"

"Yes, sir."

Marshal Coggins spoke up. "Your Honor, I've spoken with Sol, and I told him the story—both sides of it—and he's decided he believes Mr. Coe. He has said he will be responsible for him so long as he works on his property."

Seth blinked, touched by this gesture from the gruff old farmer.

Judge Twilley shrugged and picked up his gavel. "I find you guilty of minor assault. The court orders that you spend one night in jail—you have already done so—and the court fines you fifty dollars. Pay your fine, and you will be discharged. You can remove yourself to Mr. Hamer's property, as it's outside town limits. You will absent yourself from town for three days." He struck the table with his gavel and nodded toward the clerk.

Carried along by a wave of relief, Seth went to the clerk, quickly paid his fine, and hurried from the courtroom, deciding that this young judge was wiser than some older ones he'd seen at work.

Outside, Slim Coggins walked Seth to the livery. It was a hot morning—it had been getting hotter every day—and the sun flashed off the street's windows with a malicious brightness.

"Marshal," Seth said, "the judge said Dubois had been up before him."

"Some years back, he was seen smacking his wife about—and was drunk as he did it. Two of the town's ladies witnessed this and asked that something be done."

"And was it?"

"He was fined. But neither I nor the court can spend our days pursuing such matters. The common law allows wife beating most places. It's thought to be good for wedded bliss and all. Not that my wife would stand for it. I understand it was outlawed in Alabama this very year. But there's no state law ag'in it in Kansas. We do have an ordnance here in town calling for the just treatment of women, and we applied that in fining Dubois twenty-five dollars. This was most of nine years ago, when I was first hired on. The lady died the next year from pneumonia. I sometimes wish—" He broke off, shaking his head. "I guess it don't matter what I could wish for."

"How about the case of a man whupping on his grown daughter? That common law, too?"

"Not as such. But there's *tradition*—and it holds that townsfolk do not usually interfere in family matters, less'n it's a case of murder."

Seth shook his head. It all went against his grain.

They reached the livery, and the marshal watched as

Seth paid the stableman and saddled Mazie. He led her out into the bright sunshine and mounted. "Marshal, thanks for speaking up to the judge."

"Don't make me regret it, Seth. Stay out of trouble."

"I'll do my damnedest. But—there is something I should mention."

Coggins frowned. "What would that be?"

"That wanted poster—that Hannibal Fisher. I know that man. At least, one time, not long ago, I played poker with him in Abilene. He was caught cheating, and Wild Bill posted him out of town."

"I see. Must've been soon after that he was jailed in Newton. Seems to have killed the jailer and run off. You know where he might be?"

"No notion of it. Just one card game between us. But I know him by sight. And the poster said he might be in Southern Kansas. If I see him . . . I'll tell you."

With that, he touched his hat to the marshal and rode out of town for the Hamer farm.

Seth was glad to be out on the prairie where there was a bit of a breeze. But the high grass crackled when the horse brushed it; it was sere, he noticed, going yellow, sometimes brown.

As he rode along, Seth tried to figure just how he was going to see Josette. Her pa surely would not allow it. Would she even want to see him after what had happened in the store? Maybe she thought of him as nothing but trouble now. . . .

I'VE HEARD THE rumbling," said Sol Hamer as Seth climbed down from the saddle, "and I know what it means. Maybe heat lightning coming or a dry thunderstorm. We could be in for a fire!"

Seth had found him plowing out on the edge of his property, wearing a big droopy hat to give him some protection from the fierce sun. He was steering the plow behind his big draft horse, deep furrowing in close rows as a firebreak.

Despite the heat, Seth felt a chill, hearing a rumble himself from the north. Picketing Mazie in the shade of a young oak tree, he peered at the northern horizon and saw sickly yellow-brown clouds accumulating there and a flash of lightning. He knew what Sol feared. Many a wildfire was caused by a dry-thunderstorm lightning strike.

"Sol, I thank you for speaking up for me to the court," Seth said.

"Why, I only did it because my Daisy imagines you're like our son, and she has a sweet spot for you."

Seth hadn't seen anyone else but Sol and Daisy on the farm. "She misses him some, does she?" he asked, bringing a canteen to the farmer.

Sol took the canteen and said, "Yes, and we haven't seen him since Christmas! We have a few letters, however. He stayed in the Army after the war. He's a sergeant in the Cavalry, down in Oklahoma, chasing renegade Cherokees." Gazing to the south, as if to see Oklahoma, he took a long, meditative drink from the canteen.

"Sounds like a son to be proud of," said Seth, taking Sol's place at the plow.

"That's a fact. Served with distinction under General Frémont in the war."

Seth commenced plowing. As he wrestled with the plow to keep it on course, he thought of his own family's experience of the war. His father, being against both slavery and secession, had refused to enlist in the Confederate Army and forbade Seth joining in the fight, though many of his young friends did. Nor did Pa Coe wish to be set against his own neighbors by joining the Union. Feelings running high during the war, it had been touch and go around the Coe spread down in Chaseman. A neighbor whose son had died at Bull Run had called Pa Coe a coward, and Pa had called him a liar. A duel was fought, and Seth's father had been greatly saddened at *having to kill poor George Finch*. He had undertaken financial assistance for Finch's widow afterward.

Seth plowed on, his hands aching. He felt blisters arise, but he kept on. Sol came behind him with a shovel to remove the dry-grass fuel the plowing missed. The rumbling quickened, and there were more flickers from the sulfurous clouds, occasioning uneasy glances from the two men.

The sun was relentless, and plowing ground dried to iron hardness was backbreaking. The two men took turns resting in the shade, and Seth was glad when Mrs. Hamer came out on the mule, bringing refreshments.

Daisy Hamer was a wiry woman with graying brown hair. At least six inches taller than her squat husband, she had a lined face but a cheerful expression. Her calico sunbonnet was sweat stained on the sides, and the long skirts of her yellow dress snapped in the rising hot wind as she slid off the mule, bringing them a basket of molasses biscuits and a jar of homemade beer.

They gathered under a tree for the biscuits and beer. "Why, the two of you look plumb worn to a nub!"

"Hot day and hard ground," said Sol. "But we're near to finished." Taking a biscuit in one hand and the jar in another, he added, "I did most of it yesterday, Seth, when the marshal had hold of you."

"I'm surely sorry I couldn't be here to help, Sol."

"You did some good work yesterday, the way I heard it from Josette," said Daisy, "protecting her from that drunken fool of a father!"

Seth looked eagerly at her, suddenly feeling better than he had all day. "That how Josette said it?"

"Lord yes! She thought you were her white knight!"

"So—she might be willing to see me, do you think?"

Sol gave him a crafty sidelong look. "So that's what it's about? More than childhood friends, Seth?"

"Oh, Sol, don't pry so!" Daisy said, feeding crumbles of biscuit to the mule. "Seth—I spoke to Josette across the fence this morning. She was aggrieved that you were jailed on account of her. That's just how she put it! She asked me to tell you that you mustn't come into the store, but she might come to see you here. Fu'thermore, she said you truly must stay out of her papa's way!"

Seth was wondering if this was too good to be true. "She said she'd come to see me?"

"Ho *ho*!" said Sol. "The boy's smitten!" He drank some beer and said, "Might be good if you took her away from that Heywood. He's been sniffing around her like a—"

"Lord in Heaven, look at that!" Daisy burst out, pointing to the north. A line of billowing black clouds gripped the sere prairie. The three of them could just make out red flames flickering where the clouds met the plain. It was still some distance off, but that didn't offer much comfort. Wildfires could travel fast—and the hot breeze was blowing toward them, driving the blaze their way.

"There's no time to finish here, Seth," said Sol, unhitching the plow horse. "I will commence making a counterfire." He tugged the horse over to Seth. "I've got six barrels of rainwater in the barn—they're in that old wagon along with a shovel and some sacks. If you're willin', hitch Goliath to the wagon, wet those sacks good—maybe that old horse blanket—and beat out the fire where you can! There's rope and an ax. Daisy, you take the mule, quick as ever you can, and make sure the neighbors know what's coming."

Seth took hold of Goliath's reins and turned to scan the prairie. The fire was visibly closer, marching ravenously toward the town that had named itself after the very thing that could now burn it down.

He cursed under his breath, unhitched Mazie, mounted up, and with Goliath's reins in his hand, he tugged the draft horse as fast as he could get him to go across the fields toward the barn.

CHAPTER SEVEN

"THE DAMN PRAIRIE'S on fire," Briggs observed, leading his horse into the camp. "It's burning like hell-zapoppin' off to the west."

Fisher nodded. "I saw the smoke. Most likely we'll be all right here." He was squatting by the stream, a heavy stick in hand, hoping to clout one of the trout he sometimes glimpsed in Black Creek. His father had taught him to catch creek fish that way, and he was pretty good at it. "We're north of the fire line. Wind is blowing south."

"Maybe, maybe not," said Diamond. He was sitting on a rock, cleaning his shotgun. He glanced up at the sky. "Getting smoky here."

The sky was indeed dulled by smoke. It itched at their noses and stung their eyes.

They'd camped about six-and-a-half miles north of the town, where the creek cut through a tree-clustered outcropping of rocks. This was the only good cover anywhere near Prairie Fire. The nearest farm was two miles away.

"Leastways," Gaines said, "the local yokels will be too busy to take any notice of us." He was using a hunting knife to cut a steak off the antelope carcass hanging from a sugar maple.

Sweeney, who was lying on his back in the grass, hands folded behind his head, said, "Less anyone knows of us, the better." He tilted his hat back and looked up at the darkening sky. "Trouble is, I'm known around here. Anyhow, them Kelmers have my name."

"When you go after the bank, you'll keep your face covered," said Fisher. "Maybe a flour sack with holes cut for the eyes."

"If we're going to rob that bank," said Bettiger, going to the creek, "we ought to do it today."

"Why's that?" Fisher tossed the stick in the water and stood up.

Bettiger picked up a pebble and skimmed it across the stream. "Because most of the men in town, probably including the marshal, will be busy trying to set up firebreaks and such. They won't even be close into town."

"If that's so," Fisher said, "the bank will be closed. We need the banker to open the vault." He was not at all sure that the bank would be closed—hard to imagine a banker fighting a fire—but he had to find out where Seth Coe was before the robbery. While the gang was robbing the bank, keeping the marshal and any deputies occupied, he would be free to kill Seth Coe without interference from the law. He had told the men that he would plan the robbery; then he'd get the additional money from Coe while they were pulling it off. Too many men at a bank robbery, he said, was just inviting a stumble.

"A year ago," Bettiger said, looking toward the fire, "if I saw a fire threatening a settlement, why, I'd ride out to help." He shook his head. "Can't do it now. The marshal might spot me."

Briggs blinked at him in honest puzzlement. "Why would you ever do a fool thing like riding out to a fire?"

Bettiger looked at him, then just shook his head and went back to skimming pebbles.

"Peanut," said Fisher, "I'm thinking that since you're already some known in Prairie Fire, you're the man to do some scouting for us. It'll settle you in their mind as something like a local man, too. Make them less suspicious of you."

"I don't know about that!" Sweeney said, sitting up and slapping his hat on his knees. "I ain't much liked there."

"Where *are* you much liked?" Diamond asked innocently.

The others chuckled at that, and Sweeney frowned. Fisher went on. "You go out there and ask around—you can get yourself a drink in that saloon, long as you don't get far drunk, and see what you can find out. Maybe somebody knows for sure if Coe is still in town and where he's staying."

"I don't like the idea. Folks will wonder at it if I go around asking questions."

"No, they won't. You do it, and I'll give you an extra hundred dollars of my share." Fisher had no intention of doing any such thing. But it was enough that Sweeney thought he would.

"When?"

"Tomorrow morning."

"I reckon I could go. But if you're looking for Coe, why, he's the type of show-off who'd be out there fighting that fire!"

"Is he, now?" This interested Fisher. If he could catch Seth Coe alone or covered up by enough smoke, he could simply kill him and rob his body. Most traveling cowboys carried their cash right on them. Likely Coe had a money belt. "Now, that's an interesting notion. . . ."

I T WAS ABOUT a quarter mile to the Dubois property on a back road out of town. Josette was walking home from the store, between stretches of yellowing prairie grasses rustling in a hot breeze. She had left the store early, Papa having informed her that Heywood was coming by to see her. She had no wish to see Heywood Kelmer and refused to remain in the store.

"You stay, or you will be sleeping in the barn tonight!" her papa had said.

"The pigs will be better company," she'd replied.

In a rage, he threatened to throw her off the property entirely if she remained so disrespectful and stubborn. Josette laughed and stepped clear of the swipe of his arms before replying, "You would have a sad time of it without me, Papa!" And with that, she'd taken off her apron and rushed out.

It was a cloudless late afternoon, yet the sky was curiously dark. Josette wiped at her eyes and wondered why they stung.

Then she smelled smoke. She stopped, staring at

the horizon. A rippling wall of black was rising up out there. How far away? Some miles but not so very far . . .

She heard hoofbeats, and a horseman came around the bend in the road, proving to be Jimmy Tupper, a lunky, pimply farmhand who'd made a couple of clumsy passes at her. He reined in, gasping, the big stock horse snorting close beside her.

Jimmy stared down at her as if she were mad. "Where the dickens are you going, Josette? There's a wildfire comin' right at us! Cain't you see it? You need to get back to the south! Go on to town, where you'll be safe! The men are already trying to head it off, but there's just no telling!"

"And where are *you* going? Shouldn't you be helping them, Jimmy Tupper?"

"I'm sent to make sure everyone in town knows! And here it seems some didn't! Get on back to town!"

Before she could reply, he spurred the horse and galloped onward toward town.

Josette hesitated, then shook her head. She would go on to their little farm. It was not a working farm, apart from the truck garden, but they had two pigs, eight chickens, and two goats—Papa liked *fromage de chèvre*—and Josette was not going to risk their animals burning to death. Papa would soon hear of the fire, and presumably he would come and protect the farm, but she could not be certain. And her home was between here and the fire.

Josette hurried onward, striding quickly at first; then she broke into a run. The breeze changed and gusted smoke at her, making her cough, but she kept on till she got to the farm.

Alternately panting and coughing, she looked around and saw that though smoke wreathed the roofs of the farmhouse and barn, the fire was still a few miles away. Soon, she knew, ashes would begin to fall to announce the fire's imminent arrival.

She decided not to let the stock out of their pens as yet. The fire might still be turned. She'd seen it before. A six-foot-wide stretch of ground would be frantically turned up between the settlement and the oncoming fire, the grass hoed rapidly away so that the naked soil was bereft of fuel. Then a backfire was lit between the nearly barren stretch of ground and the wildfire. The two fires would meet and extinguish each other, for each was consuming the other's fuel. But a firebreak thrown up in haste wasn't likely enough where a whole town was concerned. The flames moved quickly and might well do a kind of fiery flanking motion around the backfires, coming in from the sides. And the prairie fire was ambitious, coming on rapaciously. Riders were needed to try to stanch or slow it between the backfires.

Seth. He was that kind of man, she knew. He would be out there, helping protect the Hamer farm, which was the property next door to hers. These fires moved so fast, he could easily find himself trapped.

What could she do about it? Probably nothing. But Josette strode off to the north, heading toward the raging wildfire.

A BANDANNA OVER his mouth to keep out the smoke, Seth drove the wagon to a spot about twelve yards from the fire line—Goliath shied from going closer. The roaring, crackling flames licked tall and seemed to go on and on to the north, like an endless sea of violent red and orange, with spewing black smoke. Ashes blew over them, swirling all ghostly toward the town. He wondered what cabins, what lean-tos and soddies on the prairie had already been consumed by the flames.

He jumped down and hobbled Goliath, for he was afraid the draft horse would panic and run off with the wagon. Then he hurried back to where Mazie was tied to the wagon bed. Fearful of the onrushing flames, she was trying to tug free of the leather line that held her to the wagon; her eyes rolled, reflecting the fire, her nostrils dilated, and she whinnied in fear.

"It'll be all right, girl," he said, gentling her as best he could. He poured a little canteen water on her mane to soothe her and rubbed it in, whispering comfort till she quieted a little.

Glancing left and right, he saw men on both sides about fifty yards off, some working on backfire cuts, others on horseback, pulling ropes dragging water-soaked blankets and gunnysacks between the cuts and the oncoming fire. Farther to the east, a wagon was coming from Black Creek, freighting hastily filled barrels of creek water.

He drew his knife and set about cutting holes in the gunnies and the horse blankets in the back of the wagon, his eyes itching as smoke and ashes wafted over him. He dropped the gunnies and horse blankets into the water barrels and tied two ropes to his saddle horn, then knotted the other ends through the soaked blankets and sacks.

Coughing, he untied Mazie, mounted, and set off,

dragging the soaked blankets and sacks from the water barrels, quick and straight as he could, toward the fire. It must've seemed to the mare that he was about to ride right into the flames, for she soon balked, digging in her hooves, and looked back at him as if to ask what the devil he was about.

"It's okay, Mazie," he said, patting her neck. "Come on, just a little closer!"

He nudged her with his knees, and Mazie trotted reluctantly closer to the fire, Seth letting her come at the flames at an angle. He felt the heat of the conflagration on his face now, and the roaring crackle of the wildfire muffled the whole world.

Seth got as close as he dared and set off fast, so close to the flames that still burning bits of floating ember struck his clothing and smoldered there as he dragged the water-soaked blankets along the edge of the fire in hopes of slowing it.

In a couple of minutes, he had to return to the barrels and start over. There was an ax in the wagon, and he wondered if he should just bust the barrels open. But if he did, all the water would rush out in one spot.

Over and over he returned to the barrels, soaking the blankets and sacks, riding out again to drag them, using a gloved hand to beat out the smolders on his shirtsleeves and pant legs as he went. Mazie's eyes were watering from the smoke, and so were his.

Despite the bandanna, he could feel the soot in his lungs, and the fire was getting closer, so he had to un-hobble Goliath and move the wagon back by leaning over from Mazie's saddle to tug at the draft horse's collar. Then he headed back to the fire. Sweat streaked through the ash coating the horse's flanks as they went about their work, and Seth wished there was time to give her some water.

The rippling wall of flames crackled and swept onward, barely slowed by his efforts. The wildfire glared bright, but the air around him was dark with soot, hiding the rest of the world, making it increasingly harder to see the others on the line. He felt alone in a world of flame and smoke, and he wondered if this was what hell was like.

Seth finished another wetting sweep and saw that the backfires were rising now. He realized he was between the two walls of fire. Nearest way out was up ahead, but it was closing off, the two fires rushing together. A sickening vision flickered in his mind: himself and Mazie caught in the fire, burning to death together. . . .

Fear licked up in him like a rising flame, and he spurred to a gallop, came to a place where the backfire, five feet high, was just meeting the prairie fire—and he jumped Mazie over the blaze, the horse screaming with pain as the tips of the flames singed her legs and belly.

They came down in the clear, and Mazie dodged left, on her own initiative, galloping away from the fire.

Close to the wagon, Mazie reluctantly let him take command and Seth dismounted, he and the mare both panting and coughing, his eyes running with smoke-induced tears. . . .

The prairie fire roared, the sky blackened, and the wind drove ashes into Seth's face as he took the hobble off of Goliath and tried to decide what else he could do to help. Where was Sol Hamer? He couldn't see anyone clearly, just smoke-blurred silhouettes.

Then he saw that the backfire was working; the prairie fire, close by, was shrinking back, running out of fuel. But there—about sixty yards to his left—it was breaking through where the firebreak hadn't been dug, coming on like the prow of a ship of fire, headed straight toward Josette's farm.

"Seth!" Was that Josette's voice calling thinly over the roar of the fire? *"Seth!"*

Gripping Goliath's harness to keep him from running, Seth turned and saw a woman's shape forming in the thin veil of smoke. It became Josette, running to him, coughing as she came. She'd torn linen from a slip for a ragged bandanna, but it was already black with soot. She rushed up to him, clasping his arms. "You have to get out of here, Seth!"

"I've got water in the wagon that needs to be used over there!" He pointed. "Where it's breaking through!"

"Those blankets aren't going to stop that!"

"If I can find Sol, he can drive the wagon, and I can bust the barrels, get the water out!"

"He's not here! I'll drive the wagon!"

"What! No!"

She ignored his protests, scrambling up onto the buckboard and taking the reins.

There was no time to argue. He shouted, "Back to the barn, Mazie!" and slapped the mare's rump. She galloped off, still dragging the ropes, vanishing into the smoke. Climbing into the back of the wagon, he wondered if he'd ever see the horse again. He heard men calling frantically to one another where the fire was breaking through.

"Go on, then, Josette!" he shouted.

The wagon lurched forward, and he almost fell out

the back, catching a barrel edge to steady himself. Josette was struggling to control Goliath with one hand, shouting furiously, *"Go, horse! Hurry!"* She used her other hand to whip the Clydesdale with a quirt.

The wagon picked up speed, trundling over the rough ground toward the place where the fire was breaking through. Seth glimpsed men running from the fire, two of them stopping to lift a man who had fallen. And Seth himself was coughing almost continuously, finding it hard to get enough air.

The wagon was close now. He caught up the ax handle, swinging the blade hard on the nearest barrel, smashing it open near the bottom so that water gushed out. Staggering to keep his balance in the swaying wagon, he swung the ax again and again, smashing barrels as Josette drove them past the fire, water running out the open back of the wagon. Smoke and steam gushed up where water streaming from the wagon struck the edge of the fire.

Two more barrels to go, and he felt dizzy, swinging the ax, coughing for air, as Josette drove the wagon close to the outrunner tip of the fire, turning the buckboard to follow the intruding flames.

Then there was one barrel left, and he kicked it over so it dumped out, the new rush of water pushing the rest of the liquid down onto the fire. . . .

And then they were past it, and she turned the wagon back toward her little farm. He climbed up next to her as Goliath, eager to escape the flames, pulled them full bore out of the smoke. They reached the northern edge of the property, and he braked the wagon.

Ashes still fell about them, but the air was almost clean here. They pulled off their bandannas, first coughing, then gulping in great breaths of air—only to cough again. Both of them spat soot off opposite sides of the wagon, and then they looked at each other and laughed in relief.

"Where"—she coughed again—"is Mazie?"

"I had to send her running, and like as not, some horse thief is sitting on her right now."

"I'll hazard she's"—she coughed and took a breath—"she's around here somewhere, looking for you."

"I don't know if she trusts me anymore. She got scorched out there. Lord willing, it's not too bad."

They both turned to look at the fire. The prairie fire looked scanty now, the flames shrinking back as if cowed.

"I believe that we stopped that breach in our lines, General Dubois."

She smiled and inspected him. "You've a lot of soot on your face, 'specially around your eyes." She put a hand over her mouth and laughed till she coughed, just managing to say, "You look like a racoon!"

"Well, you look like a lady racoon, so we're suited, I reckon."

"Oh!" She put her hand to her face and looked at the soot on her finger. "Oh, but *no*!" And she swore softly in French.

"What'd you expect, Josette?" He cleared his throat, leaned away to spit, and said, "You were driving a wagon hell-bent through a prairie fire!" He felt awash with emotion then, remembering the two of them working together on the wagon, so close to death. What he felt was too strong to express. All he could say was "It was—quite a sight." He looked at her in wonder. "You are some woman, Josette. You are a woman to ride the river with."

She blushed through her soot and climbed down off the wagon. "You'd better go find your horse. And I'd better find some soap." She gazed up at him for a long moment and said softly, "You're some fella, Seth Coe." Then she turned away; hitching up her skirts, she ran toward her farmhouse.

As the smoke began to clear, he saw at least a hundred people coming out to gaze in awe at the remains of the fire. Flames were still licking up here and there. The land was burned black for quite a piece, but the fire seemed to have stopped short of the farms and small ranches near Prairie Fire. A cloud of black smoke hovered over the prairie, and where the occasional lonely tree had stood, there remained only a smoking black sketch of a tree trunk.

Seth felt some pain in his right arm, looked down to see holes burned in his shirt. The flying embers had burned through in a few places, and he'd been seared, but he hadn't felt it in all the excitement.

"Damn it," Seth muttered. "That was a new shirt." He sighed. "Come on, Goliath, let's go back to our barn. You and me need a rest. 'Specially you. And I want to check on the boss and his Daisy." He turned the wagon toward the Hamer farm, watching for Sol, hoping he was safe and sound. He wished Franklin were with him. He'd have been a big help in the emergency. Franklin would have been impressed by Josette's part in controlling the blaze, too. He'd have seen in her what Seth saw.

Riding through thinning streamers of smoke, Seth

had nearly reached the Hamer place when he saw the dark figure riding toward him. Coming through a veil of smoke, the rider was just the silhouette of a man on horseback. Ashes, some still flickering with fire, fluttered past the rider—who was wearing a bowler hat.

Seth braked the wagon, tugging on Goliath's reins as Hannibal Fisher emerged from the screen of smoke.

Seth had no pistol on him, and his rifle was in Mazie's saddle. The weapons hadn't been needed for plowing nor for fighting a fire. Maybe the man meant him no harm.

But Seth doubted that. Fisher was wanted for two murders.

There was the ax in the back of the wagon. Seth supposed he could jump back there and take cover and take hold of the ax. It was all he had.

He noticed another horseman cantering closer about a hundred yards beyond Fisher. Maybe one of Fisher's men.

Seth glanced around and saw no one else close by.

The man in the lavender bowler came closer, reined in about thirty feet away—and Seth saw him draw a six-shooter.

Seth jumped up, half rolled into the back, and grabbed the ax.

"Seth Coe!" the man called out hoarsely. "What you got there, an ax? How's that going to help you? I'll tell you what you do. You throw your money belt down over here, and I'll let you go without a scratch!"

The chances of Hannibal Fisher letting him go seemed slim to none. Fisher wasn't going to let Seth go to raise an alarm.

"I don't use a money belt!" Seth called. That was the truth. "What money I have is put away somewhere!"

"Then take me to it!"

"And then you'll shoot me dead, Fisher! I've seen the posters—you've got nothing to lose! You can come over here and take your chances with my ax!"

Fisher raised the gun, took aim—

"Hannibal Fisher!" the other horseman called, riding out of the smoke. "Drop your weapon!"

Seth did not recognize the man, but he felt his heart leap when he saw the badge on the rider's vest.

This is what Franklin would call a lucky draw, Seth thought.

Fisher lowered the gun to his right side, turned his horse about to his left, shouting, "I'm dropping the gun, Sheriff!"

"He's still got the gun!" Seth shouted, but as he was saying it, Fisher was firing.

The gambler fired twice, and the lawman jerked back with the impact of a round, his horse shying as the other bullet struck the saddle's cantle. Gray gun smoke added itself to the black smoke of the prairie fire.

Seth stood and threw the ax; it spun through the air past Fisher, missing—but distracting him so he turned to level his weapon at Seth.

Fisher's bullet cracked over Seth's head as he threw himself flat in the back of the wagon. Another shot boomed then, sounding like a heavier pistol. Must have been the lawman firing at Fisher. Seth lifted up enough to see Fisher spur his horse hard, galloping away into the smoke.

The lawman's horse trotted nervously nearer, tossing its head, and Seth jumped down, taking it by the bridle.

"You're hit!" Seth said, seeing the lawman half slumped in the saddle, clutching his middle. "Let me help you onto the wagon. I'll take you in to a doc!"

The lawman, early middle age, lean, and grim faced, winced with pain as he swung from the saddle. His knees buckled when he planted his boots, and Seth caught him around the waist, then helped him to the wagon. Groaning, the lawman climbed in and lay down among the shattered barrels.

Seth tied the lawman's horse to the wagon, jumped up to the seat, and quirted Goliath, starting off as quick as the big horse would go.

Heading into Prairie Fire.

CHAPTER EIGHT

Only now, with the wounded lawman lying on the padded table, did Seth ponder the peculiar coincidence of the doctor's name he'd noticed on the signboard outside the little house. The surname was Twilley, same as the judge's. Looking at the young physician, he decided the two must be closely related. The face was almost the same, except young Doctor Twilley was clean-shaven, and they seemed much the same age.

The doc had administered laudanum, and now as he cut away the lawman's shirt so he could get at the bullet, he asked, "Sheriff from Newton, I take it, sir."

Eyes closed, the lawman spoke for the first time. "Dawson. Name's Dawson . . . Had a good shot at the son of a—" Here he stopped and emitted a groan of pain as the doctor poured spirits on the wound. "But the other fella was right there past him. . . . Coulda killed that man and . . . I took too long to try to . . ."

"Sorry you got hit, looking out for me, Sheriff," said Seth.

"Did I . . . did I get him?"

"Maybe you grazed him. He rode off east. Probably headed for the state line."

"Him and Diamond, they . . ."

"Sheriff," the doctor interrupted sternly, "you take this leather bit in your mouth here and bite down. This is going to hurt past what laudanum can help."

He placed the leather strap between Dawson's teeth, and the lawman bit down. Dawson cursed unintelligibly as the doctor cut into him, opening the wound just a little to make room for the forceps.

"Hold him down there, cowboy," the doctor said. "He's bleeding badly, and I need to get this damn thing out and close the wound quick as ever I can."

Seth stepped in close behind Dawson's head and got a good grip on his shoulders. The sheriff's back arched—though Seth sensed he was doing his best to keep still—as the doctor probed the wound, found the bullet, and worked it out, talking all the while.

"Judging by the bubbles here, it's nicked your left lung, Dawson, cut a pulmonary vein, and generally wreaked havoc. You're going to have to take it easy. You move around too soon, you could collapse your lung, maybe get blood up your bronchial tubes. But if you don't start chasing badmen right away, and if we can keep it from going septic, why, I believe you'll do all right."

Doc Twilley worked swiftly, cleaning and closing the wound. When the worst of it was over, Dawson turned his head and spat out the leather strap. The sheriff was gasping, but he'd relaxed some, and Seth let him go.

He put a hand on Dawson's arm. "Sheriff, my name's Seth Coe. I'm obliged to you. Way I see it, you took a bullet for me. If you hadn't been there, he'd have killed me sure. I had nothing with me but an ax."

"You . . . just get the Town Marshal. Let him know what's happened. Tell him Fisher's close by." Dawson looked at Doc Twilley, who was now cleaning his instruments. "Doc, how about some more of those hops?"

"Being as you've got a hole in a lung, I daren't give you another dose of laudanum so soon, Sheriff. Later on, maybe. But how's about some whiskey? I've got some Overholt in the cabinet there. Coe, you can get it for us. Three glasses if you want some."

"Not much of a whiskey drinker," Coe said, fetching the bottle and glasses. "But it's been a hell of a day. I believe I'll have me one. Say, Doc—you related to Judge Twilley?"

"Yep! He told me all about your case! Fact is, he's my twin brother. One to the law, one to medicine. That's what my father asked for as he was dying, and we could not say no. Father was a judge himself, and his father a physician."

Seth lifted Dawson up enough so that he could take a double whiskey down.

Dawson lay back with a sigh. "That's a little better now."

Seth poured himself a drink, clinked his glass with Doc Twilley, and the two of them drank.

"Say, I've got some burns, Doc," Seth said. They were feeling raw.

Twilley nodded. "Take off your shirt. I had two burn cases earlier, but neither too bad. We got lucky—well, that and some good men managed to turn the fire."

"One good woman, at least, was part of that," Seth said, taking off his shirt. "Josette Dubois. She drove a water wagon right up to the fire."

"Did she? She's a spunky one, always has been. Was I not engaged to be married, I would court her myself." He cleaned Seth's burns and bandaged them. "Not bad, not bad . . . Keep 'em clean is all . . ."

Seth put his shirt back on, drank the last of his whiskey, and asked, "Will you keep the sheriff here a while?"

"I've got straps on this examining table, and he'll spend the night there. Tomorrow I'll ease him onto the bed in my extra room. He can stay right here long as he needs it. Can't have a valuable lawman dying from neglect."

"I've got to vamoose," said Seth. "I'll have a word with the marshal and see if I can find my horse. . . ."

M ARSHAL COGGINS ARRANGED a horse for Seth at the livery and gave him a shotgun.

Seth climbed up on his tall sorrel gelding, the marshal was already aboard his paint stock horse, and the two of them went in search of both Fisher and Mazie. Seth had offered to help with the one in return for help finding the other.

They stopped at the Hamer farm, partly so Seth could tell Sol that Goliath was safe and sound, resting at the livery. Seth was disappointed to find that his own horse wasn't on the farm, but glad that Sol and Daisy were well and the farm untouched.

Standing by their horses beside the farmhouse's porch, Seth and Slim Coggins each drank a cup of coffee and ate a couple of molasses biscuits. Daisy offered them pie, but Coggins said, "Nothing I'd like better, but we'd better head out, ma'am."

"Seth," said Sol, "I thank you for what you did today. You done more than your job."

"Proud to help," said Seth, handing the coffee cup back to Daisy.

Coggins nodded. "I seen him taking on that fire. He got burned some, too."

"Not much of a much," said Seth.

"And he and that Josette Dubois—I was arguing with folks about what to do about the fire breaking through, but Seth here and Josette, by God, they just did the job while we were braying like jackasses!"

Sol and Daisy laughed at that. "Josette's a brave girl!" Daisy said.

"You were out there, too, Daisy," Sol pointed out, "warning folks, bringing water. . . ."

"You haven't seen a man riding hereabouts?" Seth asked. "Fella wearing a kinda purple-like bowler hat? Face like an undertaker?"

Sol shook his head. "No one like that. Lot of confusion out there today. Folks riding back and forth."

"I ran into him a little while ago—he's wounded a lawman from Newton."

Daisy's eyes widened. "He did this here?"

"You see him, best to let someone know. He's a wanted man."

"Let's see if we can pick up his trail, Seth," said Coggins, handing the cup to Sol. "I thank you, folks."

Seth and the marshal remounted. It took almost an

hour, with the ground all blackened from falling ashes and marked by a good many horses, but they cut Fisher's trail. It seemed to circle back, as if Fisher had returned to the scene of the confrontation and then headed east. They lost it at Black Creek just as the sun was setting.

"I'll try to pick him up tomorrow," said Coggins. "Likely gone south for the state line, howsoever. Maybe he'll take the long ride to Mexico. I'll send a message to Newton, let them know we've had a run-in with Fisher."

Seth heard a whinny and looked across the creek to see Mazie, still dragging those ropes, trotting up to look at him. The mare shook her head and whinnied again.

"She doesn't look too much the worse for wear," said Coggins.

Seth waded the gelding across the creek and caught up Mazie's reins. "You're a durned good horse, Mazie girl. I knew you wouldn't run far off. Let's get you to the barn. . . ."

JUST FOUR MILES north of the place Seth had found Mazie, Fisher was standing by the creek, drinking corn liquor with Curt Diamond. "I believe I killed Dawson," said Fisher, speaking to Diamond in a low voice. He took a sip from his tin cup and shuddered. The two men were standing alone, the others playing poker by campfire light. It was a dark night, still smelling of the wildfire smoke. "We might not want to mention that to the others. They might think it's too hot around here. But I thought you'd want to know."

"Glad to see Dawson go down. You sure?"

"Got him square in the chest. He grazed my hip with a shot, and my horse decided to take the better part of valor—but thinking about it, I decided he was killed. I went back to see if I could find his body—and Seth Coe. But they were gone. I expect Coe carried the body off."

"Coe saw the shooting. He knows who you are! Come to think of it, Hannibal, it seems to me it's too hot around here. And I don't mean that damn prairie fire!"

"You and me, we're already wanted men. Coe mentioned a wanted poster."

"Hell, I knew there'd be posters on us. I was thinking we should've knocked that old fool out instead of killing him."

"And risk him coming to and setting up a howl before we were clear of town? We had to do it dirty and fast. What use is looking back, anyhow? We got to look ahead! We need money to get us to Mexico—and to set us up there, Curt!"

Diamond finished his drink and looked wistfully into the empty cup. "'Bout at the end of our whiskey."

"I'll have Sweeney get us something to drink when he goes to town. No one's looking for him. He'll find out if there's a posse forming in Prairie Fire."

"You're shooting lawmen not but a few miles from where we stand—"

"Damn it," Fisher growled, not much above a whisper, "keep your voice down."

He glanced at the others and saw Bettiger toss down his cards in disgust. Briggs guffawed and scooped in a handful of silver. Seemed like they hadn't heard what Diamond had said. Fisher didn't want them to know what had happened.

"Well, what we going to do?" Diamond whispered. "Coe is bound to raise the alarm. There's a Town Marshal in Prairie Fire."

Fisher shrugged. "I'm going to ride out tonight. I've got a plan to make the law think I've ridden south—but I'll double back up the creek here. Then we'll move off to the east a piece. There's always Buffalo Junction."

"Buffalo Junction?" Diamond mused. "I don't think anyone there's gunning for me. Not as I recollect. But won't the Town Marshal look for us there? That's a regular robbers' roost."

"Won't look for us there if they're looking elsewhere. And no one goes there who doesn't have to. We'll wait till things cool some so they're not looking for me. Then we'll come back here and take that bank. Seth Coe has my money, and that bank has a lot more. You tell the men I'm just scouting the countryside for the best trail after the bank business. The time comes, we'll send Sweeney in to see what he can find out."

WEARY TO THE bone after plowing, fighting fires, and tracking outlaws, Seth was in the barn with Sol Hamer, the two of them working by lantern light, Sol holding Mazie still and petting her as Seth applied salve to her burns.

"You boys come in and have some supper," said Daisy, coming to the barn door, where the two men were working over Mazie.

"We'll be in quick as an owl diving for a mouse," Seth said. "I've got a powerful hunger."

"You shall have the season's first sweet corn, taters

pork chops, and cherry pie. Will that do you for a start?"

Seth grinned. "It'll do me fine, ma'am."

Daisy said, "Sol? You coming?"

"We're coming, Daisy."

"How's the mare?"

"I think she'll do," Seth muttered, looking Mazie over again.

"She's got some blisters," Sol said, peering at Mazie's belly and legs, "and some raw skin. You can't ride her for maybe a week. But I calculate she'll mend."

"She can use the rest. I'll have to hire that gelding out."

Sol patted the horse. "Friend of mine, Bone Hawking, lost his barn to the fire, off northwest. I'm going tomorrow to help him start a new barn, maybe give a hand with his stock. Soon's I get Goliath back." He glanced at Seth, waiting expectantly.

Seth didn't disappoint him. "I'll help with the barn raising gladly, Sol."

Maybe, he thought, Josette would be there.

He wished he could talk things over with Franklin. Where was Franklin now?

"Sol!"

"Coming, Daisy!"

FRANKLIN WAS STRIDING through the busy little town of Seaver, Texas, just south of the Oklahoma border. It was jumping in Seaver that warm evening; a good many cowboys were in town looking for fun. The stores were open late, the three saloons were hopping,

and a couple of girls waved silk kerchiefs out the upstairs windows of Loopy Lou's Libations and Enter-
tainments.

But Franklin was thinking he'd stayed over in this
town too long. He hadn't planned to stay but a night,
only he'd gotten sweet on a bar girl. Carla was her name.

*I'm worse than that durn fool Seth, mooning over
girls,* he thought. He decided he needed to get back on
the trail to Chaseman.

He was passing the sheriff's office when under the
oil lamp hanging over the announcement board, he
saw something that startled him.

~WANTED DEAD OR ALIVE~

$1500. REWARD
Hannibal Fisher

He read the remainder of the poster and whistled to
himself. "Ain't that the bunco steerer in Abilene? And
Seth took the shirt right off that man's back!"

"Did I hear you say you're taking off a shirt, Franklin?" said a familiar feminine voice behind him.
"Bueno! It's about time you put on some clean clothes!"

Franklin turned to her, pretending annoyance. "No,
that's *not* what I said, Carla, and no, I don't need clean
clothes—these here are clean. More or less."

She laughed. Carla was a Mexican girl with long
black hair. She was plump, voluptuous in a Mexican
blouse loosely gathered at the top and a long floral
skirt with a slit up one side to her hip. She was very
short compared to Franklin, but she looked up at him

bold as brass. "Well, are you going to buy me a drink, or ain't you?"

"I will at that." He looked once more at the poster. "That killer there—you ever see him?"

"No. Oh! He has such a cold, hard face!"

"I saw it just that cold and hard when he told Seth he'd see him again. Didn't like getting kicked out of Abilene when Seth showed him up to be a cheat!"

"Seth—your pal you talk of so much?"

"That's right. This man, when Seth faced him down over those cards, why, I saw killing in this Fisher's eyes. And now they say he's in Southern Kansas, right where Seth is."

"Kansas is a big place."

"It surely is that—anyhow, maybe Seth's tired of Prairie Fire, and he's on his way to Texas."

But no . . . Seth said he was staying at least two weeks. When Seth Coe said he was going to do something, he did it. He'd still be there.

"Did you say Prairie Fire?" Carla asked. "That the town?"

"Sure it is. He's sweet on a girl there."

"But it's so funny about Prairie Fire! Oh, not funny but . . . ."

"What's that?"

"After you went off to sleep, I went over Loopy Lou's last night, and Dusty said that town was most on fire! And it was 'cause of a fire off the prairie! Everything burning all round that Kansas town! And what is its name? Prairie Fire!"

Franklin looked at her in shock. "Knowing Seth, he'd be right in the middle of it. . . ." It was too much.

First this business with Fisher, then this tale about the fire. "Now *I'm* the damn fool because I'm going to have to go back!"

"No! Don't go, Franklin!"

"I'll think about it some tonight, Carla. But I need to know Seth didn't get himself burned up in that fire. Even if he didn't, Seth might need me to side him with Hannibal Fisher close by. Tomorrow, like as not, I'll head north. . . ."

THEY WERE LUCKY the weather had shifted. It was overcast, somewhat muggy out, but it was thought there'd be rain—much-overdue rain—and a cool breeze eased the work of clearing the burned debris.

It was getting close to noon as Seth walked beside Goliath, one hand on his harness, guiding the big draft horse to pull the last of the wreckage out of the way. The barn had caught fire from still glowing cinders blown from the north, and it had gone up before Hawking could do anything about it. Much of the barn had been burned past dragging away, and they'd had to carry out chunks of charred wood by hand. Some of the local men were wielding shovels, helping Bone Hawking carry clear the last big pile of ashes.

"We might get the frame put in today," said Sol, walking up as Seth unchained the timbers.

"Bone told me he's got plans for a bigger barn this time," said Seth, straightening up and stretching.

Sol chuckled. "What he had before wasn't much more'n a cowshed! Room for two cows, two horses, a pig he's already slaughtered, and a mule. The sly old dickens saw his chance to get his neighbors to build him a real barn!"

Seth grinned. "I don't mind. Nothing much else doing."

Nonetheless, he did want to look in on Sheriff Dawson and Marshal Coggins later on. Seth was not easy in his mind about Hannibal Fisher. Coggins might have news about the outlaw.

Many times, during the morning, Seth's gaze had strayed to the improvised table—a barn door laid over sawhorses—where the ladies had set out some food. Josette was there now talking to Daisy and Mrs. Hawking as she set out the dishes. As if she sensed him watching, Josette glanced up and quickly looked back at her chore, but with a demure little smile.

Was that smile for me? Seth wondered. She'd arrived about an hour earlier, and he'd wondered if Dubois had tried to stop her from coming.

"Ain't that Heywood Kelmer?" Sol asked, nodding to the east.

Heywood was riding in on his palomino, flanked by Vince and Blackie mounted on sorrel and gray stock horses. He was wearing the same outfit he'd worn when there'd been the trouble in the general store. He had his usual look of smug self-satisfaction as he trotted his mount up to the vittles table.

Instinctively, Seth let go of the tow chains and walked straight over to Josette. He warned himself not to get into any kind of tussle with Heywood, not even the kind that was just talk, but a strong impulse to protect Josette had hold of him.

"You know I didn't mean anything by it, Josette,"

Heywood was saying. "My father raised a gentleman. But when he—"

Seeing Seth, Heywood broke off, his smug smile tightening into a hard line.

"We—" Josette licked her lips. She smiled at Seth. "We'll have some lunch ready in a pinch, Seth," she said.

"Just looking for a drink of water," said Seth.

"You should be hungry," said Molly Hawking. She was a hefty woman in a pink-and-white calico dress, her button nose almost lost in her wide face. Her smile, showing gaps in her teeth, was big enough, however. "You've been here since not much past dawn."

"I do believe I am getting peckish, ma'am," Seth said, accepting a tin cup of water from Josette.

"What brings you fellas here?" Bone Hawking asked, walking up to the table to squint up at the horsemen. He clapped his hands to clear ashes from them. A bowlegged man with a straw hat, ash-soiled overalls, and a seamed face almost as florid as his beard, Bone was almost a head shorter than his wife.

"Vince and Blackie here are volunteering to help out with the barn raising," Heywood said, getting down off his horse. "Thought I'd see what we could do."

"You could help with those burned timbers yonder, Heywood," said Bone. There was a certain mischievousness in his voice as he said it, knowing that it was the very last job Heywood Kelmer would undertake. "Might get some cinders on that fancy coat there, I speculate."

Seth smiled and winked at Josette. Heywood's scowl deepened, seeing that. He reached into a pocket, and drew out two double eagles, giving the twenty-dollar coins to Bone. "That's to help you with the timber costs."

"Thankee," said Bone, almost grumbling the word as he slipped the coins into his pocket. "Lost ten acres of new corn to the fire, too," he added, perhaps thinking that might trigger another contribution.

Heywood ignored the hint. He turned to Vince and Blackie. "You two fellas go on over and help with that burned timber there."

Vince smiled ruefully, and Blackie rolled his eyes, but they walked over to the pile of charred wood, taking leather gloves from their back pockets as they went.

Heywood gave Josette his most condescending smile. "Now it seems that you and I have much to talk about. Maybe we could take a walk . . . ?"

Seth cleared his throat. "Heywood—"

"Seth," Josette interrupted, "would you help me carry the preserves from the kitchen?"

"Oh, I could get the—" Molly started. But Daisy gave her a nudge with an elbow. Molly cleared her throat, realizing that Josette wanted a chance to talk to Seth alone. "Yes—would you help Josette, Seth?"

"Surely," said Seth, setting down his cup. He walked side by side with Josette to the farmhouse.

"You know, he figured you were here," Seth said as they went into the kitchen. "That's the only reason he came."

"I know." She took four jars from a shelf and set them on a cutting table. "Seth—I don't want you in jail again. Do not get into it with that man."

"I didn't say a durn word to him, Josette!"

"You were fixing to!"

"Only if he tried to bully you."

"You just let me handle that! If you're in jail—well—" She turned away, before she went on. "What good are you to me in jail?"

Seth's heart lifted at that. He stepped closer, took her hand in his, and gently drew her to face him. "Just tell me straight out, Josette. If he asks you to marry him, will you?"

She looked at him in surprise. "Don't you know?"

"Can't tell. Last time we spoke of it, you seemed to be considering him as a . . . as . . ."

"I *consider* him an *oaf*! I almost laughed when he called himself a gentleman. I will not dance a step with him, let alone marry him!"

"That being the case, will you—"

She took her hand from his and placed it over his mouth. "Hush! Don't rush me, Seth Coe!" She picked up two jars of pickles and put them in his hands. "You take those out to Molly! I'll take the strawberry jam!"

"Suppose I was to ask for a kiss?"

Josette compressed her lips and narrowed her eyes. "You behave yourself! Till I tell you not to!"

She turned and bustled out of the room, and feeling strangely encouraged, he followed with a light step.

When they stepped outside, Heywood was there; he had mounted his horse and was blocking their way.

"You and I had an understanding, Josette," he said.

"No, Heywood, we did not."

"We did. Your father agreed! And here you are, acting like a soiled dove with this—"

"What did you say, mister?" Seth said, bristling, stepping toward Heywood. He had every intention of dragging Heywood Kelmer from the saddle so they could fight it out here and now.

"Seth, no!" Josette stepped in between them, holding her hands up to block Seth. "Don't! Please!"

Heywood gave one of his smug smiles. "You see that, Coe? She's ready to fight for me!"

Josette spun on her heel, planted her hands on her hips, and snapped, "Heywood Kelmer—I did that for Seth!"

"Then you're a—"

"*Get out of here*, Kelmer," Seth interrupted, the words coming between clenched teeth.

Face twitching, Heywood backed his horse up. "You fail to understand who you're tangling with, Coe," he growled. Then he turned the palomino and rode away.

CHAPTER NINE

IT WAS DUSK when Fisher got back to the camp. "How long we going to set around here, breathing them ashes?" Sweeney asked as Fisher tied his horse to a scrub oak. "Wind's been blowing all them cinders off the prairie all the damn day."

"That's a real good question," said Bettiger. He sat on a log, paring a thumbnail with a buck knife.

The camp was leaden with ashes, blown there in the aftermath of the fire. Black Creek was all murky with ash, living up to its name, and the restless men seated around the dead campfire looked like a parcel of Confederate soldiers, with the ashes graying them.

"We won't stay here any longer," Fisher said, coming to stand by the dead campfire. He took off his bowler and brushed ashes off it. "We head to Buffalo Junction soon's we get our gear loaded. Except for Sweeney. He goes to Prairie Fire, makes some inquiries for us. In a few days, why, we hit that bank. And I finish my business there, too."

"It's not just your business," said Diamond. "We get our share of Coe's money."

"Most assuredly," Fisher said with all the conviction of a practiced liar.

"Buffalo Junction?" Smiley Briggs shook his shaggy red mane. "I don't like it! That grasping cuss Feathers Martin—he'll squeeze every last penny out of a man needin' to hide out there."

"That's right," said Gaines, tamping tobacco into a pipe. "He'll do just that. Besides which, everyone knows half the wanted men in Kansas pass through that place. Be our luck to get there just when the US marshal brings in the Army. That's what they're doing some places! Cavalry instead of a posse!"

"We won't stay too long," said Fisher. "And what I've heard is Martin has men watching the roads. There's half a dozen ways out before anyone can close in. Then he goes back to pretending it's a country tavern!"

Gaines smacked his lips at that. "By God, he does have liquor, anyhow. Beer, too!"

"And beds!" Fisher pointed out.

"I'm ready for one," Bettiger admitted. "Tired of sleeping rough."

"When do I meet you there?" Sweeney asked, sitting up straight and stretching his arms.

"Soon's you find out what I need to know," said Fisher.

He commenced loading his few goods into his saddlebags. He knew he was only the nominal leader of these men. He had to keep them moving, doing, or they'd

wander off on their own—maybe even pull a gun on
him. Plain truth was, they mostly stuck with him this
far only because they had no place else to go. They
were all wanted, except for Sweeney—and maybe him,
too, if you looked far enough afield. They had little
money and few ideas. Fisher was filling the vacuum
for now.

He was playing some of it by ear. Ideally, their num-
bers would be pruned down before the money was in
hand for an easier split. He'd have to figure out how to
do that. He thought Diamond was steady enough to be
counted on to shoot Gaines and Briggs in the back if
need be. No one much cared for Sweeney. He could
find any old excuse at all to kill him.

In the end, just he and Diamond—whom he needed
to watch his back—would head for Mexico flush with
cash.

"Compadres, let us delay no longer," Fisher said, tying up the saddlebags. "Let us head east to Buffalo
Junction. I'm buying two rounds of drinks soon's we
get there. And who knows? Maybe it'll be a profitable
journey. That Feathers Martin—how much gold has he
got stored up somewhere? Maybe it's time the old thief
was robbed himself."

"Maybe," said Gaines, standing up and slapping
ashes from his trousers. "All right. I guess I'll look in
on ol' Feathers. But tell me this—where you been all the
long day, Hannibal, off on your own?"

"Making sure no one was on my trail, is where."
They knew he was a wanted man, and that explanation
would likely hold them. "Ran a trail down south like
that's where I was headed, doubled back, came most
the way here riding up in this creek. All the time

watching for lawmen and townsfolk. Most of these yo-kels are busy shoveling ash and rebuilding sheds and such. Saw no lawmen at all."

"Always smart to check the back trail," said Dia-mond, dusting ashes off his hat. He stood up and went to his horse.

The others—a certain grudging slowness in their motions—were packing up now.

"I'm ready to head east," Gaines said. "But we'd best not lay over too long at Martin's place. You seri-ous about taking his money, Hannibal? You'd have to kill him for it."

"Would that break your heart?" Fisher asked.

Gaines made a high-pitched hee-hee-hee that was a wicked mock of laughter. "Not one bit. But Feathers ain't there alone!"

Fisher squatted to fill his canteen from the creek, a little upstream from where his horse was thirstily drinking. "We'll see what can be done and what can't."

Fisher was concerned about one thing. That Seth Coe, having had a close scrape that day of the fire, would have hightailed it down to Texas already. But it was his judgment, based on Coe's nerviness, even bra-vado, that the cowboy would not flee Prairie Fire, Kan-sas. He had driven a wagon; he'd clearly been fighting a fire. Must have business in town. Odds were, Coe was still there.

And Hannibal Fisher was more determined than ever to see Seth Coe dead.

J OSETTE WAS FEEDING the pigs from a bucket of mash when Heywood Kelmer rode up.

The sun was thinking about setting, the long shadows across the barnyard striping Heywood as he trotted the palomino up. "Your pa here?" he asked brusquely. No smile this time.

"In the house," she said. "Just got home."

She turned away and used the wooden scoop to spread the mash for the grunting hogs, as if they were of more interest to her than Heywood.

"You are going to change your way of thinking, girl," he said. She glanced over her shoulder, saw him ride the horse over to the house. He dismounted, tied the horse to the hitch, and knocked on the door. Papa let Heywood in and closed the door.

Bucket in hand, Josette walked over to the house, posting herself in the shadows near the open window. She wanted to know what Heywood's business was but was loath to be in the same room with him.

"I tell you true," Heywood said, "that saddle bum all but attacked me! If he'd had a gun on him, I'd have called him out!"

Josette smiled to herself. Heywood was more bluster than bravery. She doubted he'd have called Seth out for a gunfight. She could not picture Heywood Kelmer fighting his own battles.

"That man," Heywood went on, "took her into the house alone, and when she came out, she was blushing! Seth Coe is trying to seduce your daughter! And she's playing along with him, too!"

"What!"

"I don't know how far it's gone, but I'm about to set her aside unless she changes her tune! I don't like to be denied, Dubois. Now, do you want that land—or do you not?"

"Yes, yes, of course! Here—will you have a drink, Heywood? Let us talk about it—"

"No, no drink for me now. I just want you to know where I stand. I do not take well to being given the wind like some farmhand! We will see what happens—but I will not stand for it! Now, you see to your daughter—or I will!"

Josette's eyes widened. *You see to your daughter—or I will!* What did Heywood mean by *or I will*?

Josette heard his boot steps coming to the door, and she quickly slipped around the corner of the house. She waited till he had ridden off, and then she set the bucket thoughtfully down and went in—out of long habit—to make supper for her father. Where else was she to go?

"You!" He was sitting at the kitchen table, his face in darkness, for the light from the windows was fading. A bottle of spirits sat on the table by his mug. "I told you to stay away from that cowboy!"

"It's so dark in here," she said, going to the oil lamp. She hoped he would just let the subject of Seth Coe drop if she didn't argue with him. Fingers trembling, she lit the lamp, replaced its chimney, and started for the stove.

Suddenly Dubois lurched to his feet.

She stepped back, wondering how bad it would be this time.

"You!" He wagged his finger in her face. "You are acting like a woman of the streets!"

"Papa! What would Mama think if she could hear you say such a thing!"

His eyes narrowed, and swearing in French, he slapped her so that she staggered back against the wall, her ears ringing, her face feeling as if it had been rubbed in nettles.

"You are not going to cost me that land!" he roared. "I need it! And he is a rich man—you should be happy!"

Josette felt like she could not breathe. Gasping, she rushed to the door, burst through, and ran out to the barn. She didn't bother to saddle the mule—she dragged him from his stall by the bridle and out to the barnyard.

Her father was silhouetted in the doorway, shouting, "You come here! Now! *Vite!*"

But Josette climbed astraddle the mule and kicked it with her heels. It clumped off, and she rode into the twilight toward Sol Hamer's farm.

S ETH SAT ON a stool by Dawson's bed, hat in his lap, listening to the sheriff's harsh breathing. The marshal was bare chested but for the bandages, covered only by a sheet. The window was open, and a waft of cool air visited the room, smelling of rain. Dawson seemed asleep, but Seth wasn't quite sure, and he didn't want to wake him.

There were voices in the outer room, and then Slim Coggins came in, opening the door carefully so as not to make much noise, followed by the doctor.

Doc Twilley came around to the other side of the small bed, turned the lamp up brighter, and took Dawson's wrist between his fingers.

Dawson opened his eyes and looked blearily around. "Seems I've got a power of visitors, but they're all the wrong sort," he said in a low, rasping voice. "Why is it you don't have a pretty nurse, Twilley?"

"My fiancée will not stand for it." He laid a hand over Dawson's forehead. "Your pulse is strong. Maybe a low fever. Been the same since yesterday night. Natural enough but not intensifying. Good signs." He bent over and pressed an ear to Dawson's chest, listening. "Take a deep breath there, Sheriff."

Dawson breathed deep and coughed a little.

Doc Twilley straightened up and nodded. "You'll do if you'll stick with the bed rest."

"If you write up a letter on the costs and send it to the clerk at Newton city hall, we'll get you paid, Doc. They'll cover my vittles, too."

"All in good time."

"Marshal," said Dawson, "any sign of Fisher?"

"I struck what I think were his tracks this afternoon, heading south. Right over the Oklahoma border and then lost them in the hills. Stony ground there. I've sent letters to law to the south to watch for him. All I can do."

"I figured he'd leave the state," Dawson said. "I'd sure like to track him down. He killed an old friend of mine, and he kicked me to the dirt."

"Slim," Seth put in, "if there's any kind of posse looking for him, I'll sign on for it. I don't like him running around free, holding a grudge and a gun."

"I'm a Town Marshal. I've got to stay round here," Coggins replied. "But if he comes back anywhere close to Prairie Fire, you'll be the first man I'll call on." He turned to Dawson. "Sheriff, I just wanted you to know I did what I could. If I see a chance to take him, I'll do it."

"I'm obliged, Slim."

The marshal came over to the bed; taking a silver

flask from his back pocket, he placed it beside the lamp. "That's the best apple brandy in the county, and there's more where that comes from—if the doc don't object."

"You bring some for me, too," said Twilley, "then I will allow it."

"I thank you kindly, Slim," Dawson said with a weak grin.

"Now, gentlemen, you're taking up all the good air in the room," Twilley said with a doctor's authority in his tone. "Out you go. Let the man breathe and rest. Don't overdo the brandy, Dawson."

"Rest easy, Sheriff," Seth said, standing. "Let us worry about Hannibal Fisher. If he comes around— we'll get him."

"I hope to be there when you do," Dawson muttered, reaching for the flask. "Why—this flask has my name on it! It's engraved real pretty!"

"A small gift from the town council," said Coggins.

"You extend my thanks to them, will you?"

"I will. I'll let you know if there's news."

Coggins turned to go, and Seth followed him to the little house's small front porch. There he paused, put on his hat, and sniffed the air. It was just past sunset, and thick clouds were draping the sky. Rain, for sure. But it wasn't yet falling. Lights twinkled from the town, a short distance to the west.

"Be a blessing if it rains," said Coggins, peering up at the sky. "Five years ago, we had two wildfires in one season! I would not care for another fire this year."

Rain began to patter down then. Seth put on his hat and said, "Seems like you've got the good Lord's ear."

"You still out there with the Hamers?"

"I am. Going back there now. Just about time for supper."

"Red Milligan said he saw some men camped up north a piece on Black Creek. Told me just a quarter hour ago. Might be anyone up there. We get cowboys camping on their way home often enough. But I thought maybe I'd ride out and have a look tomorrow. The law is looking for Curt Diamond, too, and there's others."

"I expect Sol won't mind if I come with you."

"I'll call for you in the morning, if"—he looked up at the sky, which was now pouring rain, and put his own hat on—"if we're not washed away in a flood!"

Seth waved, put up his shirt collar, and hurried to the other side of town to pick up the gelding, Mazie not being healed up enough to ride as yet. The rain clattered on tin roofs and rattled shingles and drumrolled on Seth's hat. Townsfolk had come out on their porches, the men lighting up pipes, to look at the downpour.

Seth's mind was on Josette. By now she'd be home. But like as not, so would Dubois. How was he to see her?

Wishing he'd worn a coat, he fetched the gelding from the livery and rode out to Sol's—and was startled to find Josette in the barn.

She was graining her mule and Mazie, and looked up with a smile that shared the glow of the lantern as he led his horse to a stall.

"Well, look who's here," he said as if talking to his horse, speaking lightly to cover his surprise. "The prettiest hostler in Kansas."

"Only Kansas?" she asked, bending to look at Mazie's belly. "She's healing up some."

He shook rainwater off his hat and came to stand beside her. He wanted to ask why she was here, but he decided she'd tell him in her own good time. "I just saw Sheriff Dawson. He's on the mend, too. You hear about that?"

"Slim Coggins told us in the store. This man Fisher was shooting at you and hit the sheriff?"

Seth winced. "Not quite the way it was." He told her the story, downplaying his own danger.

"So he knows you, this wanted man?"

"I took some money off him in a poker game, and that led to Hickok posting him out of town. Does not seem to have forgiven me for it. He murdered a man and escaped from jail."

She shivered. "There are some evil men afoot in this state."

He wanted to take her in his arms—but he was soaked, and anyhow, he was not within his rights to act so boldly.

"You are one wet cowboy," she remarked, making a show of looking him over with disapproval. "You should go put on a dry shirt. It is foolish to ride about in the rain without a slicker."

"It's not cold. Maybe it'll finally get all the ashes washed off me." She was standing so near him—was that the warmth of her body he felt or just the way she made him feel?

They were silent for a long moment as the rain drummed on the roof.

A thought occurred to him. "Are you here at the Hamers' because— Well, was it your father?"

Her lips buckled, and she closed her eyes. "Yes.

Heywood came and . . ." She gave that curiously evocative shrug of hers.

Anger rose up in Seth, hot and pervasive. "Did Dubois hit you?" he demanded.

Josette opened her eyes—and instead of answering his question, she said, "You asked me for a kiss in the Hawkings' kitchen. If you are still desirous of it, you may have it now."

The anger was swept away by another feeling—just as she'd intended, he guessed—as his arms went around her, and his lips found hers. It was a short kiss, just a handful of seconds, but he felt it all through him. Then she pressed her face into the hollow of his shoulder, and he held her close.

"Seth . . ."

"Now . . . now, you heed me good, Josette. I have twenty-six-hundred dollars saved, some of it at home in a bank, some hidden away right here in this barn. I believe I can make a deal for that land in Chaseman. It'll be some considerable work, but me and Franklin, we'll build the cabin and the outbuildings. There'll be a lot of work for all of us. I'll hire out to keep the cash coming in until—"

"Seth?" Josette leaned a little away from him but stayed within the circle of his arms. She looked up at him in wonder. "What are you asking me?"

"I'm asking you to be my wife, of course! You know I love you, and I always have, Josette. No man could ask for a better woman. It was a power of luck, running into you here—I couldn't hardly believe it. We can't let that go, Josette. It was meant to be."

"Luck?" She raised her eyebrows. "Running into

me got you tossed into the pokey, Seth Coe! I don't call that luck!"

"Seeing you in that store—luckiest thing that ever happened to me, bar none."

She smiled—at the same time looking as if she might cry. "I'm . . . I don't know . . ."

"You don't have to decide this minute! But, Josette, you said yourself you would not have Heywood Kelmer. Now, there are other good men, I know, but you and I, why . . ." He ran out of words, trying to figure out why he should ace all those other men out.

She cocked her head and lifted her chin. "And suppose I choose not to get married at all? I remember Amy Lou Smith—she was a spinster and seemed quite happy that way. I could get a job, perhaps in Kansas City. Or I could go to San Francisco or . . ."

He looked at her closely to see if she was in earnest. "Are you so soured on men now?"

Josette sighed and nestled against him once more. "My mama, she—" She broke off and shook her head. "I don't want to speak of that just now."

"I can take you far away from Dubois," Seth said, "and Heywood Kelmer. You never need be troubled with the likes of them again!"

She gave a little laugh that seemed to melt seamlessly into a sob. "Oh, Seth—I don't care to be rushed. But it feels so good when you hold me. It feels . . . like I can't let go of you, Seth." She leaned back and looked him in the eyes. "I will not ride with you to Texas unless we are married first. Here in town, it might not go well. Papa might interfere. We shall go to the county seat. And there we could . . ."

He grinned quite involuntarily. It was such a wide

grin, he could feel it on his face. "Am I hearing right? You'll marry me?"

"Haven't I just said so? But you still need a dry shirt. You're getting my blouse wet. Give me another kiss, and I'll go tell Daisy we're betrothed! She'll be so pleased! Oh, and I've got to ask Sol if he'll take that poor mule home to Papa. . . ."

He watched her go and then went to take the saddle off the gelding, thinking that sure, Daisy would be pleased they were to be married, and certainly Seth Coe was as pleased as punch.

But Francois Dubois and Heywood Kelmer . . .

Who knew what they would do when they heard?

CHAPTER TEN

IT HAD BEEN a long ride for Fisher and the others, first through the dusty evening and then through the rainy dark. Sometime past midnight, the rain finally eased into occasional drizzle, having finished its job—it had soaked them all to the bone, despite their slickers. The driving rain had left the roads muddy, so the five riders, with Gaines leading the way, trotted at the side of the road in the grass; no one wanted to risk a horse stumbling in the mud, maybe to break an ankle.

The five outlaws were almost as weary as their horses as they came in sight of Buffalo Junction. Fisher was glad to see it, but he was cautious, too. He'd been here only once, but he knew it could be a powder keg.

It was a dark night, but the lights made Buffalo Junction visible. Feathers Martin kept lanterns and lamps lit all round it, on posts around the house and along the road from the gate. There was a wooden fence, half fallen in places, around the fifty-acre property, and it was pretty well lit up so they could see anyone approaching—especially lawmen, for Buffalo Junction was a hideout for men on the run.

Sticking out like a sore thumb on the flat, mostly empty prairie, Feathers's establishment consisted of two shabby buildings set on the diagonal from each other where two roads intersected. Across from Feathers's so-called Traveler's Inn, an ancient chestnut spread its foliage over a sprawling one-story structure where horses and mules and sometimes even oxen were put up in long, narrow sheds to either side of the blacksmith. The stable was dark but for a stall at its center glowing hellishly in the blackness, the red shine marking its farrier at work. As they rode up, they could hear his hammer clanging on an anvil beside the white-hot brick forge.

The inn itself was a two-story building, once a handsome farmhouse, the upstairs divided into three rooms, two for the girls, one with bunks rented to men on the dodge. The downstairs sitting room had been converted to a saloon. The place leaned, just a little, and it'd been shored up with sunken timbers. There was a small barn out behind, where meat animals spent their short lives.

Both roads converging at Buffalo Junction were dirt, one of them little more than a trail heading south into low foothills and eventually to Oklahoma.

"I don't like this place much," Fisher said as they rode up to the farrier. "But on the other hand—it's a godsend on a night like this. Feathers does make sure the roof's kept sound."

"Howdy there, Whistler," Gaines called as they rode up.

Whistler broke off from a perfect-pitch rendition of "The Yellow Rose of Texas," dropped a horseshoe into a tub of water where it sizzled, as a red-hot horseshoe ought to, and turned to gawk up at the rider. He tended to have his mouth open when he was getting a good look at something. "That you, Buster?"

"It is," Gaines said. "Worn out, wet, but too warm and needing a drink—but it's me. Here with Hannibal Fisher and Smiley Briggs and a couple fellers I don't think you know."

Whistler, so called because he whistled a good many quite distinctive tunes as he worked, was a brawny, shirtless man who'd kept his lantern jaw shaved since the one time his departed beard had caught fire over the forge. No one dared make jokes about that occasion, for he was six feet six, and Gaines reckoned him at about three hundred pounds, most of it muscle. He was not only the blacksmith; he was an executioner on those occasions when the boss wanted a special example made. Because Whistler would get it done ugly.

Gaines climbed down and the others followed suit. "You got room to put up our horses?"

"Sure 'nuff. There's only four fellas in the house besides Feathers. There's alfalfa and water there, too." He pointed his tongs toward the other riders and said, "That's four bits a man for the nags, paid in advance however long you're like to be here."

The money was paid over—with some grumbling, since all but Fisher and Diamond were running short on cash—and they put the horses away. They removed the saddles, but only Bettiger remained to rub down his horse. The horses steamed, the night having cooled but little in the summer rain.

"Who do you suppose are the four men holed up here?" Fisher asked as they walked up to the main house, their saddlebags and bedrolls over their shoulders. "Hell, I should've asked Whistler."

"They ain't the law, and that's all you need to know," said Briggs.

"Is it? I'll make up my own mind about that."

The door opened before they got to it, for they'd been seen a quarter mile off. There were two men, Fisher knew, who watched the roads from up in the attic windows. Cletus Spence and Attic Bird Henderson. They were equipped with spyglasses and long-range rifles. Henderson, who was at least half mad, didn't like coming down from the attic unless the job required it.

Cletus Spence answered the door, shotgun in his hands—but it wasn't pointed at them, for he knew Gaines, Briggs, and Fisher. Cletus's round face was mostly hidden in beard; he had tiny piggish eyes and hands that looked like they hadn't been washed since childhood. He wore a red undershirt and suspenders holding up grime-blackened trousers. Under pressure of Cletus's swag belly, the suspenders struggled to keep hold of his pants; Fisher had won a bet with a fellow traveler, the last time he was here, suggesting one of the suspenders would lose its grip before midnight.

"Where's Deef Harry?" Gaines asked as Cletus grunted at them something that might have been an invitation to enter. He recalled the old doorman as an unusually well-bathed man and mostly deaf but courtly in his manners, all things being relative.

"He's daid."

"Dead!" exclaimed Gaines as he came into the front hall, peeling off his rain slicker. "What happened?"

"Feathers kicked Boris Hepps out for beatin' on Cindy. Boris, he come back angry, saying he'd left his poke hidden away, and when Harry opened the door to him, why, Boris shot the first man he seen."

"That being Harry? I am grieved to hear it. I liked ol' Harry. What become of Boris?"

"I knocked him down when he come a-runnin' in past me, and Feathers, he gave him over to Whistler so's to get it done ugly."

"I see! Oh, hell, I expect Boris deserved it right enough. Where's Feathers?"

A bellow from the saloon answered the question. "Come in, boys, come in!" roared Feathers. He rarely talked under a roar. He was standing in the door to the makeshift saloon, waving a whiskey bottle at them.

Feathers was a heavy man; in this humid warmth he wore cutoff rawhide pants and a sleeveless undershirt. The source of his moniker was obvious to anyone, for he sported eagle feathers and buzzard feathers in his long, matted hair, some curious variant of an Indian headdress, and there were grouse feathers sticking out of his long, curly black beard. His weathered face, sunken eyes, and gappy teeth made him look older than the forty he was. "Boys, come in and pay your money down! The drinks are lined up!"

Fisher and his men hung up their hats and coats and

were soon gathered in the saloon, where a narrow barrier of boards, topped with tin, served as the bar. A hollow-eyed, sunken-cheeked woman with bad skin and a great deal of rouge stood behind the bar, a drink in her hand, dully appraising them as they came in.

An oil lamp in each corner of the room scarcely dissipated the fog of cigar and pipe smoke. Pictures of pretty girls from magazines haphazardly adorned the walls, their figures scarcely to be seen in the murk. An unlit potbellied stove stood on the far wall. A hodgepodge of wooden chairs was scattered about, two of them occupied by rough-looking characters sitting near the bar.

A settee, a missing leg replaced by a chunk of sawn log, stood against the wall to the right, occupied by two men; one of them was a man Fisher had known in Wichita before the town constable had put him on a midnight stage out of town. The wide-bodied little man, affecting a merchant's suit, was Chugs Calloway, a bunco steerer, cardsharp, and pickpocket, also implicated in two stage robberies.

Fisher's memory of Calloway was bitter. Not wanting to share the suckers, he had argued with Fisher over the pickings, Chugs trying to claim the Little Goldie Gambling Hall for his own. Chugs had brought in his cousin Hound Pitney, a known killer, and Fisher had to back down. He'd always wanted to punish Chugs for that humiliation.

The taller man sprawled on the rest of the settee had long dirty brown hair framing his thin, stubble-bearded face and wore the pants from a sack suit and a nice golden-threaded silken vest—over nothing but bare skin. Fisher found this sartorial incongruity annoying.

He himself had taken off his coat and bowler, due to the muggy heat, but he wore a respectable white shirt under his vest. But then, he reflected, his company these days was entirely slovenly. He privately vowed he would get rid of most of them, make himself wealthy, and surround himself with a better class of criminal.

Gaines and the man in the shirtless vest were staring at each other with a kind of angry shock of recognition. The man in the vest wore a cross-draw pistol holstered aslant his belly, and his fingers crept toward it now as Gaines put a hand on his own six-shooter. Both he and Chugs, with an empty whiskey bottle on the floor between them, were bleary drunk.

"Well, boys!" boomed Feathers. "I see you know each other!"

"I know Driscoll there well enough," Gaines growled. "He stole my money and my horse!"

"That's a dirty lie!" said Driscoll in a tight, reedy voice.

"It's a cryin' shame how old, best-forgotten grudges and differences can haint a man!" said Feathers. "You boys remember our rules here! *There is no killing on the premises!*"

"What about in self-defense?" Gaines asked, his eyes on Driscoll's gun hand.

"As to that, I'd make a judgment," allowed Feathers. "I will keep an eye on Driscoll." So saying he patted the hog's-leg pistol tied up on his right hip—at which Driscoll took his hand from his gun. "Right now," Feathers added, "you just keep to the bar."

"I'm buying two rounds," Fisher reminded them, not wanting to be caught in a cross fire.

Gaines grudgingly turned away from his old adversary and went to the bar with Fisher. Briggs, Diamond, and Bettiger eagerly followed.

"Whiskey for my five friends here!" Fisher said.

"Howdy, Cindy!" Sweeney said, grinning at the gaunt woman behind the bar.

"Hey, Peanut," she said glumly. She wore a cut-back ball gown, once a cream-and-blue color, its colors now blurred in dinginess. It was a little too big for her skinny frame; its sleeves had been removed at the shoulders, and its skirt was partly cut away to reveal her thin legs.

Cindy began pouring whiskey from an unlabeled bottle into glasses that were not quite empty of whatever had been in them before. "Pay as you go, boys. Four bits a glass." Fisher paid and they drank.

Feathers leaned on the end of the bar. "You gents staying the night?"

"This night and maybe some more," Fisher said. "Here's for tonight. . . . We'll see about tomorrow. . . ." Regretfully, he counted out the cost of the bunks and gave it to Cindy, who tossed it into a cigar box she kept for room fees.

It irked Fisher to pay for these men, but he had little choice. They hadn't the money, most of them. He regarded it, however, as a short-term investment. This payout would serve to keep them in his train, and he'd get it back in time. Maybe in a week, two at most.

"Hannibal, you can stay till noon tomorrow. Then you got to pay up again," said Feathers. He waved to Cindy. "I'll have some of that beer in the floor crock," he told her.

She gave a faint nod and went down on one knee,

opening a trapdoor to reveal a hole down into the clay earth under the building, in which, Fisher knew, a stone crock of beer had been lowered by rope into a small tub of water. This kept the beer cool, which made it three times as costly as the whiskey. It cost Feathers nothing, of course, and Fisher watched enviously as Cindy gave him a steel mug of beer.

Fisher turned to Gaines and spoke in a low voice. "There something I should know about this Driscoll?"

Buster Gaines snorted. "Only that he's a lying, thieving snake."

"Steal from you, did he?"

"He did." Gaines downed the rest of his drink and signaled for another. Cindy poured, and he had drunk half of it away before she had stoppered the bottle. "We robbed three miners of their wages. They was on their way to town to spend it. He collected the money while I held the gun on them. He pocketed part of my share."

"How'd you come to know that?"

"I know what they was paid. It was even in the newspaper, how much was taken! We had our faces covered, and we got away fine. We stopped at an old shack for the split, and he just kept lying to me about taking my share and— Well, I was kinder drunk at the time, and seeing he stole from me, I pulled my sixer and fired, and I missed; he fired back, and *he* missed, and I ducked down behind a table, and when I looked up to make another shot, he was ridin' out, with all the money, towing my horse along with him, the bellycrawling son of a . . ." The cussing went on for quite a while, and Fisher turned to appraise Driscoll.

Driscoll was pointing at Gaines and talking to his partner, Chugs. Probably telling his side of the story.

Fisher didn't much care who was in the right of it. He might well have pulled the same trick if he'd been in Driscoll's place. But he didn't want Gaines shot in the back while he was here. Buster Gaines was part of the plan. He was useful.

"Stole my horse," Gaines was saying. "Stole my share. I can't see how I can stand him being here, Hannibal."

"Like as not he'll move on tomorrow."

"He's liable to sneak up and cut my throat as I sleep!" Gaines declared far too loud. Feathers looked over at them, frowning.

Gaines suddenly swung around and jabbed a finger at Driscoll. "Here's your choice, you snake! You can give me what you owe me and the price of the horse you stole, or you can meet me outside!"

"Go to the devil and kiss his red rump!" Driscoll replied, his face contorted with drunken fury.

"Outside it is!" Feathers roared. "No shootin' in the house! You go on out, both of you! Whoever lives, they bury the other. There's a field for that not fifty rods off! If you both die, your friends bury you! Now, take it outside! That's my rulin'!"

"Good enough!" Gaines snarled, spittle spraying with the words. "You comin', Driscoll? Or you going to skin out like a yellow coward once more?"

Driscoll's face went stony. He stood slowly up and said, "Sure I'm comin'. But I'm not turning my back to do it." His friend Chugs stood up at his side, hand going to his percussion revolver.

"You go on out first, Buster!" said Feathers. "You're closer to the door! They won't try nothin' in here!"

Gaines hesitated—then he turned toward the door

to the hallway. Gaines took two steps—then Driscoll snatched at his pistol. Chugs pulled his own a split second later.

Seeing Driscoll was about to shoot a valuable man in the back, Fisher felt compelled to pull his own pistol—and Briggs and Diamond drew their own. Driscoll fired, and Gaines staggered, as four guns thundered. Fisher, Diamond, and Briggs fired at Driscoll; Chugs's spasmodic shot went into the floor, and he screamed, bouncing against the wall, with the impact of the slug Fisher sent into his breastbone. Gaines was still on his feet, firing as he turned; Diamond and Fisher and Smiley Briggs were now firing at Driscoll, and the three bullets sent him into a raggedly spinning dance.

"Hold fire, damn you!" Feathers roared as gun smoke choked the room.

His ears ringing, Fisher squinted through the smoke at the two dead men slumping over the settee. Driscoll had flopped facedown across Chugs Calloway.

Feathers commenced roaring curses, banging a fist on the bar in emphasis, as Gaines, panting—eyes wide, gun muzzle trailing smoke—leaned back against the wall.

"You hit, Buster?" Fisher called.

Gaines looked down at himself in puzzlement. Then he shrugged. "He always was a bad shot. Cut through my holster, felt like I was hit, but just a graze, I reckon."

"Open the damn window, Cindy!" shouted Feathers. Cigar smoke was one thing, gun smoke another. He spun angrily to Gaines. "Here's my ruling—"

"Now, hold on, Feathers," Fisher broke in. "Driscoll tried to shoot him in the back!"

"I know he did! That's why I'm ruling you bunch can stay. But after you catch your breath, you get them bodies out of here, leave 'em out back, bury 'em in the morning! Right now you can have *one* drink on the house—only because I'm fining you whatever money them boys had on them, *and* I'm confiscatin' their horses! Their saddles and tackle, too! And you will clean up the gore unless you want to pay Cindy to do it." He nodded toward her. "Pay her four bits to clean up blood."

Growling to himself, Gaines dug a half-dollar piece from a pocket and tossed it to Cindy. She caught it neatly in the air and went for a mop and bucket. The expression on her face had not changed since they'd come in.

Feathers went to search the bodies, and Hannibal Fisher, his hands shaking just a little, finished his drink.

NOW, THAT'S A mighty fine morning," Seth said, coming out of the barn to gaze at the sun-washed, rain-scoured farm. There were only a few white clouds, like fluffy sheep driven through the bright blue sky by a shepherding light breeze.

His remark was for Josette's benefit, as she was walking up with a wooden coffee cup in her hand. She handed him his morning coffee, as if acknowledging their new status as betrothed, and accompanied it with a sweet, shy smile. "How'd you sleep out there, cowboy?"

"Never better. They make you comfortable in the house?"

"They pulled out a cot for me. I was just fine. Gravy and biscuits and bacon coming up. If you clean yourself up, I believe Daisy will let you eat in the house. But I warn you. She will question you closely about our wedding plans."

"I was thinking of a justice of the peace, and I expect the court in Freeman will have someone who could be a witness."

"But when?"

"I was pondering on that. I feel I have to do the right thing and at least ask your pa for your hand. He'll say no, but I got to ask. Could be if he hears we're bound and determined, he'll give in."

Josette shook her head. "He's mule stubborn."

"He's going to come round here, looking for you," Seth pointed out. "We could get married right away and ride out. But . . ."

She sighed. "I'd like to be settled in my mind about Papa. I don't know if I will ever be." She looked toward the south and said, "Could we really just . . . ride out?"

"I promised Sol some help. He's helped us some . . . and I want Mazie to heal up. But right soon you bet we can." He sipped a little coffee and said, "Still and all—I am going to talk to your pa, Josette. Maybe you should go with me. It's best our intentions be plainly told. I don't want him lyin', saying we married without even telling him."

She reached out and took Seth's hand. "Let me turn it over in my mind. At least till tomorrow. Sol and Daisy seem to be strangely tolerant of my staying here." Then as if wanting to change the subject, she said, "Go on, now. Wash yourself under the pump, best you can, and come in to eat."

"I'll do it. I'll have to ask Sol for some time away today, as I've promised to ride out and look around with Marshal Coggins."

Josette's delicate eyebrows knit. "Are you going out to look for trouble with that man Fisher?"

"I don't expect he's anywhere around. But . . . I'd like to know for sure. I don't want to be watching my back trail my whole life. The marshal don't seem to mind bringing me along, so . . ."

Josette shook her head and went into the barn to visit Mazie—she'd grown fond of the horse and liked to see she was healing well—and Seth turned to watch her go, enjoying the sight.

He had a parcel of troubles, it was true, what with her pa and not knowing for sure about Hannibal Fisher. But it all seemed lost in the glow he felt when he thought, *There she is—my bride.*

Nothing much was decided at breakfast, except that on the morrow, Seth would be helping with the corn harvest. Two days of that—he couldn't say no to Sol after the Hamers had taken Josette in—and then he'd try to settle things with Dubois.

Shortly after breakfast, the marshal rode up. Hearing the horse, Seth went out to meet him. "Coming with me?" Slim asked.

"I am, Marshal. Let me get my hired horse, and we're on the way. Unless you need some breakfast first."

"I loaded up on hotcakes and eggs. Let's head out. We'll do a circle around town, watch for any new tracks. Then we'll trail north along the creek, see if we can find that campsite Red Milligan spotted."

Seth saddled his horse, and they were quickly on their way. There were countless tracks around Prairie

Fire, but the men struck nothing unusual. Hannibal
Fisher's horse had a crack in his right front horseshoe—
Marshal Coggins had made that determination when
he and Seth had gone back to the location of the affray
between Dawson and Fisher. Today they couldn't find
any shoe prints with that mark.

"Doesn't prove he wasn't here," Slim said, "what
with the ash fall and the rain and all the new riders
through here. Let's trail up the creek."

They were soon on their way north along the creek,
peering into the scrub and the trees along the stream.
They stopped every time they came to a likely spot for
a recent camp.

They found nothing till they were many miles from
town. Here they came across a campfire circle of river
stones. They dismounted and searched it carefully,
hunched to look at the ground. An empty liquor jug lay
on the grass; following a set of drag marks, they found
the skeletal remains of an antelope off in the brush. It
appeared coyotes had gotten to the carcass and
dragged it off; the bloody rope it'd hung from was still
dangling from a tree limb. There were several cigar
stubs around the campfire circle, too.

Most convincing were the boot marks of a number
of men and the sign of their horses. It was Seth who
spotted the hoofprint in the clay beside the creek—the
mark of a horseshoe with that distinctive crack.

"Seems like they've been gone for a while, all night,
at least," said the marshal, looking at the campfire
traces with a professional eye. "Now, I don't find tracks
heading out west, south, or north. . . ."

"That leaves east," said Seth, grinning. "You see—I
can work out a thing or two myself."

"Most impressive! Come along."

They led their horses across the creek to the east and found the tracks, partly erased by rain, but enough remained to convince the marshal and Seth that the men had ridden in a group due east and a little south.

About five miles into following the trail, the marshal reined in. "Seth—let's head back. I think we've done what we can today. I can't go too far from town and . . . Well, I think they're headed for Buffalo Junction."

"Don't know it."

"It's said to be a robbers' roost. A crusty owlhoot name of Feathers Martin runs it at an old farm. Lots of rumors about it, nothing much real clear. It's a long ways—and I'll tell you, at least two bounty hunters disappeared, poking round there, and a US deputy marshal, too."

"Seems like the Army or someone should bust in on it!"

"It'll happen sometime. But it's mostly hearsay—and you can't get a US marshal nor the Cavalry out after hearsay." He shook his head grimly. "I sure ain't going out there, with just the two of us. But it's something to remember. I'll talk it over with Dawson. Come on. Let's get back. The day's getting worn to a nub. . . ."

I T WAS WELL into the evening, and the only saloon in Prairie Fire was already pretty lively. There were several men at the bar, loudly disagreeing about grain prices—one saying they were going down, the others saying they were going up. Two men at the far end argued politics, one condemning the policies of Ulysses

S. Grant, one defending them. But the noisiest individual, Sweeney noticed, was Heywood Kelmer.

"He's not often seen drunk," said the bartender of the Gypsy Saloon in a kind of wonder as he looked past Sweeney at Heywood Kelmer. "But when he is, fireworks ain't in it. He's a full-on powder keg. His father don't approve of him drinking, not a drop. James Kelmer, now, he's a teetotaler. Wouldn't be pleased if he could see that boy now."

The bartender was having a drink himself, with Peanut Sweeney's encouragement, and eating from a wooden bowl of pork rinds. Sweeney turned to have a gander at the table where Heywood Kelmer, wearing his fancy riding suit, sat with his two companions, Chance Grogan and Blackie. Heywood had been alternating beer and whiskey this last hour, and he was gesturing wildly, raising his voice from time to time. There were half a dozen farmhands in the little saloon, along with Heywood and his men. Two of the farmhands were playing what appeared to be a deadly serious game of checkers; the other four were nursing beers as they played poker.

Heywood and Blackie had ignored Sweeney when they'd come in; Chance had nodded to him and taken no more notice.

"What's Kelmer all worked up about?" Sweeney asked in a low voice.

"Something about that Seth Coe and the Dubois girl. Heywood's sweet on her, but she's keeping company with Coe. Stays on the same farm with him—he's in the barn, they say, and she's in the house."

"Seth Coe! Why, he's an old friend! I ain't seen him for a good spell. And she's with him? Where at?"

"I heard he was working for a farmer over on the north side of town. Don't know who."

"You don't say." Sweeney had been gathering information since he'd arrived in the midafternoon. He'd managed to work out that the bank did not have an armed guard, that there was a sheriff in town who'd been shot—said to have been shot by Hannibal Fisher. But the sheriff was on the mend at the doctor's office. The Town Marshal, Coggins, was somewhat beholden, it was said, to the Kelmers and did not like to ride far from Prairie Fire. Nor was anyone hereabouts working hard to find Hannibal Fisher. The story Sweeney had heard was that Marshal Coggins had followed Fisher's trail to the Oklahoma border and there had given up, sending word on to lawmen to the south.

Sweeney ordered another drink, then ambled over to stand near the checkers players, their table being next to Heywood's. He stood with his back to the men from Black Creek Acres, pretending a fascination with the game and listening up sharp as Heywood groused about Seth Coe.

"Marshal says that wanted man tried to kill Coe," said Heywood. "Boys, I tell you, if Coe doesn't leave Josette alone, I'll kill him myself!"

"Now, I think that might be regarded as what they call illegal," said Blackie dryly. "Even a Kelmer ain't free to just kill a fella he doesn't like, boss."

Heywood slapped the table hard, making everyone in the saloon look over at them, and yelled, "I'd let him draw first and shoot him dead! I'll nail him into his coffin!"

Sweeney snorted at that improbable vision as Heywood went on. "When I make up my mind I want something, that's an end to it! I'm going to get it! And I decided I want Josette Dubois!"

Blackie groaned, softly. "Your pa won't like you talking loose about women in a saloon, boss."

"Don't tell me how I can talk, Blackie! I'm telling you that if Coe tries to elope with her, it's as good as kidnapping! I'll raise a posse and go after them!"

"Not sure that'd work, Heywood," Chance said, sounding apologetic for having to point it out. "Posses are decided by the law—"

"Then I'll hire some men to get it done! I'll see to it—one way or another!"

Would he go that far? Sweeney wondered. Might be a way to get Seth Coe and get paid for it, too.

A quiet meeting between Heywood Kelmer and, say, Gaines and Briggs could be set up if Heywood was willing. . . .

CHAPTER ELEVEN

"S ETH," SAID JOSETTE quietly as they rode up to the Dubois farmhouse, "I have a presentiment about this."

It was just going from dusk to full dark. Josette sat on Seth's horse right behind him, clasping his waist, and now, as Seth reined in, she clambered quickly down and put her hand on his knee.

"Let me talk to Papa first!" she said, looking wide-eyed up at Seth.

"Let's go in together, honey," he said gently. "He needs to see we are together in everything." He swung out of the saddle and tied the gelding up on the hitching post.

She bit her lip, looked at the house, and then at the horse as if thinking they should just ride away. Then she let out a long breath and took his hand. "Yes."

Holding her hand he led her to the door and knocked.

"Shouldn't I just go in?" she whispered.

"Do you still live there, Josette?"

She hesitated. Then he saw the determination come into her eyes. "No. I do not live there."

There were footsteps and creaking boards; then Dubois opened the door. "You!" he snarled at Seth. He was in an undershirt, the sleeves cut away, and his suspenders were off his shoulders to droop about his hips. He looked at their clasped hands. "Take your hand off her!"

"Mr. Dubois," Seth began, "we—"

Dubois reached out, grabbed Josette's wrist, and pulled her off balance so she staggered into the house and Seth lost his hold on her hand.

"Papa—stop!" she said, struggling to get loose.

Dubois tried to slam the door in Seth's face—but Seth blocked it with his shoulder and forced his way in.

His voice grating, Seth declared, "She and I are betrothed, Dubois, and she is of age! Let go of her!"

Josette pulled away from her father and rushed to stand beside Seth. "Papa—he's here to ask for your blessing! We are going to get married!"

"You don't even know him!" Dubois said, his hand shaking as he picked up a mug from the table. "How long is this courtship? One week? Ten days? Nothing! You have known Heywood far longer!" He took a gulp of whatever was in the mug.

"Papa—I simply do not like Heywood Kelmer!"

"It is not necessary to like!" He slammed the mug on the table. "Only to marry!"

"She can't stay here, Mr. Dubois," Seth said, trying

to soften his tone. "She's wanted to leave for a long time. We knew each other as kids and— Well, sometimes folks just meet up and they *know*. Anyhow, it's not safe for her around Prairie Fire. Heywood's making threats—"

"Not safe? *You* make her in danger! What will you do, drag her off to Texas to be killed by the Cherokee on the trip? Killed by a bear?"

"I'll keep her safe," Seth said calmly. "I've taken that road to Texas many times."

"I'm not afraid to go to Texas, Papa!" Josette said. "And I will not marry Heywood! If you will not give your blessing, Seth and I will marry in Freeman when the court opens on Monday!" She added something in rapid French that Seth couldn't make out and went on. "Papa—please! I would like to have you at the wedding— here in town!"

"I will be at your wedding with *Heywood*!" he shouted, throwing the mug aside. "Now, you"—he pointed at Seth—"will go!"

Dubois spun on his heel, stalked across the room, and threw a cabinet open. A shotgun stood in an otherwise empty rack inside.

"Seth!" Josette cried. "Run!"

Dubois swung the gun up, and Seth realized he was standing between Josette and the muzzle of the double-barreled shotgun. If Dubois fired now, some of the shot spread could hit Josette.

Seth vaulted over the table, shouting, "*Here,* Dubois!"

The shopkeeper tracked Seth with the gun and, face contorted, fired both barrels—a split second after Seth threw himself flat. The gun roared like a cannon and part of a cabinet exploded just back of where Seth had been standing a heartbeat before.

Josette screamed, "No!"

Shotgun smoke billowed, and cursing, Dubois cracked the weapon open, fumbled the spent shells out, and reached for two more from the cabinet.

Seth got to his feet and rushed Dubois, grabbing the gun crossways and using it to force him back against the gun cabinet. Dubois bellowed, "You see, Josette! *Regarde ça!* He attacks me!"

Seth twisted the gun away from Dubois and stepped back.

Reaching deep for self-control, Seth took a long breath, then spun on his heel while swinging the gun and smashing the breech on the stones of the fireplace.

Dubois cursed him in French. Seth tossed the broken shotgun aside, and keeping the table between himself and Dubois, he strode over to Josette, took her by the hand, and went out the door. She came willingly along, closing the door behind her.

"Let us go—quickly, Seth! He has an old pistol!"

Seth untied the horse, stepped up and into the saddle, then helped Josette up behind him. They rode off at a good clip and in grim silence as Dubois shouted from the doorway, "You are a bad man! You steal my daughter; you will go to jail!"

IT WAS A warm, muggy night as Heywood Kelmer, smoking a cigar, paced the porch that wrapped two sides of the big house. Crickets sang, and the crescent moon was silvering the white fence around the garden plot in front of the house. Heywood was brooding, having fallen out of favor with his father for coming home drunk; rumor had reached James Kelmer of Heywood drunkenly firing his gun at the ceiling in the Gypsy. "Like the lowest drunken saddle bum!" his father had said, each word dripping with disgust.

Heywood was then given a choice: cease the imbibing of spirits altogether or find his own place in the world, far from Black Creek Acres.

Restless and all too sober, Heywood paced, thinking of Josette and how she'd snubbed him—*him!*—for that plain-faced cowboy who was scarcely taller than she was. The insult was still twisting its knife in him.

Now Heywood winced as he heard the squeak of the screen door. He knew it was his father, coming out to drag him once more through the dust. Pa rarely settled for one tongue-lashing.

"You get any work done today?" his father asked, coming to stand in the lamplight a little too close to Heywood. James Kelmer was in his shirtsleeves now, but the tie he'd worn to a meeting in town was still taut at his throat. He was a man of medium height but sharp angles, with hard planes on his face, and a black mustache cut close to his thin lips; his blue eyes, fractionally too close together, were perpetually peering about, ferreting for problems.

"I did all my work today and more, Pa. We finished the branding, and we brought the herd into the lower pastures. They're set to move to the buyer."

"That's something, anyhow. There's another matter. . . ."

Of course there is, Heywood thought.

"Heywood, I've been thinking on this matter of you and that Josette Dubois—and her cowboy." He lit a cigar and asked, "What did I teach you about letting people ride roughshod over you?"

"I stood up to Coe—told them both what I thought about it in plain talk, Pa."

"Not enough! If you want something, go and get it, long as you can do it in a way that does not land you in jail. But sometimes . . ." James Kelmer drew on the cigar and blew a stream of blue smoke out into the night. "Sometimes you can make your own laws."

Heywood nodded. He'd heard his father say it more than once. He remembered when they'd cut off the water to the Henshaw place, forcing Turk Henshaw to sell out cheap and giving Black Creek Acres another big swatch of grazing land. The law wasn't clear on it, and no one had challenged the Kelmers.

But this? "Not much I can do if she's got her mind set, Pa."

"You can make up *your* mind!" his father snapped, pointing the red eye of his cigar coal at his son. "You either walk away, and let it be one more failure—or you act! Maybe she's just waiting for you to show you're man enough to take what's yours! You ever think of that?"

Could it be true? Was that in fact what Josette wanted? Heywood found himself remembering how his own mother had ridden out one day in her buggy and had never come back. She sent her thirteen-year-old son a letter declaring that his father was too high-handed, too rigid, too heartless, and she couldn't stay and watch him ruin her son. Confused in his feelings,

Heywood had not responded and had never heard from her again. Certain papers were signed, and it was said that she had remarried, was now wedded to a prominent lawyer in San Francisco.

Why hadn't Pa gone after her? Heywood had an impulse to ask, but he knew his father would backhand him for the impertinence, so he held his tongue.

And what right, after all, had Josette to spurn a Kelmer? He had stepped down from his own social position to suggest that he might court her. She should have been grateful.

A cold anger rose in him then. "I expect you're right, Pa."

"You keep your head about you and don't let some drag-riding, dust-eating cowboy cut between you and what's yours!" His father tossed the half-finished cigar into the rose bed, where it struck out a spray of red sparks. He put his hands in his pockets and strolled back into the house.

Heywood went back to pacing. What exactly could he do about Josette?

He tossed his own cigar over the railing as his father had, and was thinking on going to the barn to see to it the hands had brushed the new Appaloosa down, when he heard the crunch of boots on the pebbly path that led past the front gate. He looked over to see Chance Grogan stalking hurriedly up.

"Hey, boss," Chance said, coming to the railing of the porch and looking up at Heywood.

The hands never came to the house unless they were summoned or had something of significance to report. "Well, what is it?"

"You remember that Peanut Sweeney?"

"What of him?"

"He's done rode in with a message for you. I got him waiting at the barn. I'd've sent him away, but it's about Josette Dubois, and I thought—"

"Yes, yes, out with it!"

"He says the man he's working for now has no liking for Seth Coe. Says maybe there's a way they can help you."

"Help me how?"

"You pay him and his boys, they'll see to it that this Coe doesn't stand in your way!"

Heywood snorted. "Who's this man?"

"Didn't say."

"*Where* is he?"

"Peanut says you'll have to meet this feller a mile north on Black Creek. Tonight!"

"Tonight? Foolishness! Running about at Peanut Sweeney's behest . . ."

There was a sound, then, hoofs clumping, wagon wheels squeaking. The two men both turned, then, looking up the entrance road to see Francois Dubois driving a small buckboard pulled by a weary mule.

"Now it's Dubois!" Heywood said wonderingly. "There's a crowd gathering!"

Dubois braked the wagon at the house's fence, jumped down, and stumped over to the porch steps. He took off his hat respectfully. "A word with you, Heywood!"

"What's happened, Francois?"

"That Seth Coe has dragged my Josette away! He attacked me in my house—he took my gun and smashed it! He snatched her hand and made her get on

his horse, and they rode away! They talk of marriage—
I said no, *jamais*!"

Chance tilted his hat back and squinted at Dubois
in puzzlement. "Jaw-may?"

"So they're getting married . . ." Heywood said, his
voice almost a whisper.

"He is *forcing* her to marry him!"

"Is that right?" Heywood wasn't convinced that Josette was being forced into anything. It had seemed to
him that she was sweet on Coe. But if Coe could be
eliminated . . .

Heywood seemed to hear his father's voice again.
*You keep your head about you and don't let some drag-
riding, dust-eating cowboy cut between you and what's
yours!*

"When is this marriage to happen?" Heywood asked.

"Josette says on Monday they will go to Freeman to
marry! Maybe you can take some men—you can stop
them!"

Heywood grunted. Freeman, the county seat. "You
been to the sheriff?"

"Not yet."

"Head on over there. Tell Slim what this Coe did.
I'll see what I can do. Go on, now!"

Dubois nodded, his lower lip stuck out with pugilis-
tic determination. He clapped his floppy hat on his
head, hurried back to the buckboard, turned it about,
and drove away.

"What you want me to tell Peanut, boss?" Chance
asked.

"Tell Peanut to set up a meeting—let's make it at the
Willow Pool along Black Creek. Tomorrow at dawn.
I'll be there. I'll meet this man and we'll see. . . ."

* * *

THE NIGHT WAS wearing on, and Seth, Josette, Sol, and Daisy were sitting around the kitchen table under a hanging oil lamp, drinking cherry cordials and toying with apple pie. None of them had much appetite.

"It could have gone bad—far worse!" Sol opined. He sipped at his cordial without much interest, probably wishing he had something stronger. "That shotgun—he could have killed you both!"

Seth nodded. He felt a sick chill, imagining Josette dying of a shotgun wound. "He could have."

Josette closed her eyes for a long moment, nodding. "I think he would have killed Seth, anyhow, if he could have."

Daisy shook her head, her eyes wide. "He'd have been hung for it!"

"Perhaps not. He would have claimed Seth was attacking him. Who would they believe? Me or Papa? He's one of the town's leading merchants. I am . . . just a girl. I'm sure that was in his mind."

Seth reached out and took her hand. "That's all over and done with. We'll be married Monday. He'll have nothing to say."

Seth had been relieved Sol had welcomed them in when he'd been told about the affair with the shotgun. He'd been afraid Sol would have sent them away in the night for fear Dubois might come around, guns blazing. But both Sol and Daisy had insisted they were welcome. Sol had sand, Seth thought. They both did.

"Would you come with us?" Josette asked.

"I can't leave the farm," Sol said, shaking his head firmly. "I've got a feller coming to talk about buying my harvest."

"I could go!" said Daisy briskly.

"Nope, my dear, I won't hear of it," Sol said, patting her shoulder. "It's a long ride. Dubois might come after them. Maybe get some of those drunken friends of his from the saloon to go, too!"

"It's all right," said Seth, smiling. "We'll be fine. There'll be someone at the courthouse in Freeman who'll witness for us."

Josette looked at the door, chewing her lip nervously. "Did you hear a rider?"

Seth got up and went quickly to the front door, reflecting that he had to start wearing his gun more often. His gun belt was hanging in the barn.

Opening the door he was both relieved and a little worried to see Slim Coggins on the porch.

Slim nodded impassively at him. "Need to talk to you and Josette."

"Was kinda expecting you."

"Come on in, Slim!" Sol called out. "Have a seat!"

Seth returned to the table with Slim, and they sat, Slim taking off his hat and leaning back in his chair a little before saying, "I reckon you know why I'm here."

Seth nodded. "I was thinking of going to see you myself. Dubois took a shot at me. If I hadn't flattened, he'd have taken off my head with a double-barrel ten gauge."

"He failed to mention that," said Slim dryly. He looked at Josette. "That what happened, Miss Dubois?"

"Yes, sir, it is. Seth wanted to ask for my hand in

marriage. That's all there was to it. Papa was drunk! He went mad!"

"He says Seth knocked him into the wall, took his gun, and busted it!"

"Knocked him into it?" Seth shook his head. "I stopped him reloading and took it away rightly enough. I didn't hurt the man."

"That's how it was," said Josette, looking the marshal in the eye.

Slim nodded thoughtfully. "I believe you. He was smelling like a still when he came to see me. I am inclined to take your word and Seth's."

"Me and Daisy," Sol interposed, "we sure believe it! We've known Dubois a good long time. He's capable of all that and more!"

Slim smoothed down his mustaches with a thumb. "Seems a case of Seth protecting himself and Josette. But I'll have a look at the Dubois place and see what I see. He couldn't hide the damage from that shotgun."

"How about some pie?" Daisy asked, brightening. "We've got cordial. Or I could make you some coffee?"

"My wife is fond of cordial, and I've come to almost like it. But . . ." Slim stood up and put on his hat. "I'll take you up on that another time."

"Can I give you some cherry cordial to take to Lou Ellen?"

"Why, if it's ready to go, ma'am, she'd like that, I'm sure. . . ."

Carrying his little bottle of homemade liqueur with him, Slim left, and Seth sat quietly with the others, holding Josette's hand and wondering if he was doing the right thing.

Dubois had said one thing that had at least some truth to it. He and Josette hadn't been reunited long before she'd agreed to marry him. Seth felt that Josette cared for him—and he knew she was comfortable with him—but it could well be that she was thinking of the marriage as a way to escape her father and Heywood Kelmer to boot.

Was that so bad? People married for all kinds of reasons. If they hung on and got to know each other, they could make something good of it.

Admittedly it was a kind of rushed courtship. But he felt the rightness of it. It was one of those things he just knew. Just as he knew the bottomland he so prized in Chaseman was destined to be his; just as he knew that day followed night and summer followed spring. He and Josette truly belonged together. He felt a solid, deep-down confidence that once they were married, she'd feel that way, too.

IT WAS STILL dark at the Willow Pool, on Black Creek. And Heywood Kelmer was nervous. He did not take to this stranger. The man seemed far too sure of himself. With his lavender bowler hat and his pin-striped trousers, this fellow who called himself Bitterman resembled a tinhorn gambler more than any kind of hired gun. The other man, Gaines, seemed mighty rough around the edges, too.

They stood around a small campfire, rustled up purely for their meeting. Chiefly, Heywood supposed, so they could see one another's faces. Sweeney was staying with the horses and keeping watch on the trail.

Heywood wondered why this Bitterman needed someone to stand guard.

"I rode with Colonel Dexter in the Sand Valley
War," said Bitterman. "Me and Gaines here, we were
regulators, protecting Dexter's land. The sheepherders
were threatening to burn his fences."

"I read something about Sand Valley," Heywood
said. "We nearly got into a range war a couple years
back, me and Pa. The other side backed away. Just in
time, too. Well, now, if you rode with Harland Dexter,
I guess you know what you're doing. Now the question
is, what can you do for me, and how much is it going to
cost?"

"We've got six men to pay. That's two thousand
dollars, half in advance. And what we do is, we take
care of Seth Coe. And we'll deliver that Dubois filly
to you."

"I'll pay one thousand." Heywood's pa was the
wealthy one. Heywood had but three thousand dollars
in the bank himself. Fine duds could be expensive.

"Fifteen hundred."

Heywood sniffed. "Twelve hundred is the best I
can do."

The man who called himself Bitterman kicked a
little dirt at the fire, frowning. "You know where this
Coe can be found?"

"I do. But he's tight with the marshal."

"You hear that, Hannibal?" Gaines shook his head.
"I don't know about this here deal."

Bitterman scowled and shook his head at Gaines.

Hannibal? Heywood puzzled at that. Hadn't he
heard recently of a notorious man named Hannibal?

But then, with Bitterman's history, no doubt he was notorious.

"Anyhow," said Heywood, "I know where he's going to be on Monday, him and the girl."

Bitterman took off his hat, fanned himself with it, then seemed to make up his mind. "Twelve hundred, it is. Half in advance by noon tomorrow."

H ANNIBAL, I RECKON the Seth Coe angle is more trouble than it's worth," said Gaines. He and Sweeney were riding on either side of Fisher, the three of them headed east toward Buffalo Junction. The crescent moon hung low over the prairie. Coyotes warbled their eerie cries from somewhere to the south. "Twelve hundred dollars don't seem like much between all us men."

"Following the plan, he'll bring a heap of money with him," Fisher said. "We don't have to hand this Dubois girl over to Heywood Kelmer. We could say, *Nope, you want her, you're going to have to come up with five thousand more!* If that sticks in his craw, why, I bet you Feathers would give us a pretty penny for her. Then we hit the bank and head south."

"I'm thinking we should just take that bank and go, Hannibal."

"See, there's your mistake—you thinking. I'm the one who does that. You're the one who carries out what I've thought up." He kept his tone affable, but he knew Gaines would be rankled.

"Is that right?" Gaines snorted. "Now, I don't think I like that kind of talk."

"There you go again! What I mean, Buster, is we all got our specialties. Now, me, I've always been a planner. I've got a plan for the Town Marshal. And then that bank will be all the easier. But, Buster—make no mistake. It'll start and end with Seth Coe."

CHAPTER TWELVE

"YOU FIGURE ON me needing to use my Colt?" Seth asked as he washed his hands under the pump. It was Saturday afternoon. The water threw a little rainbow on the ground in the slanting light. "I'm pretty good with a rifle."

Slim Coggins gave a grunt of assent. "That Hannibal Fisher—from what Dawson tells me, he's a man who doesn't forgive. He'll come back looking for you, and not alone. You'll need all the firepower you can muster. Then there's Dubois and Kelmer. How far will they go—I can't say. But just in case."

"I expect you're right, Marshal," Seth said. "I'm game, long as we don't stray far from Josette. I'm not sure she's safe here. Sol does enough already—don't want him to have to pick up a gun, too."

It was a hot late afternoon. Seth was just back from the fields. Since close on to sunup, Seth had been walking along behind Goliath and the McCormick reaper, Sol guiding the machine along and Seth raking the stalks into piles that he made into shocks. It was hot, demanding work and Seth was about worn out. His back ached, and his hands burned. But getting shooting lessons from an old hand like Slim Coggins was a chance he couldn't pass up.

"Slim, how about we get some biscuits and coffee, and I'll rest my bones some, and then we can go out to that windbreak? There's a stump out there we could use. . . ."

They were soon sitting at a worktable under a little plains cottonwood behind the house, and Josette brought them coffee, biscuits, and jam.

"Slim, it's sure comforting to see you here," she said, pouring the coffee.

Slim smiled and gave her a long slow look, at last saying, "Is it unfitting for me to say . . ."

"What?"

"That you are going to make the prettiest bride Prairie Fire has seen since my Lou Ellen. And that's been a good long while."

"Oh, not at all!" she said, waving dismissively, but blushing all the while. She hurried back into the house. She was helping Daisy replace the ticking on a mattress. Seth had noted her taking up more than her share of Daisy's chores. She'd cooked a meal for them all, too, and Seth had been able to give her a hearty compliment on it without a word of exaggeration.

"Lord, she'll look pretty in a wedding dress," Slim said.

"I don't know if there'll be time for a wedding

dress," Seth said, "but Josette would shine in a gunny-sack."

"Is that how you're going to clothe your wife?" Slim asked, grinning.

"Franklin would say so. He thinks I'm a penny-pincher."

"Never could put much by myself. Nor does the town pay me well. But we grow a good deal of our own food. And I hunt. We don't go without. Bullets, now . . ." He put his Smith & Wesson Model 3 revolver on the table. "Good cartridges are costly. Don't want to waste any. Wild Bill, he makes his own. I saw him do it in sixty-seven. Mine, the town ships in for me. I used to carry a dragoon, but I decided I needed a lighter gun. Now, here's something you got to think of—how to reload quick if you're under fire."

"Had to do it once with my rifle on a drive. We were trying to drive off a raiding party of Comanches. Only man I ever shot was a Comanchero. He was firing in the air to drive the cattle, and they were like to run the camp down so—I had to stop him."

"Sounds like you'd rather not a-had to."

Seth nodded. "I don't like to think of ending a man's life. I shot that fella off his horse with my Winchester—most like a lucky shot, too—and went to see if he was alive. There he was, stone dead, and I just thought, *Here's a man went on a long trail to get to this spot*. He was born and grew up and lived his whole life, travel-ing here and there, doing all kinds of things, like any-one else. Trying to make his way in the ways he knowed year after year. And me, I cut it all short with one pull on the trigger. He wasn't much older than me." He shook his head. "I'll tell you straight, Slim. I was sorry to do it."

"I understand," Slim said, unloading the gun. "But sometimes killing one man—or even a few men—can save a lot more lives. And it can make things more peaceful, too." He spun the gun's cylinder. "Now, let's see you load 'er up without taking too much time, and we'll see if you've got your skills right. Then we'll head over to that windbreak and find us a target. . . ."

A little while later, they were standing in the shade of a tall ash about twelve yards from the target, Seth bracing himself, hand hovering over his holstered gun. It was just a tree stump, a snag in the screen of trees along the property line. On the other side of the windbreak, the ground sloped up enough to catch any stray bullets. There was no one around but a flock of blackbirds twittering in the foliage of the windbreak.

The stump was a tall one, broken off jaggedly; it had belonged to a lightning-struck tree that had burned, its upper part keeling over into the windbreak.

"You don't really need to be ready to quick draw there, Seth," Slim said, chuckling. "Relax. Just let your hand fall to your side any way normal. Not even on the gun. When you pull, take your time. Better to move smooth and to shoot true. And to stay cool and calm."

Seth relaxed, and Slim said, "Now, I know you've pulled your pistol and fired it many a time, maybe at a wolf, maybe at a tin can, but that don't mean you've done it right."

"My pa only showed me the rifle and the shotgun. Never could hit much with a pistol."

"Just pull it and point it. Don't fire it yet."

Feeling awkward and self-conscious, Seth did as he was told, over and over.

"Just keep a-going till you can do it smooth and with no wasted motion," said Slim.

It felt like an hour, making that same draw over and over, but it was probably only fifteen minutes. In time it came more naturally, more quickly. Seth's gun was unloaded, and next they practiced aiming and dry firing till Seth was right sick of it.

"Now, young Seth, load the gun, holster it—then you'll pull, extend it full, point 'er like you're pointing out some damn thing, cock, and fire. Later on, you can cock as you pull it, but that's a mite dangerous at first."

"Never tried that," Seth said. "I was afraid I'd shoot myself in the leg."

"You might, too. Those gunsmiths in Europe over there, they're working on something called double-action. You just have to pull the trigger, and it cocks for you and fires. Not even up for sale yet. Us, we got to go the slow way. Now, let's load 'er up."

Seth loaded the gun, trying to do it in the quick, efficient way the marshal had shown him at the table, but still dropping one of the bullets. Embarrassed, he picked up the bullet, blew a bit of grass off it, and chambered it, closing the cylinder. Then he holstered the gun.

Slim nodded. "Here, you see that place at the top of the snag where the wood forks? Right below it, there's a big ol' drip of tree sap. Point at that. Don't even aim, not yet. Pull, cock as it comes up level, look at the spot you want to hit, point at it—and shoot."

Seth nodded, drew, cocked, and fired—the whole cycle seemed to take forever—and the gun bucked in his hand. The blackbirds were startled by the gunshot and rose to whir about overhead. There was no effect on the tree snag whatever.

"Missed the whole durn thing!" Slim said, grinning. "Which is about normal right now. Do it again. We'll just holster, draw, and fire now. Later on we'll fire all the rounds without holstering. . . ."

Five shots, and two of them took a splinter off the side of the snag.

"Now reload 'er and do it again. This time, line up the sights with what you're aiming at, but don't fuss about it. Just take 'er easy. . . ."

They went through it over and over again, the marshal bringing endless boxes of shells from an old railroad mail sack. Seth's wrist ached from the recoil, and so did his right arm, but he began to relax more, to find his focus.

"Just stay calm and cool," Slim said maybe half a dozen times. "That goes for being in a gunfight. If you want to live, stay calm, line up on your target, and fire."

The sun was getting low, and the revolver was getting hot by the time they quit, but Seth had started hitting the tree snag close to the sap mark he was aiming at.

"Gettin' there for sure," said Slim. "Just remember, if you want to live—"

"Stay calm, line up on your target, and fire!" Seth interposed, grinning.

"That's it. Calm is half of what you need in a fight! You keep your cool, you'll outshoot the man who's angry and flustered! Maybe we should use up another box . . . ?"

"My arm's about to fall off, Slim."

"Well, then, pick up all that brass there. That can be

taken to the gunsmith. He's got a use for it. He'll give you a penny a shell. We'll be back tomorrow, after you've done your farmwork, and see if we can cut that big splinter sticking up there right in two. . . ."

T HE NEXT DAY Seth and Sol finished harvesting wheat and moved to the cornfields. Normally Sol would take Sunday off, but the harvest was pressing him. They were joined in the afternoon by Daisy and Josette, armed with bushel baskets. They twisted off the ears of corn, sometimes picking armyworms out of the corn silk. They dumped the corn, not too roughly, into the back of a wagon. There would be another harvest of corn, later in the season, Sol predicted, as he and Daisy climbed up on the wagon to take the corn to storage sheds. Sol handed Seth's rifle down to him— the young man kept it close now—and Seth and Josette walked, holding hands, back to the farmhouse.

"Going to be around for supper?" she asked.

"I'll be doing a couple hours of target shooting and such with Slim when we get back. If we're late, why, if you can ask Daisy to put something aside for me . . ."

She sighed. "Seth—all this shooting! Is that so you can protect me?"

"Partly," he admitted.

"*Mère de dieu!* Do you expect a fight on the way to Freeman?"

"No. Not to say expecting. But it's a long ride. And it's not just your father and Kelmer to think of. It's . . . just in case."

"Let's not go to Freeman, then! Let's try to get married in Prairie Fire!"

"We talked about this. Your pa would try to stop us. He'd tell the judge lies to do it! At least he'd delay us for a good while. He's not so like to try his guff on the justice at the county seat."

She grimaced. "Yes. I suppose he could stop the marriage in Prairie Fire. How long to get to Freeman?"

"Riding cross country, most of a day. There's a stage, but it's not for three days. We could hire a buggy, but it'd take twice as long to get there. And if there was trouble . . . I wouldn't want to be in a buggy."

"I have no horse, Seth."

"I'll hire one for you."

"I have ridden—but never so far. . . ."

"Best get used to it. It's a long ride to Texas." He gave her a close look. "Is Texas too far for you to ride? There's no stagecoach all the way there."

She tugged him to a stop, and he turned to look at her. "Kiss me, Mr. Coe."

"Happy to oblige, Miss Dubois." He kissed her.

Then she stepped back and said, "I just wanted to be sure."

"Of what?"

"If Texas is too far to ride with you, will you give me more of those on the trip?"

"As many as you'll allow," Seth assured her.

"Then it's not too far to ride."

Josette smiled at him, her eyes sparkling with merriment, and he kissed her again.

IT WASN'T FAR off midnight when Franklin rode into Sublette Station. He was just thirty miles from Prairie Fire, but he was worn out and decided to stop over at the old Sublette relay station. Ned Sublette had built the station in 1861 when there was an east–west stagecoach route that went through here, but the route had been closed down. Only Ned's widow, "Ma" Sublette, remained, along with two of her sons. They kept something like an inn and stable and a three-sided open-air shed that passed as a saloon. Behind the old relay station was a small cabin. There was a small, overgrown orchard of apples and pears and a long water trough fed by a pump. All water at the relay station, for horse or man, cost a nickel a pint.

Franklin watered his horse at the trough, and Ma Sublette promptly waddled out of the relay station, listing a little to one side, the sawed-off double-barrel twelve gauge she nearly always had with her in both her hands, aslant her heavy bosom. Franklin had been here a time or two before, and he knew she stayed till midnight, watching for travelers. A squat woman in an ankle-length red dress, she had gray-streaked blond hair tied back in a ponytail, only a few teeth, and beady blue eyes now fixed on Franklin's horse.

"How much that horse drunk so fer?" she asked in a voice like a squeaky hinge.

"Oh, let's say a quart," he said.

"That'll be twenty cent. And how much you drunk?"

"Only from my own canteen. But I'll be buying some of that hard cider of yours, and tomorrow morning I'll have some bacon and slumgullion, if you have any." He knew from experience those were the only palatable foodstuffs on offer at Sublette Station.

"Be closing the saloon at midnight. You'd better get over there. I do have a pot of slumgullion, and we got fresh ham. Slaughtered an old pig two days ago. Had to chase her across the farm. Like to've fallen on my own ax. You sleeping here?"

"If there's a clean bunk."

"Always clean."

That was not Franklin's experience, but he didn't argue. "Still two bits to stable my horse?"

"It is. And two dollars for the bunk."

"Two!"

"It's gone up." She chortled at that. "Be glad it ain't three."

Franklin growled to himself, paid over the money, shaking his head the while. She kept chortling as he paid her.

He put up his horse, fed with grain he'd brought from Seaver, and trudged through the thin moonlight to the open-air bar. A single lantern spread a pool of bluish light over the interior of the shed. There were barrels to sit on, and a couple of planks over two more barrels stood in for a bar. There were a couple of dusty men standing together at the other end of the bar, drinking something that brought grimaces with every swallow. He didn't know them—but then again, he thought he knew their like. One of them, a shifty-looking fellow in a black frock coat, vest, and striped trousers, said, "We ought to go back to Feathers's place. Fisher'll be back."

"We don't have to do what he says, Diamond," the other man said. He was shorter, a tubby man with a mane of red hair. He looked drunk enough, he seemed at risk of falling off his barrel. He scratched in the mass of red chest hair showing from his open shirt and snappishly declared, "We don't have to follow him like a pack of trained dogs!"

"Briggs, don't use my—"

The man called Diamond glanced around, and Franklin was careful to occupy himself with waving at "Possum" Sublette, the elder of the two boys. "Hard cider!" Franklin told him.

Mouth agape as always and one eye crossed, Possum brought over a pitcher and a wooden cup. He poured the cider, then stuck out a dirty hand and said, "Two bits."

Franklin paid it over, but his mind was on what he'd just heard from the other two at the bar. The man called Diamond had mentioned a Fisher. And he didn't seem to want his companion to call him Diamond in public. Now where had Franklin heard those two names together? That wanted poster . . .

Hannibal Fisher . . . For Murder of a Jail Employee . . . May Be in the Company of Escaped Murderer Curt Diamond.

And he'd heard of "Feathers," too. Buffalo Junction. Story that went around the campfires was that Buffalo Junction was a hideout for outlaws.

This man Diamond, who seemed like he was going to meet Hannibal Fisher, was here in Southern Kansas, where Seth was. Could be Fisher was indeed going after Seth up here.

"We need to go back, Smiley," Diamond was saying. "We did the scouting. No law dogs on this trail. And he'll be looking for us. There's money waiting, and soon."

"I'll believe that when I see it counted on a table! Anyhow, I ain't riding that far east tonight."

"Well, let's get us a bunk. I can't stomach any more of this belly wash. I'm hitting the hay."

"Yeah, the hell with this here swill."

Briggs got off the barrel, teetering, catching the bar to keep from falling, and then staggered off toward the old station building, Diamond close behind.

Franklin waited a minute, then slipped away from the drink shed and made his way to the old relay station. Diamond and Briggs were just now going into the low adobe building. He'd seen no other horses but theirs and those belonging to the Sublettes, and Franklin figured no one else was staying here tonight.

A lantern flickered alight, visible through the open shutters of a window. Moving in deep shadow, Franklin went as quietly as he could up to the window and stood just to one side. The window had no glass; there were shutters in case of storms, but they were wide open, and he could hear the two men talking.

"I still think this chasing after some cowboy is foolishness." The drink-slurred voice sounded like Briggs. "Buster and me both think so."

"It will pay off," Diamond said. There was the sound of a boot hitting the floor, then another. "You wait and see, Smiley. We'll track down this Coe, likely tomorrow, or the next day. Maybe use him to lure that marshal off where we can dry-gulch him. Take care of them both at once."

Holy hell, Franklin thought. *Got to leave here tonight and warn Seth.*

He heard boot steps behind him and turned to see the other Sublette boy, Sam, coming at him. The tall, gangly, bearded young man had a dragoon pistol in one hand and a lantern in the other. "Sneak thief! Ma, get out here! I caught the thief!"

"What have you been drinking, you damn fool?"

Franklin said. Angry at being snuck up on and braced, Franklin slapped the gun muzzle aside; closing his hand over the gun barrel, he snatched it loose and used the butt to crack Sam a good one on the jaw so that he fell over backward with a hoarse yell.

"What do you mean by coming on a man like that?" Franklin demanded, taking the gun into his right hand and pointing it at Sam.

Groaning, Sam sat up and howled, "Ma! Possum!"

There was a shuffling sound behind him, and Franklin turned around in time to see Ma Sublette jab her sawed-off shotgun at him. She was only three paces distant.

"Drop the gun and throw up your hands, or I'll cut you in half!" she hissed.

Franklin dropped the pistol. "He came at me with that old dragoon, and I got no idea why!"

"You surely know why—he caught you! We were wondering which one of you cowboys was sneaking around, stealin' folks' goods out of here! People been missing things! And my boy there caught you fixing to steal!"

"Now, how would anyone steal anything from outside the building here?"

"He was looking in the winder, Ma!" Sam called.

"I was just gettin' a breath of air!" Franklin insisted. "I am no thief!"

"Liar!" said Sam, getting up.

"Sam, get that gun!" she yelled, her shotgun's muzzle not wavering. ·

Sam picked up the gun and jabbed the muzzle in Franklin's back. "He hit me, Ma! I'm hankering to kill him!"

"We will keep him for the sheriff over in Short Tracks! I'll send Possum to get him!"

"That'll take a couple days, Ma. We ought to—"

"Shut your stinky mouth, boy! Take him to the smokehouse! We'll tie him up there! I'll get the padlock!"

CHAPTER THIRTEEN

MONDAY MORNING, SETH woke at dawn, hearing the rooster crow. He'd always liked the sound of a rooster in the morning. He stretched out in the hay, yawning, then sat up, thinking that his new home with Josette would include some chickens and a rooster to call him to work.

Right now he had to spruce up for his wedding day. Daisy had washed his clothes for him the night before, and she'd left them to dry on a line in the barn.

Wearing only an old pair of Sol's overalls, he went to the pump outside the barn and washed in the faint gray of earliest morning, using the cake of soap left there for the purpose, and rinsed off. He dried himself on a linen cloth and went to the clothesline, bringing along a bucket of water for shaving. His clothes were still a touch damp, but he didn't mind. They'd dry enough later. It would be hot today.

He returned to the barn, put on a clean shirt and the only pants he had without holes. Then he dug his straight razor from his saddlebags, lit the lantern, and set to shaving, using an old piece of mirror glass Sol had given him. And all the time he was wondering if he had figured things right, if they were right to take this trip to Freeman today. Josette had as much as told her pa their plans. That worried him some.

There were lights in the house now. Daisy was up making coffee, and like as not, Josette was at the kitchen pump, washing her hair and getting ready herself. Soon they'd live in the same house, and he'd see her washing her hair, getting dressed in the morning. It would be another kind of life.

Seth mounted the gelding, rode into town, and woke the grumpy stableman to hire out a horse for Josette: a roan riding pony. He had to pay an extra dollar for the interruption in the stableman's sleep.

He returned to the farm, leading the pony, and had a quick cup of coffee, eggs, biscuits, and bacon with the Hamers and Josette—who ate very little. She seemed excited, worried, and a little stunned.

"Well, Josette, shall we go?" he asked when breakfast was cleared away.

Daisy and Josette shared a glance of amazement.

"Seth Coe," Daisy protested, "the girl's got one frock and the dress I loaned her, which don't fit, anyhow. She's got to have something suitable to get married in!"

"Ha!" Sol said, grinning. "Now you're gettin' a foretaste of marriage, Seth!"

"A wedding dress?" Seth scratched his head. "Why, that requires sending away for, don't it?" he asked.

"It need not to be out of a catalogue," Josette said hurriedly. "Just something that doesn't make me look like a scarecrow! Mary's shop has a pretty dress, yellow with pink trimming, that I think would fit me. Oh, I know I should have gotten one before, but I was afraid to run into Papa. He drinks a good deal on Sunday night, and his practice is to open late on Monday. I will need two other dresses, too. I can get it all done before he gets to town! I do have to stop in at the apothecary and . . ."

Seth sighed. He had planned an early-morning departure for Freeman, but it was not to be. He reached into his pocket. "How much do you need for that dress, darlin'?"

It was two-and-a-half hours more before they were on their way to the county seat, Josette riding the hired roan pony, Seth the gelding. It was already hot as they cantered along the northwest road. The prairie still showed the signs of the wildfire, with great swatches of blackness. Occasionally they saw the remains of a ranch house or cabin, mostly just the blackened chimneys remaining, sticking up like tombstones. They passed the burned bones of several cattle and a charred antelope and many a leafless blackened tree. The slight breeze fluttered the cinders, sometimes sending black dust across the road so that at times they had to cover their mouths.

"Such a melancholy sight," Josette said, gazing sadly out over the blackened plains.

"But look there!" Seth pointed out new plants already poking through the ash. "It's known that after a fire, the grass, the flowers, the trees—they all come back greener and fuller than before!"

Josette smiled, reached over, and squeezed his hand.

Three hours more in the saddle and then they stopped for rest and water at a little stream wending crookedly across the plains. Josette was already saddle sore.

The fire had jumped the narrow stream, but the green of the water plants was a refreshment to the eye. Walking his horse to the water, Seth discovered himself to be in rising spirits and absently sang a snatch of a song he'd offered up at many a cattle drive campfire:

Well, I'm a fiddle-footed cowboy, and I always will be.
I'm a fiddle-footed cowboy, that's the life for me. . . .

Josette chuckled. "What is that song! Sing some more!"

"It's not all of it quite fit for a lady."

"Well, sing the part that is!" she insisted, sitting cross-legged by the stream.

Refilling his canteen, Seth sang,

Well, I'm a fiddle-footed cowboy with raggedy drawers.
Don't make much money and I might die poor.
Just a fiddle-footed cowboy with broken spurs
Till a gal loves me'n makes me hers!

Josette laughed with delight and said, "Raggedy drawers! We'll soon fix that! And I shall make you mine this very day, you poor cowboy!"

But Seth was starting to worry they wouldn't get to Freeman on time to be wedded this day.

Once more on their way, he gently asked, "That horse of yours—did you take it on any long rides?"

"Oh, surely I did—sometimes an hour."

"An hour! You're not much used to long rides, then. Feeling sore?"

She shrugged. "But of course. My legs ache, my . . . my backside—is not happy. But the rest of me is happy, Seth."

"Riding all day is something that takes getting used to. And this here's nothing compared to the ride to Chaseman. We can take our time heading there, but even so . . ." He shook his head.

"You will see! I am tougher than I look."

He winked at her. "That I never doubted."

In early afternoon they had passed the burned region and were back among knee-high grass of yellow and green and prairie flowers of scarlet and blue. Reaching a small pond lined with rushes, they stopped for a bite of the food Daisy had packed for them. Seth reckoned they were not even halfway to Freeman. Had it been he and Franklin setting out early and riding at a good clip, they'd have been two-thirds of the way there. But then, he reflected, a man had to learn to accommodate himself to his bride, as she would accommodate herself to him.

On they went, passing through a couple of small settlements with a good deal of cultivated land round about. Josette, doubtless thinking about the new home they planned in Texas, appraised the local farmhouses. "Now, that one there looks to have started small, Seth, and then they added onto it."

"That's often the way of it, and if one builds sturdy,

you can stack a second floor on or extend it out to the side."

She lapsed into a reverie, doubtless thinking of how she would like her house to be, and Seth looked at the cattle and sheep, the orchards and fields, imagining them on the ranch he and Josette would create together.

There was yet a considerable stretch of wilderness to cross, and by the time they reached it—a marshy, shallow valley divided up by converging creeks—the sun was well past zenith. Their route took them up the middle of the long valley.

"Do you think we'll get there on time, Seth?" Josette asked, rubbing her backside with one hand as they stood by a creek, enjoying the shade of the willows.

"Can't tell, Josette. Not sure how late the courthouse stays open in Freeman . . ."

It was almost dusk by the time they got into Freeman, Josette saddle weary, the horses tired, and Seth worried. The town was surprisingly noisy, with a great many wagons bustling in the amalgam-paved street and small crowds talking on the walkways. Some sort of celebration banner was being put up across the main street by several men in fancy firemen's uniforms.

The courthouse was a two-story structure of brick and neatly ornamental wood, right in the center of town. A little man with a gray goatish beard and a blue constable's uniform was just locking the front doors when they rode up.

"Now, hold on, mister, if you please!" Seth called, handing Josette his reins and climbing down. "Wait!" He rushed up the steps to the constable.

The wizened constable turned to him, frowning, and asked in a high-pitched voice, "What's all this commotion now?"

"We need to get married—right away!"

The constable squinted at Josette, who was now tying their horses to a fireplug. "I don't see any urgency there. If she's with child, no one will know if you wait a day—"

"Mister," Seth snapped, "careful what you say!"

The constable gave him an amused smile. "Maybe I spoke too quick. But, son, the justice has gone home for the day. We open tomorrow at eight thirty. He'll be in at nine. And there's paperwork to be done, too!"

Seth growled to himself, and, remembering that he'd need to get past this constable on the morrow, said, "Much obliged. We'll be here tomorrow at eight thirty. Where might be a decent place we can get a couple rooms for the night?"

The old man gave his head a firm shake. "All full up! Every last room in town is rented! People are even renting out their sitting rooms! Folks is coming in from all over the county for the big hoot'n'holler!"

"How'd they know we were coming?" Seth asked dryly as Josette joined them.

"As I reckon you *know*, young smart aleck," said the constable, "it ain't your marryin' they're excited about. It's Mayor Huffings's wedding to the governor's niece! Huffings owns half the property hereabouts, he's a man whose pockets are fair stuffed with cash, and he's throwing a big to-do! The wedding will be in the Baptist church on Elderberry Street. Afterward there's a band playing in Freeman Square, with dancing, free beer—everyone's invited!"

"Where will we stay tonight?" Josette asked, looking down the busy street. "It does look quite crowded."

"We'll see what we can find. . . ."

They asked up and down the street and nearly everywhere else, but could find not even a single bed for rent. At last, Josette gave a Gallic shrug and said, "I camped rough as a little girl, and I can do it again. We have two blankets we can lie on. I am sure I can trust you to be a gentleman."

"Why, of course you can!"

He thought she seemed a little disappointed at his certainty, but she spread her hands, gave another shrug, and said, "Let us find a quiet place near town with some water. The night will be warm. We have some food left. . . ."

T HAT THEM?" GAINES asked.

"It is," said Heywood grimly.

The six men—Briggs, Gaines, Dubois, Bettiger, Sweeney, and Heywood Kelmer—were gathered on the balcony of Dolly's Dance Hall and Saloon. The enormous wedding banner was tied, at an upper corner, to the railing of the balcony whence it stretched across the street. Fisher and Diamond were camped out in the countryside, not wanting to come in because there were wanted posters on both of them and far too many lawmen in this fairly large town. Heywood had been dismayed, hearing of the wanted posters, but he wasn't sure if it was safe to back out now. And after all, there was Josette riding past right below him alongside Seth Coe.

"Looks like it's how you thought, Buster," said Bettiger. "They're going south. Couldn't find a place in town, so they're heading home."

"Or they plan to camp," said Sweeney. "They got here after courthouse hours, seems to me."

The noise from the street covered their talk: the chatter of the crowd, the clatter of buggies, the calls of bullwhackers shouting at the oxen towing wagons loaded with beer barrels.

"Yes," said Dubois. "They come so far—they will not go back. We must stop them before they marry."

"What do you plan to do?" Bettiger asked nervously. "I mean—how you going to stop them?"

"We take them prisoner," said Gaines. "Fisher wants to ask Coe where his money might be. He sees us planning to skin that girl, he'll talk."

Dubois gave him a sharp look. "What is this?"

"Just a little playacting is all it'll be," suggested Sweeney.

"Then, once we're satisfied he's told us true," said Gaines, "we finish Coe and stick him in a shallow grave. The girl—well, we'll finish our arrangements with Dubois here."

Bettiger stared at Gaines as if seeing him for the first time. "I don't think that's . . . I thought we were just going to give her back to her father and have done with it!"

"Did you? You seem to be a weak reed, boy," Gaines said, looking at him thoughtfully. "You want to stay aboveground, you'd better play along." He cast a dark look at Heywood and Dubois. "That goes for all of you."

* * *

FRANKLIN HAD WORKED the ropes off his wrists with the help of a nail sticking out of the wall, but getting out of the smoke shed was another challenge entirely. The floor was of stone; the walls—smelling heavily of smoked pig—were logs cut roughly into squared-off timbers. The door was of heavy wood and was padlocked on the outside. He'd tried throwing his weight on the door to break the lock, but it was too firmly secured.

The only light came through cracks, a thin reddish sundown glow angling bladelike down, illuminating dust. He'd been given no food, not even water, and his throat was starting to close from dehydration. It was stuffy in here, stifling hot. But for hour after hour, Franklin dug away at a lower back corner of the shack, using the dull meat hook the Sublettes had left hanging from the ceiling. He'd found a weak spot in the shed's back corner where one of the logs along the floor hadn't reached far enough. The empty space had been filled with a shorter cut. The space it had filled might be big enough for him to wriggle through if he could remove the shorter log they'd used as a plug. But the chinks were plastered, and the wood was firmly stuck in place.

Hands aching, wrists burning, Franklin felt like he was nevertheless making progress. He'd gotten most of the plaster out and weakened the pressure on the lumber by scraping away a layer of wood.

Suppose they did get a lawman in here? Who would the lawman believe? Probably the man would trust Ma Sublette, she being a local.

Grimacing at the thought of getting taken out of here and moved to yet another kind of cell, he bent more eagerly to his work.

But a minute later, Franklin heard muffled footsteps. He set the meat hook aside and leaned up against the wall to cover up his efforts in case they should look in on him.

"You ain't stinking up my shed in there, are you?" came Ma Sublette's voice at the door.

"Ma'am, I've neither ate nor drank!" Franklin called, his voice a croak. "I've got nothing to eliminate! Now, if you want to keep me alive, you'll give me some water!"

"I'll think on it!" she said. He heard her shuffling away.

He went back to work and, in another minute, felt a breath of cool air come through the chinks. Encouraged, he labored feverishly—and in a few minutes more the lumber was almost loose. He set to tugging at it, to using the hook as a pry bar with one hand, his other gripping the wood at the end. It came free—and he pulled it into the shed.

"Thank the good Lord," Franklin muttered. He picked up the meat hook, took one long breath, then lay down flat, thrust his arms through the gap, and wriggled forward. He was not a small man, and he reflected that it would be mighty humiliating and downright maddening were he to get stuck partway through. The back of the smoker was up against the log cabin, and his escape route was out the shed's exposed side, around the corner from the door. If he didn't get out quick and find some cover, they'd see him.

Feeling like a caterpillar, Franklin inched forward, us-

ing his elbows and the meat hook in his left hand, which
he dug into the hard ground. A couple of inches, a couple more—then his shoulders caught partway through
the gap, compressed by the wood to either side.

He groaned, then cursed under his breath. Then he
blew all the air from his chest and tried to relax his
muscles to make a little room. There—it felt less con-
strictive. Feeling about with the fingers of his right
hand, he encountered the base of a branch that had
been roughly sawn off on a log on the cabin. He
gripped it and pulled, at the same time levering with
his left elbow where it dug into the dirt. He began moving again. Inch by inch.

He got his shoulders and chest through and wriggled faster. After that, it was fairly easy.

Before long, Franklin was getting to his feet in the
darkness outside, panting, feeling dizzy but elated.

He heard footsteps and pressed back into the shadows, holding his breath.

"All righty, Mr. Sneak Thief" came Possum's voice.
"Ma's a Christian woman, so's you get this here canteen. I ain't sayin' if it's been spat in."

Franklin knelt by the hole in the shed, put his head
partway through, and shouted, "I'm dying of thirst,
Possum! I can't even sit up!"

"Hold on, hold on. . . . I'll toss it in!"

Franklin crept to the corner of the shed and heard
the big key turn on the heart-shell lock. The door
creaked open.

"Where are you? Step into the damn light!" Possum
said. Franklin eased from cover, circled behind Possum, reached out—and snatched the dragoon from
Possum's gun belt.

"What the holy—" Possum turned around and met the gun muzzle shoved up under his chin.

"Be quiet, or I'll see if this ol' pistol still fires," Franklin growled. "If it don't, I'll use the barrel to crack that pea brain of yours right in!"

Possum froze, gaping at him.

"Now," Franklin said in a hoarse whisper, "you took fourteen dollars off me. Where is it?"

Hand trembling, Possum dug in a pocket and pulled out a wad of cash.

Franklin took it. "Turn around!"

"What you gonna do?"

"Depends on what *you* do! Turn around!"

Franklin stepped back, looked at the money, squinting in the dim light. He picked out fourteen dollars, pocketed it, then pressed his boot against Possum's back and shoved.

Possum staggered through the open door and turned to face the doorway, hands raised. "Don't shoot!"

"Shut your mouth!" Franklin hissed. "And take this money!" He threw the remainder of the bills into the shed. "I took fourteen dollars and no more," he went on, whispering. "Because *I am no thief*! If I ever see you and your brother again, I'm going to call you out, and I'll shoot you one at a time! Now, shut up in there—if I hear any noise, I'm going to shoot through that door!"

Franklin shut the door and locked it, then hurried off to the horse sheds. There he found his horse, saddle, canteen, and saddlebags. He took up the canteen and drank deeply.

Then he saddled the horse, slung his saddlebags, mounted, and rode off at a gallop toward Prairie Fire, hoping he was in time to warn Seth. . . .

* * *

THE NEAREST PLACE that seemed suitable to Seth, where they could be screened from road agents and the like, turned out to be on a flat, grassy spot under a willow tree drooping over a thin stream. He and Josette were screened from the road by a stand of cottonwoods, and there was no one else in sight. Their horses were close by, contentedly cropping grass. Seth wore his gun belt and had the Winchester at hand.

They sat on a blanket, between two tree roots, eating corn cakes and salted venison and watching the shadows from the setting sun stretch over the stream. Dragonflies skittered through the rushes, and frogs plopped into the eddies. There was a smell of some blossom in the air, a flower that Seth couldn't identify.

"I think I might prefer this to a lonely hotel room," he said. "But I'm sorry I couldn't get you a bed, Josette."

"I am perfectly content," she said, picking up her canteen. "But tomorrow, how shall I prepare myself? I have to bathe and brush my hair at least! Here? I don't know. I need a mirror! And some privacy!"

"We passed a farm coming out here. It had a civilized look. Maybe I can ask them if they'll let us use their pump, borrow their barn for a few minutes to get ready. If we tell them we're—"

He broke off, listening. Was that the sound of horses coming through the trees?

"Yes, if we tell them we're getting married, they will help us. I'm sure of it!" Josette said. She frowned, hearing the hooves now herself.

Suddenly her father was there, trotting a hired horse

through the willow trees, about twenty yards down the stream bank, followed by four other riders draped in the thickening shadows of evening: Heywood Kelmer, Peanut Sweeney, and two men Seth did not recognize. Dubois was riding in front, and the others were lining up behind him, in the narrow opening between the trees and the stream.

"Get on your horse quick as you can, Josette!" Seth said, grabbing up the Winchester. He stood up, tucking the butt of the rifle into his shoulder, aiming square at Dubois. "Hold right there, you men!"

"Seth—" Josette said.

"Unless you want to go with them, Josette," he grated, *"get on the horse!"* He heard her running to her horse.

Staring at Seth's rifle, Dubois reined in, and the others were forced to stop behind him.

"Get out of the damn way!" yelled the big bearish man blocked behind Dubois.

"Don't you try it, Dubois!" Seth shouted. "I don't want to shoot you, but I'll do it!" Seth began to back up toward his horse.

"Surrender!" Dubois shouted. "I want my daughter!"

"She's with me of her own free will!" Seth replied.

Cursing in French, Dubois started his mount forward. Seth fired at the ground in front of Dubois's horse, making it balk. It twisted, backing up.

"Seth!" Josette called, her voice breaking. "Don't kill him!"

The big bearish man started his horse into the stream, going around Dubois. He had a pistol in hand and fired, the shot cracking past Seth's right ear. Seth fired back, and his target jerked in his saddle, his face contorting, his horse rearing.

"Go, Josette!" Seth shouted. "I'm right behind you!" He bolted the five paces to his mount, stepped into the stirrup, grabbed the saddle horn with his free hand, and then he was in the saddle riding after Josette. She was heading upslope, following the thin trail they'd used to come down to the stream. As he stuck his Winchester in its saddle holster, Josette looked back at him, and he waved a hand toward the south. "Go! Quick! I'll be right with you!"

Horses whinnied behind them, a bullet cracked, and Seth felt a vicious dig at his left arm, a searing pain above the elbow.

Then they'd reached the road, and Josette was galloping to the south, with Seth close behind her. They quickly came to a sharp switchback, and Seth spurred the gelding up close to Josette as they rode hard around the sharp bend. He recalled that the road straightened out after this—a stretch where their pursuers would have a clear shot at them. He had to get Josette off the main road.

"Josette," he called, passing her, "follow me!"

Off to the left, a ravine opened up, leading down to a marsh. He rode into the ravine, and she swung to follow him. They had to force their horses through the brush choking the ravine. In a few moments, they were down in the cut and screened by underbrush.

Seth grabbed the reins of Josette's roan, and they halted on a stretch of clay ground just short of the marsh. He put a finger over his lips, and they listened. A few seconds passed, and then they heard the riders drumming by on the road overhead.

"Seth, what'll we do? They'll come back here looking for us!"

"It'll take 'em some time to work out where we are," he said. His heart was pounding, his breath coming fast.

"Your arm—you've been shot!"

He looked at his throbbing left arm. A bullet had grooved through the left side of it, cutting in a quarter inch deep. Didn't seem like a bad wound, but it was bleeding freely.

"Get down off that horse instantly!" she commanded.

Surprised at this sudden outburst of authority from Josette, he climbed down, wincing at the pain in his arm. She was quickly beside him, unbuttoning his sleeve and rolling it up. She tied a handkerchief over the wound and then used another from her saddlebag to make a simple tourniquet above it. "You'll have to loosen that in a while. . . ."

She broke off, startled by her own bloodied hands, and went quickly to the marsh water. She crouched, laving the blood off, and, voice trembling, said, "We can't stay here long, Seth, can we?"

"No. Maybe we can ride across country, then circle back to Freeman. Look for the marshal there."

She stood up and looked at him, her face pale. "You shot one of those men!"

"Only when he almost shot my head off!"

She squeezed her eyes shut at that. "Oh, God. They'll testify that you murdered that man."

He went to her, took her in his arms. "I think I hit him in the shoulder. He'll live, most like. And—the truth'll come out, honey. No one will jail me for it, I promise."

* * *

"D ID YOU HEAR gunshots a minute or two ago,
Hannibal?" Diamond asked, coming back to the
camp. He'd been answering the call of nature in the
scrub brush nearby. Awaiting word, Fisher and Diamond were camped around a small fire on a clay bank
a short distance from town. They were on the same
little creek Seth and Josette had camped on but a quarter mile upstream.

"Sure seemed like shots," Fisher said. He was stuff-
ing supplies back in his saddlebags. "We should ride
out and see what we can see."

"You suppose it's Gaines and them others?" Diamond asked. "Might be they ran afoul of the law."

"Might be. Or they found Coe. That's more likely."

"Going off on this here wild-goose chase after Coe
out here—it sure tangles things up, Hannibal. Not
what you'd planned."

Hannibal shrugged. Once Coe had been spotted in
Freeman, he'd had to send the men after him. "The
opportunity come on up at me, had to take it."

They heard a rustling in the brush and a horse
neighing. Diamond pulled his pistol, cocked it—and
lowered it when he saw Gaines riding in, face twisted
in pain. There was blood running down his right arm.

"You hit?" Diamond asked, holstering his gun.

"Now, there's a smart question," Gaines snarled,
climbing off his horse beside them. "Of course I'm hit,
you damn fool! Took a round in the shoulder. That
Coe plugged me."

"Where are the others?" Fisher asked.

"They're chasing Coe and the girl. I can shoot with

my left most well as my right, but I'm no good till I get this damn ball out of me."

Fisher took a pint of whiskey from his saddlebag and handed it to Gaines. "Pour that over it. Stanch it good, ride into Freeman, and find a doc. Tell 'em your friend was hunting and mistook you for something useful."

"And what then?" Gaines asked, uncorking the bottle. He took a long swig as Fisher answered.

"Once you're patched up, head out to Feathers's place. Meet you there. Unless you're too poorly to ride. Then you'll miss out, and that's all there is to it."

"I'll be there," Gaines growled.

"Where they heading to?"

"South on the main road. Half mile from here, last I saw."

Fisher nodded, climbed into the saddle, and said, "Come on, Curt."

Gaines looked balefully after them as they trotted their horses up the slope to the road.

CHAPTER FOURTEEN

ARM THROBBING BUT feeling steady on his feet, Seth led the horses to the marsh water and let them drink. They could ride cross-country, but it was dark, and who knew what they might run into? He decided that the best course was to take the main road, behind their pursuers, and ride hard back to Freeman as fast as the horses could go. They'd find the Town Marshal, tell him their story. Only Seth wasn't at all sure they could get on the road before Dubois and the others came back this way.

Josette walked up to him, took the reins of her horse, and said what he'd been thinking. "They'll be here, Seth, anytime now."

She then slapped his gelding's rump hard so it sloshed off into the water as she mounted her horse—and Seth blinked up at her in confusion. "What're you doing, Josette?"

"They're coming, Seth—I heard them just now. They'll find our tracks down here. There's no time to run. And they'll kill you, Seth. They tried once, and they'll do it again. I'm going with them—I'm going to tell them I'll marry Heywood. I'm not going to be the cause of your dying!"

Then she shouted *"Yaw!"* and slapped her horse's rump and galloped off as Seth tried and failed to grab her reins.

He stared after her for a handful of stunned seconds as she raced back up the ravine to the road; then he turned and splashed after his horse. He could hear voices from up on the road now—Josette's voice and men replying—but he couldn't hear what they were saying.

At last he got hold of the gelding, mounted, and started off—but by the time he got to the road, Josette and the men with her were gone.

THE NIGHT WAS upon them, and Josette's heart felt like a lump of lead within her as she rode toward Freeman with Heywood and the other men.

But she rode with her head held high. *I had to do it,* she told herself defiantly. *There were too many of them. There was no time to get away. They'd have killed him. . . .*

Heywood rode to Josette's right, her father to her left. Behind her were three men, one of them called Briggs, another they'd called Peanut, and a younger man, seeming quietly troubled, who was as yet nameless to her.

"He lit out for Prairie Fire, did he, Josette?" Heywood said gleefully.

"That's right," she said. "Just left me there. Rode off on a deer trail, cross-country."

"Just proves he doesn't give a fig about you!"

"Are you lying, girl?" her papa asked, frowning. "That is not like this man Coe."

She shrugged. "Believe what you like."

"He probably passed us in the dark, maybe fifty feet away!" Briggs said.

"Fisher won't like Coe getting away," said the younger man riding beside Briggs.

"You can tell Fisher about it yourself, Bettiger!" Peanut said. "Here he comes!"

Two men rode swiftly toward them, meeting them on the road. Everyone halted, and the horses milled nervously about as the men talked.

"Fisher," said Bettiger, "the man Coe has bolted. But we have the girl."

"You let him get away?" Fisher shook his head in disgust.

Fisher? Josette stared at him, trying to see his face in the thin moonlight. Where had she heard that name? He had a long, cadaverous face. His curious lavender bowler and his three-piece suit suggested finery, but the clothes were dusty and threadbare, and the man had a patchy beard growing out.

Then she remembered. Seth had told her about the encounter with him and Sheriff Dawson—and that face, even the hat, matched the wanted poster in front of the marshal's office. This was the man who'd tried to kill her betrothed!

The rider in the black frock coat said, "Bettiger—what're you boys doing here? You should be chasin Coe down!"

"We thought we'd ought to escort this woman to Freeman," Bettiger replied nervously, "so's she can get married to Heywood here. That was the deal, wasn't it?"

"The deal is what I say it is," said Fisher. He moved his right hand languidly, reaching under his coat, and drew a gun. He kept it in his hand casually, as if toying with it, and said, "The deal *now* is that the girl belongs to me unless someone pays her ransom."

"What!" Heywood burst out.

"Ransom?" Dubois said incredulously.

"How much money you carrying, Heywood?" Fisher said, looking Heywood in the eyes.

"Why—not much."

"I heard him talking to the old Frenchy here," said Briggs. "He's planning to take her on a trip to San Francisco. Have them a honeymoon! Get her away so she can see what money can do. He's got a power of money in his money belt there."

"Now, that's what we need to hear," said Fisher. "Smiley, get that money belt and bring it here."

Heywood began, "Now, look here—" But he broke off when Fisher pointed the pistol at his head.

Josette had to remind herself to breathe. Her pulse thudded as she wondered if they would simply kill Heywood and her father and take her away and . . .

She refused to imagine anything more.

Briggs got down off his horse, drew a knife, and reached under Heywood's coat. In a few moments, he'd cut the money belt loose. He tossed it to Fisher, who caught it with his free hand.

"Keep these two covered," said Fisher. He holstered his gun and lit a match with one hand, then opened the money belt. Humming to himself, holding the belt up to the light, he did a quick count. "I make it about two thousand four hundred dollars!"

Smiley Briggs whistled at that.

"Do you know who it is you're robbing?" Heywood demanded, his voice quavering.

"It's not robbery," said Fisher mildly, extracting some cash from the money belt. "It is a fresh negotiation. You will have a shorter honeymoon, is all, unless you can have your rich daddy wire you some more. I'm keeping two thousand two hundred dollars for delivery of the girl. Give this to him, Smiley." He handed two hundred dollars to the pudgy red-haired man.

"Cain't I keep none of it?" Briggs asked.

"You will share in what I've taken from him—and you'll have your cut of the down payment he gave us, too. We'll split the money later."

"That girl could be more valuable was we to keep her," said Peanut.

Shivers ran down Josette's spine at that.

Fisher shook his head. "I want no more trouble than I have already, so we will let him have the girl and his life and two hundred dollars. If Kelmer here speaks against me anywhere at all—" He looked Heywood in the face and said, "I'll find him and kill him."

Heywood's mouth quivered. He looked away.

Briggs grumbled under his breath but handed the two hundred up to Heywood, who took it with an ill grace and stuffed it in a coat pocket.

"Fisher," Heywood began. "If you think—"

"Heywood!" Josette said sharply, cutting him off. "You'd best keep your mouth closed and be glad he doesn't kill you."

"A very sensible young lady," said the man in the frock coat, chuckling. "She'll make you a fine wife, Heywood!"

"You want me to take his gun, Fisher?" asked Briggs.

"Nope." Fisher stuck the money belt in a saddlebag. "He might need to pawn it."

Briggs laughed at that.

"Off you go to Freeman, Heywood," Fisher said, moving his horse aside. He lifted his hat. "Felicitations on your nuptials."

Hands trembling, Heywood reached out and took the reins of Josette's horse. He whipped his horse into a canter, and they started toward Freeman. Josette's papa followed, cursing as he went.

Josette half expected that the outlaws—for such they surely were—would shoot Heywood in the back. But Heywood, Josette, and her father rode around a curve without incident and headed for Freeman, with Josette feeling sure Fisher and his men would try to track Seth.

And if they found Seth—they'd kill him.

D OWN ON ONE knee, his horse's reins in his hand, Seth was puzzled by the tracks in the dirt road. He was pretty sure the daintier tracks belonged to Josette's roan pony. It was smaller than many horses, and Josette didn't weigh much. The hoofprints, just visible in moon- and starlight, were fairly clear. But they were going the wrong direction. He'd figured Heywood would head back to Prairie Fire. But those tracks, and the others grouped around them, were heading north.

Maybe Kelmer didn't want to ride all those hours south in the dark. And maybe he knew a way to get married after hours in Freeman. His father was a powerful man, after all, who probably had friends up there.

Seth seemed to hear Josette's voice again. *I'm going to tell them I'll marry Heywood.*

Josette would marry him, Seth thought bitterly, and she'd just have to get used to being wealthy, spoiled, and comfortable and having a handsome husband.

But would she really do it? Maybe Seth could find them and change her mind.

He stood up, mounted, and set off at a canter for Freeman.

He could hear Josette's voice, whispering in his mind. *I'll marry Heywood. . . .*

Seth spurred to a gallop and leaned forward in his saddle. He had to know.

The twilight deepened. He galloped around a curve—and saw five riders coming toward him, spread across the road, silhouettes in the gloaming. They were only a hundred yards away. He couldn't see Josette. Most likely she'd gone on with her father and Heywood Kelmer.

But that rider in the middle, he was sure, was Hannibal Fisher. And he'd brought a whole damn gang with him.

One of the men pointed at him, and another drew a gun.

Seth swore to himself and turned his horse off the road and down a slight trail between a couple of cottonwoods. He heard the riders coming after him. A bullet cracked past, striking low on a tree.

They were shooting at his horse, Seth reckoned. Fisher would want him alive, if possible, to find out where his money was. He glanced over his shoulder and saw the men riding down the embankment behind him.

Seth drove the horse through the cottonwoods, trying to keep them between him and the gang. In a few moments, he reached the marsh, where several streams came together. He reined in, unsure which way to go and with but a second to make up his mind. If he rode to the right, they'd have a clear shot at him between the stream and the trees. They were coming down on his left, so he couldn't ride that way. There was a good deal of brush and a grove of trees on a small island in the marsh, not far off. At least some of his pursuers might get mired coming after him.

"Coe, hold on, now. Let's talk!" called Fisher, behind and left.

Seth applied his spurs, and his horse splashed into mucky water and through a stand of rushes. Mosquitoes rose around him, dragonflies darted away, and his horse balked at the deepening water.

But he shouted, "*Go*, ya hammerhead, *yaw*!" and the gelding thrashed on. A bullet cut the water close by; another cracked past his left ear.

Josette . . .

He urged the horse on, slanting to the right behind a screen of tall reeds. A mallard flew up from a nest, angrily quacking. Behind them, the men shouted at one another, and he could hear their horses snorting, their legs splashing into the marsh.

Seth's horse struck a deeper place in the sluggish

stream and floundered, neighing, its eyes rolling. The water was coming up over his boots. He thought about quicksand and figured maybe he was going to have to jump in the water to keep from going down with the horse.

But then the gelding got its hooves onto something solid, and they were moving, and in a few steps, they reached the farther bank. If he could get to the trees . . .

They were climbing the clay bank when he heard a gunshot mingled with the gelding's scream. The horse sunfished in pain, and Seth jerked his feet out of the stirrups and vaulted free in a motion he'd learned from riding broncs. He came down on his boots, and the horse fell heavily on its side, squealing piteously.

"I'm sorry, fella," he said, pulling his Winchester from its saddle holster. He started up the bank toward the trees, wishing he could do something for the gelding. But glancing back, he saw blood pumping out of the horse's neck; someone had hit an artery with a rifle shot. Death would come quickly.

A bullet kicked splinters from the trunk of a silver maple as he dashed by, and then he was in the screen of swamp dogwood brush, thick and a little taller than he was. It scratched at him as he pushed between the brush and a big sycamore bole, looking for an escape route—or a place to take a stand.

"Sweeney, Bettiger!" It was Fisher's voice somewhere behind Seth. "Get south of him. We'll catch him between us!"

Seth paused by the upturned roots of a fallen tree and looked back through a gap in the brush. He couldn't see Sweeney; he must have been on the other side of the little island, behind him. But a stocky, red-haired rider was coming up the bank about twenty yards north. Beyond him Seth could just see Hannibal Fisher riding into the trees, along with a man in a long black frock coat.

Hannibal Fisher, Wanted Dead or Alive . . .

Seth brought the Winchester up—but then Fisher passed from sight in the trees, the man in the frock coat with him. Seth swung the Winchester around to point at the man with the red hair—and hesitated. This hombre could be anyone, even some fool who thought he was on a posse. Seth shook his head. More likely he was an outlaw.

But he couldn't quite bring himself to shoot this stranger down without knowing for sure.

"Son of a . . . Oh, the hell with it." Seth turned and moved off alongside the fallen tree, hunkered as he went to keep its trunk between him and the gang. His heart thumped, and there was a metallic taste in his mouth.

Hearing horses coming, he rose to look over the fallen trunk and spotted Fisher about fifty feet away, visible in the thin light from the moon and stars streaming between the trees. Without hesitating Seth propped the rifle on the tree trunk and aimed. The man riding up beside Fisher said, "Look out, Hannibal!" and fired a pistol at Seth. The bullet kicked up sawdust and splinters, stinging Seth's cheeks, and his own pull on the trigger was more of a twitch. The shot went wild, and then Fisher was firing back. More bits of bark spat and Seth ducked down behind the thick bole. He scurried in a crouch alongside the fallen tree—and then he saw Sweeney and a younger man riding out of the brush on his right.

They'd seen him and they had a clear shot. Sweeney was taking aim.

Seth looked for cover and, not finding any, fired the Winchester from the hip. The shot hit the younger man in the side so that blood splashed and the man groaned.

"Surrender in the name of the law!" bellowed a familiar voice from the trees to the south.

Sweeney and the other man turned, startled— Sweeney bringing his pistol around to fire—

A rider came bursting into the little clearing by the fallen tree, firing a shotgun from the saddle. It was Franklin.

Hit square by the shotgun blast, Sweeney shrieked and fell backward off his horse—one foot caught in a stirrup. The other outlaw turned his horse; hunched in pain, he rode off into the brush to the east.

Franklin's shotgun let loose again, and someone yelled on the other side of the fallen tree.

"Hannibal, I'm hit!"

Seth swung his rifle around and saw Fisher sitting on his horse just ten paces off, trying to aim at Seth— but the gambler's horse was balking, rearing, and he was having trouble steadying his gun.

The man in the frock coat was just behind Fisher, backing his horse up, firing at Franklin. Seth fired the Winchester without having much chance to aim and saw a piece of Fisher's coat sleeve fly apart. A pistol banged to Seth's right—Franklin popping the pistol at Fisher and the other man. He fired three times, and Seth jacked another round into the chamber and fired again, hitting a tree close beside Fisher.

Hannibal Fisher turned his horse and spurred off

into the trees, the man in the long black frock coat following.

Seth fired after them—but he didn't have a clear shot and doubted he hit anything but tree bark.

Shaking, he stood up straight and turned to Franklin, who was getting down off his horse.

"You hit, Seth?" he asked, leading his horse over to him.

"Not this time." Seth's heart was still pounding so loud, he could hear it. He felt light-headed. "Got creased some in my arm earlier. How'd you find me?"

Franklin squinted at the brush, looking for Fisher as he spoke. "Marshal in Prairie Fire told me you headed up here—said Fisher was in the country round here, looking for you. And I heard a couple fellas in that gang talking at Ma Sublette's place. I come up to warn you—about killed my horse doing it. I was heading for Freeman, and I heard the shots. Had a look-see, and I caught sight of that no-good Sweeney . . ."

"Sure glad to see you, Franklin. He'd have nailed me to this log here if it weren't for you."

"They're not going to give up so easy."

"You got buckshot into one of them, and I nearly hit Fisher a couple times. Sweeney's dead. The other fella ran off. And you said"—Seth managed a weary laugh—"'Surrender in the name of the law!'"

Franklin grinned. "It worked, didn't it? They didn't know if I was part of a posse! I expect that's why they've done rid off. How many of them were there, you know?"

"Well there was— Holy cow!" Seth remembered the red-haired man. And the owlhoot would be somewhere behind him.

He spun around in time to see a round, florid-faced man with red hair, mouth open, staring at them from the brush by the marsh. Franklin saw him, too, and fired his pistol—the man instantly vanished. They heard the brush rustling as he ran off, then the sound of a horse moving away.

"That was close—he like to have shot me in the back!" Seth said. "That's two I owe you!"

"And I won't let you forget it! Seth—let's get the hell out of here! Say—where's your horse?"

"Dead. They shot him."

They heard a snorting nearby and a whicker—and turned to see Sweeney's horse dragging the dead man along by the stirrup just thirty paces away.

Seth jogged over to the horse, calling soothingly, "Hey, pal, I've got you. It's all right! We'll get that load off you right quick!" He caught the horse's bridle, and Franklin tugged Sweeney's booted foot from the stirrup.

"You think we should bury Sweeney?" Seth asked.

"Nope. We need to get out of here before they flank around on us."

Seth mounted Sweeney's horse, feeling a stab of pain in his injured arm. Franklin swung up into his own saddle, and they set out south quick as they could go in the brushy woods—heading away from Fisher.

"Maybe we should circle them and shoot that murderin' cheat!" Franklin suggested as they rode along. "With him dead, the others'll likely run off."

Seth shook his head. "They gather up, why, there'll be four of them against us. We're lucky to have got out of that shooting gallery!"

"Say, where's Josette? Marshal said you two were getting hitched up!"

"Rode off with Heywood Kelmer to Freeman. He and her pappy were partnered up with Fisher. She said she was going to keep me from getting killed even if it meant marrying Heywood."

"Well, I'll be damned! You're saying—she surrendered to him?"

"Or maybe changed her mind about living with a cowboy planning on scratching out a living in Texas."

Franklin looked at him, frowning, but said nothing.

They came to the edge of the trees and reined in, looking around. They saw no one, but the outlaws could have been hidden in the brush.

Seth was thinking about the way Sweeney had looked when he'd tugged the other man free of that stirrup. The dead outlaw had stared up at the sky, mouth open, looking startled, as if amazed he had ended this way. "It bother you any, killing Sweeney?"

"Him? No. He was trying to kill you. And he'd have killed me if he could. Anyhow—I was in the war, Seth. I don't like killing. But I got used to it."

Seth nodded. Franklin had served with the Army of the Confederacy for a year as a teenager and had killed his share of men. "I expect that's natural enough. But—I hope I never do get used to it, Franklin."

"Where to now?" Franklin asked.

"Guess I've just got to know for sure . . ."

"About Josette?"

"Yep. So I'm going to Freeman. Have to find another trail to get there. We'd be sitting ducks on the main road." He cleared his throat. "I won't ask you to come with me. You and that horse of yours both look about rode out."

"What I've been through with Ma Sublette—" Franklin shook his head. "I'll tell you later. Hell, I'm going to the nearest town, and that's Freeman. Let's ride."

CHAPTER FIFTEEN

THIS JUDGE WILL not come," said Dubois sourly. He flapped a hand toward the growing celebration in the main square. "He is there, drinking and dancing!"

"The justice is an old friend of my father's," Heywood said, looking impatiently at the locked door of the courthouse. "And he owes us a favor. I know just where I can get a room for tonight, too. There's a ranch a mile south does a lot of business with Black Creek Acres. They'll loan us a nice bedroom."

Josette, standing between the two men on the top step of the courthouse, hoped the judge would not appear. She glanced over her shoulder and thought of running, but they would probably catch her.

She might have run, anyway. But it could end in Seth being shot down. Heywood would give those horrible men some more money and have his revenge.

Poor Seth. What was he feeling now?

It was dark out, but there were a good many lights from the square down the street where the mayor's celebration was ginning up, with lanterns hanging about the stage erected for the occasion, and all the gaslights alit, showing off the bunting. A noisy crowd was milling about, waiting for the newlyweds to show up.

Josette sighed. It was someone's grand wedding celebration—for a bride who was happy to be married. It made a mock of her own imminent marriage.

The band chose that moment to play its first tune, which Josette recognized as "Vilikins and His Dinah," a drippily sentimental song she found oppressive to hear—she was more in the mood for a dirge.

There was the sound of the door unlocking, and it swung open, revealing the wizened little constable who'd sent her away but a short time ago.

"You the Kelmer marriage folks?" the little man asked dourly, one hand on the door, the other tugging his goatish beard.

"We are!" Heywood said, straightening his string tie. "Where's Justice Hopkins?"

"He's inside, and he needs to get this done lickety-split. He's done been to the wedding, and now he's expected at the reception. Coming over here for this was mighty inconvenient."

"Just take us to him if you please," said Heywood.

The constable grudgingly stood aside, and they went into a large drafty hallway of heavily lacquered wood. They found the judge standing in the courtroom in front of the bench, his hands in his trouser pockets. He was a middle-aged man, his heavy jaws going jowly, bags under his impatient eyes. He wore a cream-colored suit and tails, and there was a rose in his buttonhole. "Let us get this under way, Kelmer," he said. "The courtroom should be closed, and I am wanted elsewhere. Was it not for your father—"

"I'm as eager as you are, Your Honor," Heywood declared.

Josette felt a tightening in her throat. A feeling of panic was rising within her. It was suddenly hard to breathe.

The constable stood to the side, arms crossed, frowning, his eyes on Josette. "Ain't you the girl who came here with another fella to marry earlier today?"

She gave a faint nod in response.

The constable shook his head, his frown deepening. "You sure are a fickle little thing, then. Something curious about all this."

"What's that, Laird?" the judge said absently, tugging a leather binder from his bench top. He turned back to them, began flipping through paperwork in the binder.

"Just that this young lady was here with a young fella a few hours ago, wanting to get married. And it wasn't this man Kelmer."

"That's none of your business," Heywood snapped.

"He was forcing her to come!" Dubois interposed. "He'd kidnapped her—"

"Lies!" Josette blurted. She was startled by her own voice—she was unable to keep quiet. She had resolved to marry Heywood, but now it all came tumbling out. "This is the abduction! I was here with Seth of my own free will! But these men sent gunslingers—murderers!"

"What's that?" The judge looked up at her, eyebrows lifted in astonishment. "Murderers?"

"She's teched!" said Heywood. "All aflutter about the marriage. Let's get on with this!"

The judge closed the folder and peered closely at Josette. "Young lady—do you consent to this marriage here and now of your own free will, or do you not?"

She felt a certainty then that she could not go through with it. "I do not, Your Honor!" she replied.

By now, she decided, Seth would be as safe as he was likely to be, with Fisher still on the loose.

"She marries who I say!" Dubois said. "It is the right of a father!"

"I am of an age to decide for myself!" Josette said, stamping a buttoned-up shoe on the floor. "I chose Seth Coe—not Heywood Kelmer! But they threatened to kill Seth and—"

"She's promised me!" Heywood growled. "She's got to do it!"

"Your Honor," said the constable, "I cannot be a party to this young lady being forced into marrying this man."

"I am of the same mind, Laird," said Hopkins, nodding.

"Look here. You owe my father!" Heywood said, jabbing an index finger at the judge.

"Owing a favor doesn't mean I'm going to break the law, Kelmer," said Hopkins, glowering at him.

Heywood hesitated, chewing his lower lip. Then he blurted, "I've been, ah, financially inconvenienced, but I can raise some money if that—"

"Are you trying to *bribe* me, sir?" Hopkins demanded. "Constable—stand ready to take this man into custody, should he make any further offer of a bribe!"

"Yes, sir!" The constable was smiling now.

The judge turned to Josette. "What's this about a murderer?"

She licked her lips and decided to just say it right out. "One of those men was Hannibal Fisher—wanted for murder."

"Fisher!" exclaimed the constable.

"Heywood Kelmer hired him to take me away from Seth—and they ended by robbing Heywood!"

"Ho *ho*!" the constable said, amused.

"Now, that's a lie!" said Heywood, licking his lips. "I . . . I asked some men to help me find the lady. The man's name was Bitterman, not Fisher!"

"So he told you," Josette said. "But I saw that face on a wanted poster. And he robbed you—threatened you with a gun! I saw that, too!"

"Where are these men now, Kelmer?" Judge Hopkins asked.

Kelmer swallowed and took a step backward, as if thinking about a quick exit. "I don't know, Your Honor—south somewhere. Or east. I don't think it's that Fisher."

The judge slapped the folder against his thigh thoughtfully. "This marriage ceremony is hereby canceled."

"No!" Dubois said, almost howling.

The judge pointed a finger at him. "You, sir, will be silent! Now, it's my ruling that this lady will depart here on her own to go where she pleases. You gentlemen will wait here for fifteen minutes with the constable—then you will go to the Town Marshal's office with Laird, and you will give your statements. I will look into this matter about Fisher tomorrow. . . ."

Feeling giddy, Josette said, "Thank you, Your Honor!" and hurried out the door. Suddenly light on her feet, she began running till she was through the courthouse door and out into the night. Swinging from a thin braided leather strap in her hand was a small purse she'd made and embroidered herself, and in it were eleven dollars, all her savings in the world. Perhaps she could use a few dollars of it to persuade some family to take her in for the night. She was scared to ride the roan back all alone. Well, probably Heywood would take the horse back to Prairie Fire.

Tomorrow she could get a stage—she had just enough to get her to Prairie Fire. She could make her way to the Hamer farm and await Seth. . . .

She prayed he was still alive.

HANNIBAL FISHER HALTED his mount at the edge of a broad, slow-moving stream on the east side of the marsh. Briggs and Diamond did the same, all of them looking about for the man who'd slipped through their fingers. Fisher saw only the dark trees beyond the stream, the sliver of moon reflected in the green-black water, the erratic flutter of bats flying over.

"We can't trail him in this here marshland, Hannibal," said Diamond, grimacing with pain. His right leg and ribs had been peppered with ten-gauge pellets. Most of the spread had missed him, and none seemed to have penetrated deeply, but he'd caught enough to feel like his right side was afire. Fisher knew that Diamond wanted to go to ground so he could dig out the pellets.

Fisher himself was churning with rage inside, and

he had no one to direct it at except Diamond and Briggs. "Curt—stop your damn whining. You are not hurt bad. We'll trail him if I say to, or you'll be on your way and miss your chance at the money."

Diamond shook his head as if about to retort, then seemed to think better of it.

"Any gate," said Smiley Briggs, "I don't think that other cowboy was part of a posse. Those two was all I saw."

Fisher took off his hat, waving away a small cloud of mosquitoes. "That other man's name is Franklin. He's just another cowboy, and there's no sign of the law. He spooked us, it's true, but he won't bluff me again." He looked narrowly at Briggs. "Smiley, tell me this—if you saw those two, why didn't you shoot that big cowboy at least?"

"I was fixing to! But they opened up on me, and my horse started to run off—I had to chase him down—and I wasn't sure if there was maybe a lawman off in the brush, and—"

"And you turned yellow and run away!" growled Diamond. He clutched his side. "Hannibal. I got to get this shot out of me."

"You will. Now, shut up and let me—" He broke off. There was motion in the trees across the water. The dark shape of a horse was barely visible. "I see somebody—maybe. Could be Peanut's horse, but it could be Coe over there." He pointed and said, "Come on!"

He started across the water, and luckily it was shallow, the mud not too deep, and they got through it and up onto the rise. They found a thin game trail through the trees, and Fisher led the way to a small clearing lit by moonlight and stars. Bettiger was sitting on a log, bare chested, dabbing at a wound in his side with a kerchief. He looked up, startled, as they rode in. Fisher dismounted.

"Just decide you'd have a little break over here, did you, Bettiger?" Fisher asked archly.

"I . . ." Bettiger licked his lips. "I was— I got shot. Just ended up over here."

"Just ended up, you say. Looks more to me like you were fixing to head off on your own somewhere. Maybe find a doc. Maybe talk to the law."

"The law!" Wincing, Bettiger stood up, his right hand dropping near his holstered six-gun. "Why would I do that? I'm a wanted man!"

"Because you've been squirming about my plans for some time now," said Fisher, feeling the seething rage rising up in him. "Because you're the son of a Texas Ranger. And blood will tell." His voice was getting louder as he spoke. "And because you are probably figuring on turning me in—making some kind of deal with the law. Maybe even get a reward!"

With that, Fisher pulled his gun, and Diamond drew his because Fisher was drawing. Bettiger instinctively drew his own—and Fisher shot him in the face, making his head rock back on his neck. He didn't get off a shot as Diamond shot him twice, the blood spurting from his bare chest. Bettiger's horse, untethered and spooked by the gunshots, galloped off into the trees.

The young outlaw went to his knees and flopped facedown, still clutching his unfired gun.

"Holy moly," Briggs muttered. Then he chuckled. "Never did trust him. Good riddance!"

Fisher slipped his gun into its hideaway holster and

went to check the dead man's pockets. He discovered only four dollars, two bits, and a silver watch. He put those slim pickings in his pocket, took Bettiger's gun, looked it over, and stuck it in his waistband. "We'll see if we can find his horse. . . ."

"And when we do?" Diamond asked, clutching at his own wounded side.

"Maybe we'll cut the trails of those slippery cowboys," said Fisher, speaking more calmly now. He felt a little better, having killed a man—and one who'd been worrying him. "If we don't find 'em pretty quick, we'll go back to the camp, and you can pry out those pellets. Then maybe head for Buffalo Junction and move ahead with that bank job. Like as not, Coe will go back to Prairie Fire. I can find him there."

"We're short men for the bank job, ain't we?" said Briggs. "Buster didn't look too good back at the camp. Sweeney's dead. Bettiger's dead."

"As to that—I have me a notion. . . ."

I T WAS IN sight of midnight when two exhausted cowboys, on two exhausted horses, rode into Freeman from the eastern road. Seth and Franklin had struggled through seemingly endless swampy ground and muddy streams before finding a trail that led them to the east–west road into Freeman.

"I suppose we should find the town's law and tell them what happened," Franklin said as they trotted their mounts through the outskirts of town. "I shot a man off his horse. And we come upon Hannibal Fisher. They'll want to know. Someone will want to go out there and look for Fisher and pick up that body."

"Be better to report it in Prairie Fire," Seth said. "They might hold me up here and could be that Josette's gone back home. I need to be free to move around. But if you want to do it, I can't stop you."

"We can wait. Sweeney can wait, too. We'll report it to Marshal Coggins."

Seth's left arm was aching, but the bullet had passed clean through, and when he touched the skin close to the wound, he didn't feel the telltale hotness of infection.

"We'll never find a doc for that arm of yours this time of night," said Franklin.

"There's a big party still going on—you hear it? If we find a doc, he'll be drunk! My arm's not so bad. It's Josette I'm here for."

"Hate to say it, Seth, but by now, she's married and, well, Heywood's got her alone somewhere."

Seth wasn't so sure. "Wouldn't be easy to get her married, it being night and with all these goings-on. But it could happen in the morning. And I don't know how to find her. I'm not even sure she'll *want* me to come get her."

"You really think she'd choose him over you—I mean, without feeling forced into it?" Franklin snorted. "Heywood Kelmer? That strutting rooster?"

"A woman has got to be practical. How is marrying me practical? Maybe what she said about wanting to keep me safe was . . ." He shrugged.

"You think it was just an excuse?"

Franklin was putting Seth's innermost fears into words. It made him feel sick to hear it aloud. "I sure don't know, Franklin."

They reached the noisy square and rode around the

edges of the crowd, looking for Josette but not truly expecting to find her here. Then they went on to the courthouse. It was closed and locked. No one answered Seth's knock.

"Seth—you want to keep looking, you can do it. But I'll have to be afoot. I got to find a place to stable my horse before he folds up under me. He's like to founder."

Seth shrugged. He was so tired, it was hard to think. "We can't find her this way. Let's see if we can get a pint of whiskey—mostly for my wound. But I believe I'll have a pull on it. We passed a livery back there; I saw the stableman watching the party from his loft window."

They returned to the stable and made a deal with the gruff, half-drunk stableman. The stalls were full, but there was room out back, with water and grass, and they were permitted, for an extra dollar, to stretch out near their horses.

Sitting on a pile of hay with his back to the stable wall, Seth tended his wound and decided to have another look for Josette. Franklin was already asleep, but Seth could get up and start walking about, asking folks if they'd seen her.

But his eyes were heavy. He'd lost some blood and . . . he was dead weary. Wouldn't hurt to close his eyes for a few minutes before setting out.

He was asleep before he knew it.

GAINES ALMOST DIDN'T make it here," said Feathers Martin. Fisher, Cletus Spence, Feathers, and Briggs were standing at the foot of the bed—a big four-

poster that was usually a kind of workshop for a soiled
dove. They were looking at the delirious Buster
Gaines. It was a hot day, and the room stank from sickness and sweat. "Seems he couldn't find a doctor in
Freeman, so he went to a barber."

"When I was a boy," Briggs remarked nostalgically,
"barbers had two jobs. They cut hair, and they dug rifle
balls out of folks. Sewed up the hole, too. Leastways
that's how it was in Kentucky."

"This barber had a bad cough, and he carved Buster
up some, getting at that bullet," Feathers went on.
"That's how Gaines told it. Didn't burn the wound or
nothin'. So's it got infected, and when he rode in here,
he was already burnin' with fever. Hadn't been that he
rides with you, Fisher, I'd have turned him away."

Gaines moaned and thrashed and opened his eyes
but didn't seem to see them. "Daddy said he'd whip the
skin off you, Buster . . ." Gaines mumbled, closing his
eyes again.

Fisher shook his head. Gaines wasn't going to be
much use. "Feathers, let's have a drink and a talk."

The four men trooped to the stairs and down to the
saloon, where Cindy poured them out drinks without
having to be asked. There was no one in the saloon
except a working girl at the bar and Diamond, sitting
in one of the chairs against the wall, playing solitaire
on a small tabletop, his chest bare except for bandages
around his pellet wounds. The whore, Fisher noted,
was three sheets to the wind, her head drooping over
her drink, her elbows on the bar. Her bright blond sau-
sage curls, gaily dyed, were beginning to lose their
shape; she wore a patchy bare-shouldered pink dance
hall frock, and in her right hand was the smoking stub

of a cigar. Her name was Rosie, Fisher knew, and Gaines was in her bed. Cindy was keeping her in free drinks.

"Hey, boys, who's lonely?" Rosie asked, slurring her words, as they took up their drinks. "I can work a bunk. Done it more'n once. How about you, Smiley?"

"A leetle later, I'll take you up on that, Rosie," Briggs said, raising his glass to her.

"Feathers," Fisher said, toying with his glass, "we're short on men. And you said you weren't making ends meet."

"These women and my guards, they eat me out of house and home," Feathers groused. He pushed the whiskey aside. "Cindy, get me the cold beer."

She nodded and opened the trapdoor as Feathers went on. "And we're just not getting much trade in here lately. Word's getting around, and the fellers are spooked that the law will come. I ain't quite down to the blanket, but I'm getting there."

Fisher suspected that Feathers had a good deal stashed away somewhere. But that was a thought for later. "Well, now, seems like you need to get the gold flowing. Maybe get you a bag of bank cash and use it to fix this place up. Make it more respectable. Fact is, I need another man for the bank. Good-sized bank— only bank in Prairie Fire, and there's no other for a day's ride."

"That's a notion," Feathers said, taking his cold beer from Cindy. He drank half of it off in one great gulp, wiped his beard with the back of his hand, and said, "I was thinking on something along them lines but figured to do it on my own."

"Safer to ride with us where we can watch your

back. There's a guard at the bank and a marshal across the street."

"Haven't robbed nobody in years."

"Then you're getting rusty!" Fisher said, winking at him. "You need to show you've still got the goods, Feathers!"

"Oh, hell, if I wanted to, I could do it. What's the split?"

"We're cutting it equal," Fisher said, though he had no intention of sharing the split equally.

"Why—shore. It gets powerful dull out here. Is Curt coming? He's some chewed up himself."

"I am certainly coming!" Diamond called, smacking a card down onto the table. "Ain't but scratched."

"How about me?" Cletus demanded. "Kin I come?"

"I do have a use for you," Fisher said, slapping Cletus on the shoulder.

"I guess I can get Attic Bird to watch the shop," Feathers said. "When's this little ball gonna open, Hannibal?"

"A few days, maybe," said Fisher. "What say we pay Cindy to slip into Prairie Fire. I don't expect she's known there. She can finish the sizing up that Sweeney started and meet us at the camp."

"I guess that'd be okay," said Feathers.

Smiley Briggs looked at the ceiling. "I want to stay some tomorrow, see if Buster's going to get any better."

Feathers snorted. "He's got that fast-moving sickness that gets deep in a man. He'll be in the bone orchard in a day or two—I'll bet ten dollars on it right now!"

"I'll take that bet!" said Briggs. "Now, I need me an-

other drink . . . and then I'm gonna take Rosie to the
bunkroom while she can still get there."

JOSETTE USED EVERY penny she had for the stagecoach trip, and she was beginning to wish she'd ridden the roan after all. She'd never traveled in a
stagecoach before—her father didn't hold with any sort
of travel unless absolutely needed—and she was
amazed at how much dust came in the open windows,
and how the metal-shod wheels seemed to find every
hole and rock in the road to bounce on, jarring her
over and over.

The two other passengers were not pleasant company. Josette sat facing the front of the coach; on her
left, overshadowing her and pressing her into a corner
with his bulk, was a great fetid bull of a man all in buckskin who had barely fit through the door. He had dozed
for most of the journey thus far, his long greasy black
hair and mustaches waggling, his bristly chin bouncing
on his chest with the jolting of the stagecoach.

Across from Josette was a middle-aged woman with
a long, sallow face; she was dressed all in black. She
seemed newly widowed, and she'd sat staring at her
wringing hands for the entire two hours they'd already
spent in this dust-choked stagecoach. The widow had
murmured, "Good day to you," on stepping into the
coach and had been unapproachably silent ever since,
looking like she might at any moment burst into tears.
Josette's heart went out to the woman, but she found
her presence oppressive, for it was a dark reminder
that she might herself be a widow now. It was true she

had not been married to Seth to the letter of the law, but she had felt married all the same. And if Fisher had caught up to Seth . . .

The stagecoach hit a particularly grievous bump, and the big man in buckskin woke up, blinking around. "Still here," he muttered. "Still here." He dug a flask from a coat pocket and swigged, then offered it to Josette with a yellow grin. "Wet your whistle?" She only shook her head.

"What's your name, little chickabiddy?" the big man in buckskin asked, leaning closer to Josette.

Completely unwilling to engage in such familiarities with this man, Josette tried changing the subject. "Do you find your living in the mountains?"

"Oh, aye, yep," he grunted. "Furs!" Then he bobbed his thick eyebrows at her. "Got me a nice, private cabin up there! Mebbe you'd like to see it!"

She ignored the invitation. "You are far from the mountains here."

"Weary of the High Lonely! Decided I wanted to see Topeka. Heard it was wild. 'Twas not! Sheriff didn't like me. The girls, now—they liked me!" Another leer.

Josette sighed at that and looked pointedly away.

The coach bounced again, and more dust swirled in, making Josette cough. To avoid the big man's steady gaze, she looked out the window, mildly curious at hearing horses riding up behind the coach. It occurred to her then that the riders might be her father and Heywood, come to reclaim her, and she cringed inwardly.

She stuck her head out a little, just enough to peer back at the riders, and caught a glimpse of one of them. . . .

"Seth!" she blurted. Then she shouted it. *"Seth!"*

But he didn't seem to hear her over the clatter of the stagecoach.

The coach was tracking right down the middle of the road, and the riders came up on their right to pass it. Looking grim, Seth had his eyes fixed on the road ahead and rode quickly past.

"Seth!" she called out with everything she had. *"Seth Coe!"*

Now he turned his head, and he saw her, his face lighting up with surprise and wonder. "Josette!"

Josette shouted up at the driver, "Stop! Stop the coach, driver!"

There was no response.

"Stop!"

The stagecoach didn't slow a whit.

The widow was staring at her aghast. Josette didn't care. "Stop, driver, or I'll throw myself out the door!" she shouted.

It seemed to her the coach sped up a touch then. But Seth was riding up close to the lead horses, flicking his lasso and catching one about the neck. Winding the rope at his end around the saddle horn, he pulled back hard on his horse's reins so it dug in its hooves. The lead horse of the stagecoach team slowed, struggling with the rope.

"Stop, damn you!" Seth shouted.

Josette recognized Franklin's voice shouting something she couldn't quite make out and then the coach's brakes squealed; she had to brace herself, and she could smell a little smoke from the friction of wood on wood as the stagecoach ground to a halt.

"Put that damn shotgun down. This ain't a robbery,

you chucklehead!" Franklin bellowed as Josette climbed out of the stagecoach and ran to Seth.

He slid off his horse, his eyes full of questions, but Josette didn't give him a chance to ask them.

She simply threw herself into his arms.

CHAPTER SIXTEEN

S HAKING HER HEAD in wonder, Daisy poured a cordial for Josette, and they sat across the wooden table near the kitchen stove. "And there he was, riding past you, thinking you were married up to Heywood back in Freeman!"

"Daisy—he was looking for me all that morning in Freeman! And all the time, I was out on a little farm to the edge of town, waiting for the stagecoach. It comes right by there. I was scarce a mile from him—thinking he might be dead, and him thinking I'd left him for Heywood!"

"Freeman is a tolerably sizable town," Daisy said, pouring herself a cordial. "Easy to miss someone. You two must've had a lot to say to each other. He had reason to think you left him for Heywood!"

"I had to do some explaining. But he was so glad we found each other again, he didn't say much besides asking me for a kiss. He settled up with the driver, and we rode up top with all the bags. Franklin led Seth's horse, and we just took our ease on those bags, talking all the way to Prairie Fire."

"Did Doc Twilley see to his arm?"

"Yes, when we came in yesterday. It seems he'll be all right. I suppose it hurts him some, but you know how men are!"

"Oh, I do. They will not tell us! Why, one time Sol fractured his wrist and didn't tell me for two days!"

Josette chuckled at that, but she knew women hid their pain, too. She thought of her mama.

She sipped her cherry cordial, thick, sweet, and with just a little kick to it. They were waiting for the men to come back. Seth had gone into Prairie Fire to see if the stableman would take Sweeney's horse, and perhaps thirty dollars, to make up for the dead gelding, and Sol was out in the fields.

"Josette—you may as well get married in Prairie Fire. Your father's here in town, sure, but word is getting around he was working with outlaws and all but kidnapped you. You've got Judge Twilley on your side and the marshal, too. If I was you, I'd get married in the wink of an eye. Maybe tomorrow!"

"Tomorrow!"

"Now, listen—we can hitch up Goliath to the buckboard. You can ride into town and make all the arrangements. Seth's not been gone long—he's got business with the marshal and Sheriff Dawson and the stableman. He'll be around when you get there. Just take him by the ear and drag him to the city hall, fix up the papers and the time for marrying. Get it done soon and there'll be no more interference from your father."

"Daisy! When did you hatch this plan?" Josette laughed, delighted.

"Just this minute. Are you willing?"

"All except for the part about taking him by the ear."

"Oh, I was joshing. He'll come along, honey, if you so much as crook your little finger at him." After a moment, she added, "Maybe you should wait for Sol; he can go in with you. After all you've been through . . ."

Josette stood up. "I'll be fine! Seth left his Winchester here—I'll take it along. I can shoot, too, you know."

Fisher and his men were back at the same camp on Black Creek. Gaines would not be coming with them to Prairie Fire. They'd seen Whistler dragging Buster's body behind a horse out to the bone orchard when they'd set out from Buffalo Junction that morning.

The remaining men had cursed Fisher every way from Sunday when he'd dragged them from their beds at ten in the morning. Fisher needed them ready, close to Prairie Fire; that way, when Cindy returned with her report, they could hit the bank, supposing the report was favorable.

These complexities were lost on men with aching heads, owing to the oh-be-joyful they'd imbibed the night before, but Fisher had enticed them into their saddles with vivid descriptions of the riches that would come if they followed his plan. And besides, they could take turns napping in camp.

As it happened, they were all snoring—except

Fisher, who was standing watch—when Cindy came riding up on her paint. She looked almost ladylike, wearing a riding habit and a feathered hat.

"She's back!" Fisher shouted. "Everybody up!"

Grumbling, the men got up and gathered around to hear what Cindy had to say.

She climbed off the little horse and said, "That Seth Coe's signed some papers with the marshal, telling what happened up north. I stood outside the marshal's office and heard some of their talk. Coe's planning to get married in a few days. Then he went to dickering with the fellow in the stables. Seems like he's going to be right on the main street there for a while."

Fisher grunted and looked off toward Prairie Fire. "Sounds like Heywood failed to hang on to his little Josette." The way things were shaping up, it seemed he wouldn't have time to capture Coe and grill him about the whereabouts of his money. He'd just have to kill him and hope it was on his body. "The marshal was around when you left town, Cindy?"

"He is. Seen him through the window, sittin' in his office."

"You can make another hundred dollars if you do exactly what I say. . . ."

SETH CAME OUT of the city hall, smiling. He was feeling good, despite the ache in his bandaged left arm. It was a hot late afternoon, but not terrible hot, and he was going to get married once he set a date with Josette.

He came upon Franklin sitting on a bench in front of the marshal's office, fussing with a knot in an old lasso. Franklin's horse was tied up at the hitching post, scuffing its hooves as if eager to be off.

"You haven't got your buckaroo knot figured, Franklin?" Seth said, ambling up.

"I'm learning a new one Cullin showed me. Anyway, he give me this, and I can't get it untied. I'm about to figure it out using my pocketknife. Like that feller they told us about in school. Alexander the somebody."

"Alexander the Great. Gordian knot, that was. He cut right through it. I've just about sawn through my own: Judge Twilley says I'm in the clear. My statement and Josette's and yours are good enough for him. Soon's I get married, and after me and Josette have a night at the inn, we can all three head south to Chaseman."

"That's fine! I'm more than ready to get out of Kansas. Seems like it should be quiet farming country, yet it's always got some trouble going. Texas is peaceful compared to this." He sat back and put a serious look on his face. "I just have one question—supposing Judge Twilley and Doc Twilley were to change clothes, maybe both shave the same. Could Doc Twilley play the judge and the judge the doctor with no one the wiser?"

Seth laughed. "Another puzzle!"

"What say we figure it out over a glass of beer?"

"You go on. I'll join you right quick. I just want to look in on Sheriff Dawson."

"Good enough." Franklin threw the knotted lasso down in disgust. "I want no more to do with that durn thing." He got up, stretched, and climbed on his horse. The saloon was just far enough away to ride to. "Don't make it too long, or I'll start in on the whiskey."

Seth watched him go, thinking he was always going

to be in Franklin's debt. Without him, he'd be vulture meat on a lonely little island in the marshes.

Whistling "Camptown Races" to himself, Seth strolled to Doc Twilley's place. He knocked and the doc called out, "Come in. Everybody else has!"

Seth came in just as two ladies in bonnets were departing, both carrying baskets. He took off his hat and said, "Ladies . . ." and stepped out of their way.

He went into the back room to see Dawson sitting on the edge of the bed, fully dressed, right down to the boots. Doc Twilley was taking the sheriff's pulse. The sheriff still looked a little pale, and there was a cane leaning on the bed next to him.

"Steady as can be," the doc said.

"Why, he looks like he's rarin' to go!" Seth exclaimed.

Dawson grinned. "Been up and walking. Some."

"Still hurts when he breathes deep," said the doc, "and will for a while. He has to stay right close to bed and use the cane when he moves around till he's got his strength back. Be a while before he can ride. Even in a stagecoach. But he's on the mend."

"Took one in the chest and near ready to ride a bronc!" Seth said. "Sheriff, you're one tough bird."

"I could ride if he'd let me!" Dawson said. "The man's a terrible tyrant."

"You'd start bleeding and choking on blood if you try to ride," declared Doc Twilley. "But you can go out on the porch, sit in the chair, smirk at the ladies."

"Always been good at all them things," said Dawson, leaning on the cane to get up. A wince showed some pain, but he seemed steady. "What I want to do is clean my gun. Didn't clean it this whole time. Got

dust and ashes in it. Where're my saddlebags? I got
some oil and a brush in there. . . ."

"You'll do," Seth said. "Sheriff—if you're up to it,
Josette and I are getting married. Not sure of the day
yet. Be honored if you'd witness for us."

"Be a pleasure."

Seth stuck his hat on his head, grinned at them
both, and whistling once more, went back to the street.
He headed for the marshal's office, having a message
from the Hamers for Slim.

A strikingly skinny woman in a riding outfit was
walking toward him. She had a lady's riding hat with a
yellow plume in it. She stared at him in a way that un-
settled him as he lifted his hat to her. He walked past
her and looked through the window of the marshal's
office. No one there. He decided he'd write the message out and leave it on his desk.

Inside the office, Seth felt someone watching him,
and he looked up. There was the lady in the riding
habit again, looking through the window at him. Then
she hurried off.

Shrugging, Seth took up a pencil and paper, wondering where Slim Coggins had got to. . . .

S LIM COGGINS CAME banging through the door into
the Gypsy Saloon, his gun drawn. He stopped,
staring around in bafflement. "Where are they?"

Franklin looked up from the bar. "Where are who,
Marshal?"

Slim looked around in confusion. "I was told someone was robbing the bar!"

Franklin and the bartender were alone in the saloon, Franklin nursing a beer and eating pork rinds. The bartender shook his head. "Nope. Who told you this?"

Slim holstered his gun. "A lady named Cindy Mc-Gill, or so she said. Never saw her around before. Said she saw two masked men running in here with their guns drawn!"

"Been peaceful as the grave in here," said Franklin.

"Little too peaceful for business," said the bartender. "Someone's been pulling your leg, Slim."

A sudden dread struck Franklin. He got off the barstool. "Marshal—seems like someone wanted you away from town!"

Slim's eyes widened. "Holy cats!"

Franklin suddenly thought of Hannibal Fisher. And of Seth being back there alone.

He bolted past Slim and out the door, shouting, "Come on, Slim!"

They were astride their horses and riding toward town so fast, Franklin couldn't remember mounting. It suddenly came to Franklin that the saloon wasn't *that* far from town. That meant Fisher would have sent someone. . . .

"Look out, Slim!" he shouted, drawing his gun as the big man stepped into the road. He was standing by the wooden fence of the stock-buyer's pen, a thick-bodied, round-faced man with a corona of bushy hair and beard round his head; he wore suspenders stretching over a red shirt. But what most caught Franklin's notice was the shotgun in his hands—the shotgun that was tracking the marshal. Franklin realized this man had been waiting for the Town Marshal to come back from the saloon.

Slim didn't see the outlaw, nor did he take heed of Franklin's warning. He was riding intently toward town.

Franklin veered his mount straight for the outlaw, shouting, *"Hi-yi-yi-yawwww!"* as loud as he could to get his attention. The big stranger reflexively jerked the shotgun toward Franklin.

But he hadn't got it lined up before Franklin started firing. The shotgun boomed, but the blast roared out between the two horses and the top of the outlaw's head vanished from the eyebrows up.

By heaven, Franklin thought, *that was a lucky shot. . . .*

He galloped on past the falling outlaw, not even seeing him hit the ground as he followed Slim into town.

S ETH WAS SEATED at the Town Marshal's desk, writing on a piece of paper, *I'm going back to the farm, Slim—Sol's inviting you and Mrs. Coggins to dinner tonight,* when he heard a gunshot and shouts from the bank across the street.

Seth dropped the pencil and drew his gun, rushing to the open door. Just as he moved out from behind the office window, it shattered, a bullet screaming past him, shards of glass flying, glittering around him in the harsh sunlight.

Seth saw the gunman through the open door. There, in the narrow alley across the street, standing in the shadows, was Hannibal Fisher, coolly cocking and aiming his gun.

Seth ducked back behind the wall between the door and the window as another bullet cracked past him.

Heart thudding, he leaned back enough to glance out the window toward the bank. Three men with flour sacks on their heads, holes cut for their eyes, were coming out of the bank, canvas money bags in one hand and revolvers in the other. They turned toward their mounts to the side of the bank, the horses shying at the gunshots, tugging at the reins tied to the hitching post. The man in the black frock coat was there, trying to get up on his horse. Beside him was a bigger man with a full beard that stuck out under his mask; the beard was festooned with feathers. Likely that'd be Feathers Martin.

Feathers ran up to one of the horses, pulled it loose from the post. The other two outlaws were trying to climb up on their own spooked horses, but they were encumbered by the bags.

"Seth Coe!" called Fisher. "Come on out! Come out and give me my money back!"

"Fisher!" Seth called out. "You have lost your senses! The law is coming!" And indeed, Seth heard urgent hoofbeats coming from the street.

"Fisher, damn it, we're going!" called one of the outlaws. The man in the black frock coat. "Leave it be!"

A gunshot rang out from down the street to Seth's right. Seth figured the law had dismounted and gone for cover. He heard Slim's voice. "Drop your weapons!"

Another gunshot kicked up dust by Feathers's stock horse. The horse reared, jerking the reins from his hands, and galloped off. The two other robbers turned to fire toward Slim.

"Seth!" It was Franklin's voice.

Seth risked a look out the door and saw Franklin

afoot, ducking into the recessed door of the milliner's shop.

"Fisher's in the alley across from me, Franklin!" Seth shouted.

Seth still couldn't see the marshal, but he heard him shout, "Drop them guns, or we'll cut you down, boys!"

Seth risked a quick glance out the window and saw Feathers fire at the marshal. Then the outlaw turned to grab the smaller one climbing on his horse, pulling him down so he sprawled on the street. The smaller outlaw, cursing, got to his feet, scooping up his fallen gun. A bullet clanged off a metal fixture on a post near him.

Seth decided he had to get in the fight, and he would simply pick the best target. He fired out the window at Feathers, who was trying to get up in the saddle. The round struck low on the outlaw's left side, and he stumbled, losing the stirrup and roaring in pain; then he swung his gun toward the marshal's office and fired. Seth fired at the same moment, letting the schooling that Slim had given him guide his hand. Feathers's bullet sang past Seth's head, but his own went home in the bearded man's big belly. Feathers staggered but kept to his feet, firing.

Seth fired once more, and the robber's head jerked— he took two steps toward Seth . . . and fell on his face, twitching.

A bullet from Fisher slashed past Seth, and he ducked back under cover.

Gunfire cracked back and forth, two of the outlaws firing at Slim and Franklin. Seth leaned over, fired out the window, hitting the shorter outlaw in the leg, the shot knocking him off his feet.

The man in the black frock coat rushed to his horse, mounted, and fired toward the marshal, then galloped off down the street—but Franklin and Slim fired at the same time, two shots close together, and the man on the horse arched his back, wounded. He turned in the saddle and returned fire as his horse galloped off to Seth's left as he struggled to control it.

The smaller one tried to hobble off, turning to fire as he went. Another gun cracked, with a heavier sound than the other two—the outlaw gave out a cry that mingled pain and despair as he toppled over backward. The sound of that gun—that was Dawson, Seth reckoned. He'd come down the street and joined in! The sheriff's revolver roared again and struck the outlaw riding away. The man in the black frock coat pitched from the saddle.

"Seth Coe!" Fisher shouted, firing.

Seth ducked back from the window. Three more shots from the bigger gun. Seth leaned over and looked toward Fisher—and caught a glimpse of him turning, running down the alley. Dawson was getting too close and had driven Fisher off.

"Fisher!" Seth shouted. He fired after him, emptying his gun—and missing.

He holstered his revolver and turned to the rack just inside the door. Seth grabbed a shotgun, checked that it was loaded, and ran out the door through a cloud of gray-blue gun smoke, vowing that Fisher was not going to get away. The man had sold Josette to another man. The man had hunted him down and twice tried to kill him. It had to end. If Seth Coe had anything to say about it, he was not going to let Hannibal Fisher live.

Seth ran through the alley, emerged on the dirt road crossing behind it—in time to see Josette.

She was standing behind the buckboard, staring at Fisher, who was running right at her, gun in hand. Leaning against the buckboard beside her was Seth's Winchester. Josette turned and grabbed up the rifle.

"Fisher!" Seth shouted. "I'm here! Turn around!"

"You'll drop your gun, or I'll kill her, Coe!" Fisher yelled. He was three strides from Josette.

Seth sprinted, shotgun in hand. He had to get to a good shooting angle—he couldn't risk hitting Josette.

Josette turned, backing around the side of the buckboard, raising the gun as Fisher came almost in reach of her. She fired, but the bullet only clipped part of his left ear away. Fisher snatched at her, and she swung the gun barrel, knocking his hands aside—

Then Seth was there, skidding to a stop, yelling, "Josette, get down!"

She threw herself down as Fisher turned to him—and Seth pulled the trigger.

The blast hit Hannibal Fisher in the side, spinning him so that he was facing away from Seth. The wound in his side smoking, Fisher took an unsteady step—then whipped quickly around, snarling, raising his gun.

Seth gave him the other barrel almost point-blank dead center in his chest. Fisher was lifted off his feet and fell heavily on his back, splashing a puddle of his own blood.

Hands shaking, Seth tossed the shotgun aside and ran to Josette, who was getting up, her hands trembling over her eyes.

He put his arms around her, and she gasped and

sobbed into his shoulder. "Are you all right, Josette? Did he hurt you?"

"No, no, he . . ." She took a deep breath and then straightened up, wiped tears from her eyes, and looked at him in a kind of defiance. "I'm all right now, Seth. We'll be just fine. He can't hurt us now."

CHAPTER SEVENTEEN

THEY WERE SITTING at the table in the Hamers' backyard—Seth, Josette, Sol, Daisy, and Franklin—finishing a light supper of cold meat and greens. It was still light out, but the sun was low enough to stretch shadows from the cottonwood. Franklin was on his second piece of apple pie; Seth was just poking at his with a fork. He had tried to eat out of politeness, but he kept seeing the same bloody images in his mind's eye. Men shot full of holes. Fisher nearly blown in half.

He had killed two men this day and helped kill a third. That was going to take a lot of digesting before he could digest food, too.

Sol was packing his pipe, frowning. Shaking his head at his own thoughts. "It's lucky no one died in the bank today," he said. "One shot fired in the ceiling. That bank guard went to his knees and put his hands up without a sound! They were wise to give over the money. And it all came back, every dollar, within an hour!"

Josette had eaten little, and now she pushed her plate away. "Still got a butterfly or two fluttering in my middle," she said.

Seth reached out and took her hand. "Me, too. Butterflies and maybe some bluebottles."

"Who *were* all those fellows?" Daisy asked. "Franklin said there were five of them."

"Slim got 'em identified," Seth said. "Besides Fisher, there was Curt Diamond and Feathers Martin. That big owlhoot that Franklin shot was Cletus Spence. The short one was somebody named Briggs. All badmen known to the law."

Franklin shook his head. "That bloodthirsty news writer fella kept on and on."

"You sure had a lot to tell him," Seth said.

"He kept askin'!" Franklin glanced quizzically at Josette. "Now, what were you doing in town, anyhow?"

She sighed. "I wanted to find Seth and go to the city hall and get the date set and all! I just . . . I don't know. I needed to see him. And then, when I was getting close to town, I heard all the shooting. . . ."

"And that's when you should have turned around and come back here!" Sol said, pointing his pipe stem at her.

Josette shook her head. "When I heard the shooting, I knew Seth was in it."

"Which is why you should have done just what Sol said!" Seth said, snorting. "Good Lord, Josette!"

She gave that peculiar shrug of hers that he loved so much. "I had a gun with me! I wanted to help you!"

He squeezed her hand. "Well, you did. You hadn't've fired that gun, kept him busy, he might've got me!"

She gave him a wan smile. "Seth—I'm hoping for some peace after this. I hear so many stories about Texas now. That after the war it changed and turned all wild and woolly."

"Texas?" Seth looked at Franklin, pretending bafflement. "Wild and woolly? What's she mean?"

Franklin shook his head. "Can't imagine. Why, you lived in Chaseman, girl! It's peaceful as a Sunday school picnic!"

Josette laughed. "I don't care what it's like. I want to be wherever Seth is."

F IVE DAYS PASSED. Cool weather for the time of year, even a little rain—a relief to Prairie Fire, Kansas.

The day before the wedding, Seth and Josette came into the marshal's office. The window was boarded over, so there was a lantern lit over his desk. The marshal looked up, smiling as they walked in. "Morning, folks!"

He came around the desk and shook Seth's hand. "I'm looking forward to that wedding! My wife is making me wear my Sunday suit. Kinda tight around the neck."

"I think you will survive the ordeal, Slim Coggins," Josette said.

He grinned at her. "Yes, ma'am." He turned and took a slip of paper from the desk and handed it to Seth. "That's for you."

"What's this?"

"It's a bank draft! From the city of Newton!"

"It's . . . Josette! This is fifteen hundred dollars!"

"Wanted dead or alive means just what it says," Slim said. "You killed him, you get the reward."

Seth hesitated. Money for killing . . .

"Oh, Seth!" Josette exclaimed. She took the bank draft from him, folded it, and put it in her purse. "This will make building the house so much easier!"

Seth had to laugh. "All right, then. Thanks, Slim."

"Don't thank me. Thank Dawson. He requested it for you."

"How's he doing?"

Slim shrugged. "Maybe Dawson shouldn't have come hobbling down the street with that big dragoon in his hand. But he was the last nail in the coffin for that gang. Fisher and those others, they weren't counting on that!"

"Or on Franklin either!" Seth said.

"Nope. There's one thing I'm puzzled about." Slim frowned thoughtfully at the lantern. "That girl. Cindy. She was with them—she sent me on that wild-goose chase. Wonder who she was to them. Fisher's girl?" He shrugged. "Never could find her again. I wonder where she is now. . . ."

I T WAS A breezy noon at Buffalo Junction.

Cindy and Rosie were sitting on the settee in the makeshift saloon, both of them quite sober. Cindy was wearing the riding habit; Rosie was in a nightgown. They were drinking tea from two cracked teacups Cindy had found on a shelf in the pantry.

They were alone in the house but for Attic Bird

Henderson, who was, as usual, in the attic. Cindy had just ridden in. She'd been hiding at Sublette Station, afraid to come back and be here with Whistler running the place. But she finally decided to go back to Buffalo Junction.

"You sure they're *all* dead? Even Feathers?" Rosie asked.

"I saw it clear. I was no more'n five rods away, watching from behind a hay wagon. They're dead as doornails. Robbed the bank, had them a passel of money, couldn't get their butts on their saddles quick enough. Had to get in a fight."

"Muttonheads!"

Cindy nodded. "Idiots! I'd have gotten out of there with that money."

"Me, too." Rosie sipped a little tea. "Whistler thinks they're still alive. I've been having to be quick and careful to keep out of his way."

"By now he's figured out they ain't coming back."

"You really going to split Feathers's money with me?"

"I am."

"And you know where it is?"

"It's buried in that hole back of the bar, right under the beer. I've known it was there for a long while now. I dug it up one time and counted it. There is upward of five thousand in gold. I put it back, and Feathers never guessed. But I kept it in my mind. Now, you can take yours and just go or—"

She broke off as they heard the front door open. There came those distinctive heavy footsteps, creaking in the front hall of the old farmhouse at Buffalo Junction. She knew just who it was. Whistler. And they could hear him whistling "Tom Dooley." She'd noticed him watching her when she'd ridden back to the house alone an hour ago. She'd been expecting him. Whistler had taken her more than once without paying and without her permission. He thought he was going to do it again.

"Are you ready?" Cindy asked.

"I am."

Both women took their pistols from their purses. Cindy went to stand behind the bar and hid the gun behind her back. Rosie put hers under her rump in easy reach. She leaned back on the settee and sipped her tea.

Whistler clomped into the saloon and paused just inside the door, looking at Cindy. He was bare chested, and he stank as richly as always so that both women could smell him from across the room.

In his right hand was an ax handle.

"Where's the boss?" he asked, crossing to the bar.

"He's dead. So are the others. I hid out for a while. Didn't want the sheriff to track me."

"Well, now, seems like this here is my place now. You come out from behind there."

"No," she said calmly, "I don't think I will."

He swung the ax handle hard, smashing it down on the timbers so that they cracked. Cindy took a step back. "I said, come out from behind there."

"Whistler," said Rosie, "leave her alone."

He turned to see her standing now, the pistol in her hand.

"You going to shoot me with that little thing?"

She smiled. "For starters." She pointed the gun at his breastbone and fired. He stumbled back against the bar, then snarled, raised the ax handle, and started forward.

Cindy shot him in the back of the head. He froze, wavering in place. Then, as she cocked the gun again, he turned toward her.

She shot him in the forehead.

This time he fell. *A big man, she noted, makes a big sound when he hits the floor.*

Cindy came around and made sure he was dead. They stared at him for a minute. Then Cindy turned to Rosie. "Let me ask you this—supposing we turned this place into a more regular cathouse? Hired some girls, treated 'em decent. Just cowboys, no men on the dodge. Run it ourselves. What do you think? Would you stick and help me run it?"

"Would I have to . . . ?"

"Nope. Nor me."

"Then I'm for it!"

There was a creaking coming from above them. "Attic Bird's stirring," Rosie said. "He'll have heard the gunshots."

"I know." Cindy could hear him coming down already.

She went to stand in the space back of the first flight of stairs. Attic Bird came down, not seeing her. He was a bald man who shaved his head and his eyebrows and his beard every other day. He was some crazy but harmless to those in the house. He came down once a week to get clean overalls and to empty his thunder mug. He had never done the girls an injury.

Cindy stepped up behind him and pressed the pistol to the back of his head. "Mr. Henderson," she said, "drop your gun, and we'll have us a talk."

Attic Bird stopped in his tracks and dropped his gun. "What's all this?" he asked, in his creaky, rarely used voice.

"The gents are dead," Cindy said. "Killed in town. The boss and all them others. Whistler, too—I had to shoot him right there in the saloon because he was coming after me with an ax handle."

"I see."

"Now, me and Rosie are taking over, and we're going to run this place more genteel-like. If you want to go in with us, you'd have to come down out of the attic more. You'll get good pay. I'll give you five hundred in gold right now in fact. If you say no, you can have the five hundred and ride out peaceful. If you stay, we'll make you a partner."

"This is my home," Attic Bird said. "I have been thinking of coming down more, anyhow. Let's do us the deal. . . ."

S ETH WAS SURPRISED by the number of people who came to their little wedding in the city hall. The courtroom was packed to the gills, everyone in their Sunday best. He'd bought a church coat, as he thought of it, just for the occasion, and Josette wore the pretty dress she'd bought to wear in Freeman.

Standing behind the bride and groom was Franklin, who was best man. Sol and Daisy, Slim Coggins and Sheriff Dawson sat in the front row. Dawson was getting his color back, and it was predicted he'd be ready for the saddle in a fortnight. Doc Twilley sat beside Dawson, smiling as he watched his brother officiate.

There was a general cheer when Seth kissed his

bride and some hoorahing when they went out to the street. Seth looked around to see if Heywood Kelmer or Francois Dubois was about. But they were not to be seen. Josette had not invited her father to the wedding, and Seth had not seen Dubois but for the occasional glimpse of him riding his mule down to the saloon.

Seth had sent Heywood Kelmer a note, carried by Franklin.

> *Heywood Kelmer: I have been informed by Judge Twilley that I can testify regarding your association with Hannibal Fisher, but I am not required to do so. If you keep away from town so long as I'm here, I will not feel that I must take such steps against you. If you approach me with violence, I will respond with the same.*

Standing on his porch, Heywood had read the note, simply nodded at Franklin, and gone into the house. No one had seen hide nor hair of him in Prairie Fire since.

Josette was expecting to ride in the buckboard back to the Hamer farm, where a general celebration and square dance was planned, but she stopped in her tracks at the sight of a white horse waiting for her at the hitching post in front of the city hall.

"There's your mount for the ride, Josette," said Seth, grinning.

"Marie!" she burst out. She ran to the horse her father had sold and hugged her; the horse nuzzled her back and whinnied softly.

"I bought her on the sly a couple days back," said Seth, walking over to check that the saddle was properly cinched. He was deeply pleased to see how happy the horse made Josette. "Had to pay twice what your pa sold her for, but she's worth it. Marie's a fine strong horse. She'll do for the ride to Chaseman. . . ."

Josette threw her arms around his neck and kissed him.

The crowd coming out of the city hall let loose with another cheer.

Seth climbed onto the buckboard, a bit squeezed between Sol and Daisy, Josette mounted Marie, and they set off for the farm. Josette rode with Franklin riding beside her, telling stories of Seth all the while.

"Now, there was one time when he tried to rope the biggest wild bull you ever saw. That ol' bull dragged him out of the saddle, and like the stubborn fool he is, he would not let go! It towed him right on through a patch of—"

"Franklin, you do not need to tell her that story!" Seth called.

Later that night, Seth and Josette slipped away from the somewhat inebriated guests. Seth borrowed the mule, Josette took Marie, and they rode to town for their wedding night at the inn.

They remained in Prairie Fire for another week, staying at the inn, making preparations, and seeing that Mazie was fully healed.

At last they set out for Texas. Franklin rode a little behind them. He camped just close enough to keep watch at night, and they stopped in towns when they could along the way. It was an arduous trip, and Josette was painfully saddle sore, but at last they arrived in Chaseman. Seth's chosen bottomland was still there and he bought it within an hour of their arrival.

They set up tents on the property, and Seth hired

workmen to help as he and Franklin began building the farmhouse and the barn—with much oversight from Josette.

She brought them hot food, took care of the new stock, and was often at Seth's side as he worked, handing him tools, carrying boards, and listening to him sing.

Well, I'm a fiddle-footed cowboy with raggedy drawers.
Don't make much money and I might die poor.
Just a fiddle-footed cowboy with broken spurs
Till a gal loves me'n makes me hers!

Ready to find
your next great read?

Let us help.

Visit prh.com/nextread

Penguin
Random
House